TH

DAY TEN

R. R. Haywood

Copyright © R. R. Haywood 2013

R. R. Haywood asserts his moral right under the Copyright, Designs and Patents Act, 1988, to be identified as the author of this work.

All Rights reserved.

Disclaimer: This is a work of fiction. All characters and events, unless those clearly in the public domain, are fictitious, and any resemblance to actual persons, living, dead (or undead), is purely coincidental.

No part of this publication may be reproduced, copied, stored in a retrieval system, or transmitted, in any form or by any means, without the prior written consent of the copyright holder, nor be otherwise circulated in any form of binding or cover other than that in which it is published and without a similar condition being imposed on the subsequent purchaser

RR Haywood

Day Ten.

Sunday.

One

Laying on his back and resting on his elbows Nick squints from the strong sunshine pouring through the plate glass windows of the café at the top of the long pier. Bathed in sweat he exhales slowly and looks over to the sleeping form of Blowers, amazed at how within the thirty seconds since he nudged him awake to take his turn on watch he has managed to get to his makeshift bed and drift off. With the lure of sleep threatening to pull him back under Nick reluctantly sits up and stretches his hands down to his feet. His hamstrings feel tight; his back muscles feel tight; his arms and just about every muscle in his body feel tight. With a low groan he clambers to his feet and stands with that sleepy fug hanging on his face for long seconds before rubbing his eyes and stretching his arms out to the sides.

The last two days have been relentless. Running, fighting, hardly any sleep, crap food, the risk of death at every point and then Lani making them sprint up that bloody hill too. Remembering the hill sprint Nick tenses his thigh muscles and winces at the onset of pain already starting to spread through the deep muscle.

With a yawn he twists round and visually checks the sleeping forms around him. Clarence's huge bulk flat on his back and snoring away like a walrus with a sinus problem. Blowers and Cookey, like he was just a minute ago, are both sound asleep. Dave, as in his wakeful hours, sleeps quietly on his back with his hands crossed over his chest. Two knives, one either side of his bedding, rest on the floor ready to be gripped and used. Nick notices that Dave has positioned himself between Howie and the entrance. Anything that enters must go through him first. Tom, the new lad curled up on his side facing away from him but he can tell from the steady rise and fall of his upper body that he sleeps soundly. Nick was unsure about Tom and Steven to start off with. Afraid somehow that the bond they had built up between them would be weakened. Steven was lost in the church fight and that's something Tom will have to deal with. Just as Nick had to when they lost Tucker, Curtis and Jamie.

Finally his eyes come to rest on the prone figures of Howie and Lani. Sleeping close together and Nick notices their hands are entwined. The sight of them lying hand in hand invokes a sudden feeling of unity, closeness, family.

The fractured society of broken family values saw Nick, as with many young men of his age; grow up without a role model. Without that alpha male to guide them and see them through the hard times. In his school days Nick had Miss Rachel, his special needs teacher. An immensely passionate woman who taught Nick that just because he couldn't read or write that he wasn't useless, that he was still a person with values and a voice. The tuition was close and exceptions made, the use of her first name instead of surname helping bridge that gap between teacher and student. It was Miss Rachel that encouraged Nick to develop his love of anything electrical and mechanical. Miss Rachel would even bring broken things in and ask Nick to see if he could fix them, but only after he'd tried a few minutes of reading out loud. With her steadying influence and the patience she showed, Nick developed as a person and saw that maybe he wasn't just destined to get labouring work here and there. But when the school years ended, Nick struggled with the day to day life without that support and quickly became one of the many young men attending the job centre to sign on.

It was the scheme to earn extra benefit and join the Territorial Army that saved his life. He remembers holding the pen over the form and trying to decide if he should sign up and thinking back to the kindness that Miss Rachel showed him and knowing this was his chance to do something different.

Meeting the other lads, and then ultimately Howie gave him something he hadn't experienced before. A life. A belonging. His skills had already been used several times and not one of them judged his inability. He'd stood on the line with these men in the most utterly terrifying of situations but Nick wouldn't change any of it.

Howie fills that role as mentor, leader, and a father figure of immeasurable kindness. Brave isn't a strong enough word for how Nick regards Howie. His ability and never failing courage. Howie would willingly give his life for any one of them to have the chance for survival. That intense look in his eyes and that quiet dark brooding nature, the fire burning away in his soul that drives them on to do things Nick never thought possible. Nick fancied Lani when she came into the group. They all did. The beautiful Thai girl became part of them within a few hours and already Nick couldn't imagine her not being there. She fought bravely with strength and courage, never failing to take her turn. Now, watching her lie hand in hand with Howie fills Nick with a sense of something, something he can't explain. Just that it's right. That's all.

He quietly opens the rear door leading out onto the outside decking area. The air outside is cooler than the humidity of the enclosed room so he wedges the door open with a patio chair and scans the view. Thick black smoke still plumes from the church fire deep in the town, smaller wisps of smoke spiralling up from the long row of burnt out houses along the seafront. The rest looks serene and peaceful. Golden beaches with the blue waters gently lapping at the shore. The houses look clean and homely. He turns slowly soaking in the view while he pulls a battered packet of cigarettes from his pocket and taps one out. Despite the air being still he still cups the flame of the lighter and inhales the smoke into his lungs. Feeling the rough bite in his dry throat and coughing gently. Exhaling the smoke he looks out following the shore line to the harbour in the distance and the long line of dark objects moving slowly into the sea.

It takes him several seconds of staring dully to realise what he's seeing. Boats moving away from the harbour. Lots of boats. His heart quickens and his face lights up with the excitement of seeing their group getting safely away from the Island. He throws the cigarette into the waters below and runs back inside, calling out and watching as sleepy forms become suddenly awake forms, leaping to their feet and grabbing weapons to slay whatever foe that has dared to disturb them.

'The boats,' Nick coughs, his voice as yet unused since he woke up, 'boats from the harbour,' he points to the windows.

The group hastily move out onto the decking and lean against the railing watching with smiles and low cheers at the flotilla of vessels moving safely away.

'Dean kept his word then,' Clarence stretches his mighty arms and leans his bulk against the railing which creaks in response.

'He did,' Howie nods with a huge grin, 'he bloody did! Well done Nick, good spot mate.' Howie grins at the young lad. The others turn to smile and clap him on the shoulders like it was Nick's own work that got them away safely.

'Does that mean we get the day off Mr Howie?' Cookey asked with a mischievous grin.

'Well I don't know about that,' Howie replied scratching his head, 'but maybe a few hours to relax before we move off. What's the time?'

'Just gone two,' Nick replied checking his watch, 'and I'm bloody starving.'

'Again? We only just had food you gutsy bugger,' Blowers says.

'That was hours ago,' Nick replies as he lights another cigarette and hands the pack round. Standing there and with the first good news in days they relax against the barrier, lounging in patio chairs and re-living the night's events.

'Tom, how are you mate?' Howie asks after nodding to the young policeman to step away to the side.

'I'm good Mr Howie,' Tom nods back quietly.

'Listen, I'm sorry about Steven. He was a good lad and it was bad the way he went like that...' Howie speaks gently, knowing Tom saw him fire his pistol into Tom's head as he lay dying. The injuries were too bad for survival and Howie couldn't risk another Darren coming back.

'I know, you had to do it,' Tom looks back into the dark eyes of Howie, holding his gaze for seconds and showing that he understands.

'For what it's worth mate, I'm glad you came with us. You fought well Tom and I don't know how we would have got through it without you.' Howie meant the words too. Tom had fought well and even when Steven fell he didn't allow himself to falter but pushed on with the same savage ferocity as the rest of them.

'Mr Howie...' Tom asked with a sudden puzzled expression, 'last night when you pushed forward in the tower stairwell...how did you do that?' He stared hard into Howie's face watching the sudden dark look creep into his eyes, that power, that hard stare.

'I don't know mate,' Howie replied suddenly with a wry smile, 'it just sort of happens.'

'Happens?' What you mean you've done that before?' Tom asked. He, along with the rest, stood and watched in rapture as Howie took the front position during the desperate battle to hold the stairs. When they were being beaten back and losing more ground than ever before Howie changed. His whole manner and being became fluid. Not like Dave, the way he moves like a dancer with grace and agility, but something else. A power poured from Howie and it was like the undead just fell before him. Every strike was where it should have been. Every step saw them wilt and fall away from him. An electric feeling passed through all of them and Tom felt the hairs on the back of his neck standing up. Witnessing something extraordinary.

'Ha! You can tell you're a copper Tom,' Howie smiled awkwardly, 'I don't know mate. It just happens. Right, there must be some coffee round here somewhere, fancy one mate?' Howie deflected the question and his easy smile meant no offence was taken. The rules had changed and whereas just a few days ago Tom would have stood his ground and questioned the man regarding his ability, now he was just glad to be with him. Glad to be with all of them. What he saw during that night was a unity that even the police never matched. The way they watched each other, pulling each other back and covering the weak points. Tom heard them say they were used to fighting alongside each other and now he understands what that means. The easy jokes, the banter and the ready smiles they keep flashing even when they were so massively outnumbered. Dave, the small quiet man that Tom and Steven already held in awe taking on the role of sergeant to Howie's officer. Blowers like a corporal, stepping in to take the lead whenever needed.

'Oi Tom, do you fancy a smoke mate?' Cookey called out. Tom turned to look at the group seated round a large table and saw Blowers motion to an empty chair in the middle of them. Lani already seated and smiling from a comment made by Nick. A small gesture but one of great meaning. An acceptance into the group and with a quick smile of his own he walked forward to sit amongst them.

Blowers watches Tom speaking as Cookey goes to sit down in the chair next to him. Blowers blocks the seat quietly and gets a puzzled look from Cookey in return, he nods to Tom indicating the chair is for him. Cookey nods in understanding and takes the next one alone.

'He did well,' Cookey says quietly.

'Yeah, shame about Steven,' Blowers replies.

'Shame about all of them,' Cookey says with a sad look at his friend, 'what now?'

'Eh?' Blowers snaps his mind back to the present.

'What now?' Cookey repeats, 'back to the fort?'

'Probably...' Blowers nods.

'Okay,' Cookey says softly.

'What?' Blowers picks up on the tone of his normally jovial friend.

'Nothing,' Cookey hesitates, 'I dunno, I just kind of like this.'

'How do you mean?' Blowers asks.

'Us, you know, just us lot being on the road and doing stuff together. Shit, sounds weird like that. I'm not saying I like it...like the whole end of the world thing but you know...being together like this.'

'Feels safer?' Nick cuts in leaning across Lani sat next to him.

'Yeah like we know what we're doing...shit it doesn't make sense when I say it but I know what I mean in my head,' Cookey screws his face up in concentration, 'it's like...well...' his voice drops along with his gaze which stays fixed to his boots, 'family or something,' he mumbles expecting a torrent of abuse from Blowers and Nick he feels the first flush of shame burning his face.

'Me too,' Nick adds quietly with his own uncomfortable shuffle in the patio chair, 'I wish Tucker was here and Jamie and Curtis. Especially

Tucker...I miss his food.' Lani smiles with sadness at the lads around her. She can feel the close bond between them. And from what they said there was quite a few before the big battle at the fort they came from. Now down to three but they protect each other like brothers under the watchful eye of Howie.

'They were the best,' Cookey adds in a muted tone, 'Oi Tom do you fancy a smoke mate,' he calls out seeing Howie move back inside and Tom left standing alone.

'I don't smoke,' Tom smiles and moves over to the chair nodded at by Blowers, 'thanks for asking though mate.'

'No worries, so you were a copper then? How long were you in for?' Cookey asks with a genuinely interested look.

'That must have been a hard job,' Nick asks before he can answer, ''I'd have loved to have been a policeman.'

'Why didn't you join up then?' Tom asked.

'Can't read or write,' Nick shrugs with a smile to show he's over any form of embarrassment about it.

'Really?' Lani asks in surprise.

'Yeah, severe dyslexia and well I just didn't really bother at school...'

'He's bloody good at electrical stuff though,' Cookey cuts in, keen to defend his friend from any shame, 'he got Tower Bridge in London all rigged up...do you remember that?' He laughs at Blowers.

'Jesus that was brilliant,' Blowers laughs at the memory watching Nick smile sheepishly, 'the bridge splits in two right, so we had this massive horde coming at us and we were getting pinned down so Nick here, he goes into the control room and gets the thing working...' Blowers breaks off laughing hard, more so because of Cookey starting to crack up... 'he gets one end going up and down like this,' he imitates the bridge with one forearm, 'and this horde were coming over it so Nick waits until they get there and whoosh he lifts it up and they go flying... then he drops it down and waits for them to all stack up against the end of the other bit and whoosh it goes up again....funniest thing you ever saw.'

'And he got the petrol pumps going at that garage,' Cookey says wiping tears of laughter away.

'Oh those rats,' Nick shudders, 'nasty. You remember that bloke on the roof?'

'Oh that was bloody funny too, we drove off with his trousers on the Saxon,' Blowers starts off again as Cookey bends over with his stomach hurting from laughing. Lani and Tom laugh as Blowers launches into a descriptive replay of the memory.

'Jesus,' Tom says after gaining control of his laughter, 'you done some things you lot.'

'We have,' Nick nods slowly, 'we'd have been dead many times though if it weren't for Mr Howie and Dave.'

'That roof we were saying about,' Blowers cuts in, 'well Mr Howie got isolated on his own downstairs. We were surrounded and it didn't look good, rats and zombie filth everywhere. The Saxon was out in the car park with the big machine gun on the top. So Mr Howie decides…on his own…to charge the lot of them and make it to the Saxon so he can cut 'em down and save us…'

'Dave though,' Cookey takes over, 'Dave thought the same thing and wanted to save Mr Howie,' he leans in speaking quieter, 'he ditched his guns and screamed "Blowers you're in charge" and launches himself off the roof, straight into the lot of them…only had his knives he did,' he leans back shaking his head in wonder.

'Christ,' Tom exclaims, 'so Howie charged them from the bottom and Dave went from the top…and they didn't know what the other one was doing?'

'No mate, they both figured one of them had to survive to protect us and get to Mr Howie's sister.'

'Fuck…' Tom whispers, 'last night when he did that thing… you know…going at them like that, so he's done that before then?'

'Yeah a few times,' Blowers answers looking uncomfortable. Tom picks up on the slight shift in position and the quiet looks between Blowers, Cookey and Nick. 'What?' Tom asks, unable to restrain the instinctive policeman habit of asking questions.

'Nothin',' Nick shrugs and lights another cigarette.

'No Nick, what?' Lani presses the question home having also picked up on the subtle looks between the three lads.

'I dunno, that fight outside the fort…he…well Mr Howie he sort of did something weird and…'

'What?' Tom asked quietly and could see the now overt shifting and fumbling between the lads now.

'Well he got beat down,' Cookey explains, 'we all saw it,' he looks to Blowers and Nick both nodding in confirmation, 'we we're fucked, I mean completely fucked. We were getting slaughtered and there was so many of them…I think Curtis went down first, maybe Tucker…I don't know anyway we we're losing. Badly. Mr Howie gets beaten down and we knew we'd lost it, we'd given them a bloody good hiding but it was over…' his voice trails off at the vivid memory playing through his mind. The sounds of screaming and the constant growling and roars of the undead as they pressed the attack again and again, the smell of blood and guts being spilled, the fear and the exhaustion.

'He was on his knees,' Nick picks the tale up with a distant look, 'Mr Howie on his knees crying, he kept trying to get back up but he was done for, Dave was off somewhere and the rest of us were getting the shit beaten out of us. We all saw it,' Nick suddenly looks up at Blowers and speaks with a firmer tone, like he wants confirmation too before he carries on, 'Mr Howie was down…but then he changed. He started praying to himself and then got back up...his face,' Nick shakes his head, 'his face was...'

'It was different,' Blowers cuts in, 'he got back up and he was saying the Lord's Prayer, his voice got strong, so loud and we all heard it.'

'Were you close to him then?' Tom probes for the details.

'No I mean we all heard it, everyone on that field heard it. Every man fighting heard that prayer coming from him... We all took it up and seeing him rise up, he was like a Viking warrior or...something from a movie...they wouldn't go for him...like they were scared or something, Mr Howie he just stood there and they cowered back...then he went for it.'

'Like last night?' Tom asked.

'Yeah, like last night,' Blowers replies, 'him and Dave were something else. Relentless. Ruthless. And Clarence...mate he is so bloody strong.'

'Yeah I watched him,' Tom replied.

Lani listens intently as the stories are relayed. The lads giving the funny and heart breaking accounts of their time together. Like the others, she gets that tingling hair on the back of the neck feeling at the memories of the big fight re-told. That quiet and softly spoken man with the easy smile, holding her hand when he could have easily pulled away or shifted position. She saw his discomfort when they were swimming this morning, how his face blushed when she made the joke about calling him Howie when they were alone. That same quiet man who held a field of undead at bay with a dangerous glint in his eye.

Her family came from Thailand when she was very young; moving to a strange country that was so wealthy but with such fractured family values. Her own family kept them close and raised her with discipline and love. Nurturing where parents should, guiding and proving that hard work and dedication paid off. She knew her parent's had to work so hard to get anything for those first few years, dealing with the stereotypes and prejudice of a mainly white population. Her own strong mix of conflicting values meant she often felt neither here nor there. Isolated from her traditions of her country but still not a complete part of the local society.

The utter terror of being left alone for those long days and longer nights. Hearing the undead howling as the sun went down and knowing her family and friends were all taken, that they would kill her without remorse if she got caught. She spent days sobbing and crying, hiding in fear as she grew filthier and more hungry. Then when she couldn't take it anymore she went out to find them. Going to her friend's house and finding him turned, she got trapped and where she thought she would freeze in fear, she didn't. She fought back and killed. Then killed more as she battled her way out of the building. The adrenalin surge left her shaking and trembling from head to toe but in that instant she changed. A switch had been clicked inside her. She no longer cried and although she still felt the same fear, it was coupled with a burning rage and desire for revenge.

She became cunning, and when she saw her hiding place had been smashed and entered while she was away she knew that if she fixed it the people would see and come back. But knowing they had already entered and found nothing she figured it would now be the safest place. Then, when Howie and Nick came in, she heard the movements and thought they were the undead. Going out to exact that vengeance she froze on seeing two armed men standing just feet in front of her and inwardly cursed her own stupidity. Lani's mind was resolute and firm. She knew men found her beautiful, an exotic difference from the mostly pale taller girls of the country. She also knew that men would try and take that beauty if they found her. She'd decided that if that happened she would fight to the death but suddenly seeing two men there, armed with guns, hard stares and dressed like mercenaries she didn't feel so brave.

Lani watched them speaking, she took in the friendly tone Howie used and the way he backed off and told Nick to do the same. As they went to leave her instinct told her to go after them and take the chance. She did and now looking back, perhaps that split second decision has given her the best chance for survival. Who knows what will happen, she may die any minute. Any one of them could. But here with these men she knows she stands the strongest possibility of living.

Howie and the way he gets nervous round her when they're alone. He's sweet and something inside her is drawn to him in a way she hasn't felt before. Strange times though and strange behaviours. She felt foolish when they woke, for having the need to hold his hand and showing a weakness but now, sitting amongst these people and feeling secure for the first time since this began she relaxes and enjoys the sunlight, but still glances frequently into the café to watch the man with the curly dark hair. He's mid conversation with Dave and Clarence, he turns, smiles, she feels her heart skip a beat and she smiles back, then chuckles softly at seeing his blush even from this distance.

Inside the café Clarence and Dave stand together with Howie, making plans while drinking warm water from bottles left in their packs.

'I'm just saying I think they need a few hours to unwind boss, it's been relentless the last few days. They're young and they've done everything you've asked of them...' Clarence rumbles in a conversational tone.

'Yeah, I guess so,' Howie nods back. The urge to press on burns inside but where to? He has accomplished what he set out to do. Saved Sarah, dealt with the threats along the way and got the women and children from the fort safely back across the water. There could be threats on the other side waiting for them, but as Sarah and Sergeant Hopewell repeatedly said, they have to be able to take care of themselves and the sea captain will probably take them straight to the back of the fort too. The constant pace. The sheer desperation of each day and now, with what he can only think of as down time he feels twitchy and like there should be another mission, another task waiting.

'Let's get some coffee going and see what food we can find,' Clarence adds. Even he feels tired after the nights ferocious fighting. He'd happily push on without complaint if the need arose, but he also knows, after many years' service, that taking time to unwind is as important as anything else in times of extreme combat and stress.

Clarence chose to come with Howie knowing they would need good experienced fighters in order to stand the best chance of getting to the women and children, and of course Sarah. At the fort big Chris accepted his decision and he set out, intending to assist and then get back to work alongside his former comrade. However, Clarence had watched the way Howie and the lads fought together as a tight unit. They sheer courage they displayed was at times, unnerving and reminded him strongly of how he, Chris and Malcolm had been when they were young and fresh recruits. After the last two days of being with them constantly, Clarence, as with the others, now felt an unbreakable bond. When he slipped from the roof climbing down from the church tower, he faced certain death from the fire raging beneath him. But those lads and Lani risked their own safety to save him and that took something far more than courage. It was unity, comradeship and every decent value that was drummed into him as a young soldier. Seeing Howie's quick reactions, his constant state of mind and ability to take information in, process it and reach a decision even in the harshest of situations had continually impressed Clarence and he felt himself slipping into calling Howie "boss". A word used by soldiers towards their ranking officer when out in the field and the need for such rigid formality wasn't so important.

As the two days went on, Clarence felt Howie's natural authority coming through and now he understood just why these men followed him

'Dave, you happy with that?' Howie asks. He glances out the window at Lani smiling at him and feels the blush starting instantly, quickly turning back to Dave in the hope they don't notice.

'Yes Mr Howie,' Dave nods with a blank expression.

'Right, that's settled then. Chill out here for a few hours and get some rest. I'll go break the good news,' he strolls out the door into the sunlight and smiles as the group turn to watch and start getting to their feet, ready to move out.

'Relax,' Howie waves an arm at them, 'we're staying here for a while so we can relax and unwind. Personally I was ready to go find another horde to piss off but I reckon I've been outvoted so...' his voice drains away, lost in the sudden cheers erupting from everyone seated at the large table. Smiling he gives thanks that someone like

Clarence has the experience and knowledge to impart at such times.

'But...we still need a constant watch on and keep your weapons close at all times, got it?'

A round of grinning affirmations come straight back, "yes sir" and "yes Mr Howie". Shaking his head and still wondering how he came to get stuck with being called Sir and Mr Howie he grins back and leans against the rail.

'We need food though,' he muses.

'Mr Howie, I saw some rods in the office when we searched earlier, we could have a go at catching fish,' Cookey asks, 'if we did it from here we could keep a watch on the pier too.'

'Good idea mate, crack on and catch us some dinner then. Nick, I need your special skills,' Nick looks up with a sudden keen interest in his eye, already excited at whatever challenge awaits. 'Is it possible to rig that coffee machine,' Howie points into the room at the shiny coffee maker on the counter, 'to a car battery? If not then how would we get power to it so we can brew up?'

'There's some car's in the car park on the other side Nick,' Blowers informs him needlessly.

'I'm on it Mr Howie, just the coffee machine or anything else?' Nick already on his feet and squeezing through the chairs, cigarette hanging from his mouth.

'Coffee first, definitely coffee first but see what else you can find.'

'Ha, I'll need a hand...'

'Im fishing,' Blowers replies quickly, relishing the prospect of a few hours idling with his feet dangling off the pier's edge.

'Tom, you any good with car's and stuff?' Nick asks.

'Yeah I'll help mate,' Tom gets up to follow Nick into the café.

'You can't smoke in there,' Cookey suddenly shouts after Nick as he walks towards the counter with his cigarette in his mouth.

'Oh shit, I forgot,' Nick turns and jogs quickly back to the open door. Stopping as realises what he's doing, 'you twat Cookey,' he shouts and goes back inside making a play of puffing away while he walks through.

'Tom, that's illegal you should nick him...Ha, get it...nick him...Nick?' Cookey laughs to himself, feeling not the slightest embarrassment at the stony faces refusing to humour him, 'oh well I thought it was funny. Right let's get them rods,' he nods to Blowers. The two lads setting off through the café shouting abuse at Nick and Tom as they pass.

A silence descends outside as Howie and Lani both realise they're alone. Nodding slowly they both look at each other. Neither speaks. Nervous stares. Slow smiles start to form and they both burst out laughing, releasing the small tension that built up within those few seconds.

'So we're alone,' Howie says, 'you can call me Howie now.'

'Well in that case you should call me Miss Lani then.'

'Miss Lani? Sounds like an Italian sausage,' Howie laughs, 'okay it's a deal Miss Lani.'

'Thank you Howie,' Lani replies with perfect politeness.

'So you okay then?' Howie asks softly.

'Fine, er...thanks for last night with the hand...thing,' she bites her bottom lip and smiles coyly; suddenly aware that maybe she didn't need to mention it.

'Ah, yes that's er...er...fine...yeah really...anytime...'

'Anytime?' She asks quickly.

'Well you know...maybe not anytime...but...'

'So not anytime?' She cocks her head to one side watching him seriously and trying not to laugh at his nervous stuttering.

'Well no of course anytime...you know...anytime you want a hand...ha a hand! No I meant that not a hand like helping you with something, though obviously I can help you with things if...if you want...but I meant...as in a hand to...er...well...hold...'

'Howie,' she laughs, 'I can't believe you're so nervous round me.'

'Oh bloody hell,' he laughs at himself, 'I'm always like it round beautiful women.'

'So I'm beautiful then?' She carries on with the merciless teasing but the jokey question is clearly loaded for an answer.

'Shit I walked into that one didn't I...' Howie grins as he runs a hand through his thick hair and drops his eyes down to the floor, 'Lani you are very beautiful,' he says softly and looks up with a sudden smile. Amazed at himself and that never in a million years would he dream of telling someone as beautiful as Lani that she was beautiful simply for fear of dropping dead with embarrassment and knowing it would sound cheesy coming from him. But his polite tone and clear nerves convey the gesture with meaning instead of being corny and clichéd. 'Lani! Are you blushing now?' Howie chuckles with delight at the tinge of redness in her cheeks.

'No, it's the sun!' she grins back at him showing her white even teeth, laughing the blush away she reaches up to take her hair band out and runs her fingers through her long silky hair.

'Oh the sun is it?'

'Okay so it wasn't the sun. So Howie, what task have you got for me?'

'Eh, for you?'

'Well Nick and Tom are going to rig up the coffee machine, Cookey and Blowers are fishing so what...' she fixes him with a steady mischievous eye, 'are you going to do with me?'

'Oh you can't ask it like that,' Howie groans.

'Sorry, I feel mean for teasing you. I promise I'll never do it in front of the others though,' she says earnestly.

'Okay,' he replies, 'thank you. Er...I've no idea. We've got to sort the kit out, see what ammunition we've got left. Get some food sorted, and work out a way of getting back I guess.'

'Right, well I'll come with you then,' she gets up quickly as Howie gives thanks for her easy confident manner saving him from a certain death of stuttering like a drunk Hugh Grant.

Two

Day Nine

Saturday.

'Look Geez you gotta pay up innit,' Maddox shouted up at the house from the street.

'I'm not paying for being in my own house now piss off,' the man leaning out of the upstairs window of the semi-detached brick built house shouted down to the gang of youths.

'You is on the Bossman's land now geez,' Maddox shouted in reply, his deep voice resonating in the still warm air.

'Look I'm not afraid of a bunch of kids so piss off.' The man shouted down. Red faced with a balding head and a stocky muscular build from spending the last twenty years as a builder alongside hard men, and he wasn't easily intimidated, especially by a bunch of hoody wearing teenagers.

'Or what?' Maddox shouted back.

'There's no feds now bruv,' Ryker interrupted to a chorus of jeers and cat calls.

'Feds? What? Fuckin' kids,' the man slammed his window shut and disappeared out if view. Maddox, after giving an irritated glance at Ryker waited a full five seconds before giving the order;

'Brick it,' he shouted and watched as the crew started throwing missiles at every window in the house. The downstairs had been boarded up from the inside and the door looked barricaded too. The Bossman had said to look for the houses that were boarded up as it meant they'd have supplies. The strict instruction given to tell the survivors they were being taxed for protection and to give up half their food. Ryker and his crew had found this house and soon reported back to Maddox; the Bossman's number two and in charge of the *street security taxing operation* as he called it. Maddox had tried reasoning with the man but he clearly didn't want to oblige with paying his due, so his house got bricked to start with.

Shouts and jeers from the teenagers screaming as they threw rocks, house bricks and anything else they could find. Windows of the first floor imploded and shouts of rage brayed out from the man inside.

'Enough,' Maddox raised his hand and listened with satisfaction as the missiles ceased, all apart from one thrown by Ryker, another act of defiance to be dealt with later.

'Oi Geez?' Maddox shouted, waiting for the balding man to slowly peer over the window sill, 'your house is fucked up blood, and we're gonna fuck it up some more if you don't give us your stuff.'

The man peeked over the sill then dropped back down staring in fury at the glass fragments strewn about the floor. 'Little fucker's,' he growled. Seething anger boiled up inside him as he stormed down the stairs holding a baseball bat and started undoing the many new locks fitted to the door.

'He's comin' out bruv,' Ryker shouted.

'Yeah I can see that,' Maddox shouted back as the front door burst open and the apoplectic middle aged man stormed out holding the bat out to one side. Sniggers and laughs sounded out in derision as the teenagers started their mocking.

'Fuck off...just fuck off now you little cunts,' the man shouted holding the bat out pointing at Maddox and then sweeping along the row of kids all with their hoods up despite the high heat.

'Look at you old man,' Maddox said.

'You want some do ya? Ya fackin' want some?' The man waved the bat round in wide circles and glared back. A gang of scrawny teenagers with skinny legs and skinny arms, dressed in baggy tracksuit trousers tucked into their socks, hoods up or baseball caps pulled down, not one of them could be over seventeen years old, never done a day's work and just sit about smoking weed all day probably. He wasn't about to be scared out of his home by a bunch of kids. The zombies were bad enough and he'd taken pleasure in killing a few of them getting supplies back to his house and then some more that shuffled along when he was boarding up the windows and doors too.

'We is keepin' the streets safe bruv,' Maddox shouted, 'we're the feds now so you got to pay innit.'

'I ain't givin' you shit boy?' The man said with a sneer.

'Boy?' Maddox flared, 'listen old man, you pay up or we will fuck you up…we want your stuff'

'My stuff?'

'Half your supplies or we gonna fuck you up bad.'

'Come and get it then…boy,' the man sneered goadingly.

The Bossman had warned him about people like this, and Maddox had met a few over the last few days. But the Bossman also made it clear that a dead survivor can only pay once, whereas a living survivor would keep paying.

The teenagers were itching to start and Maddox knew he only had to give the word and this old man would be done for.

'Bunch of fuckin' nigger kids, paki's and cunt Muslim's. This ain't your estate…so fuck off.'

Silence descended as the insults embedded into the young ears. Maddox paused for a beat then growled 'Have him.'

Within seconds the front garden was littered with bricks and stones launched by the youths. The man dodged a few and made a few quick steps back to his door before a well-aimed shot to the back of his head brought him down quickly. Bleeding and seeing stars he stood back up shaking his head and grasping the bat tightly. The youths moved in, drawing batons taken from the zombie police they had taken down, sticks, chains and knives gripped by the hands of teenagers advancing en masse. The man, realising the missiles had stopped, foolishly stood his ground. Bringing his bat up to shoulder height with a two handed grip and watching to see who would be first to come at him. One good shot to a head would scare these little shits. Crack a skull open and they'll be running off quicker than anything.

But they didn't go at him one at a time. These youths, almost feral from years spent running riot and living on council estates knew their greatest strength was in numbers. Young, quick moving and with no remorse they acted like a pack of hyena's and converged at once. Chains whipping out and striking the man across his back and legs as he swung the bat out wildly. Hit after hit, strike after strike, chains whipping and limbs being struck as the youths darted in and out quickly. All the time laughing and mocking the old man. He fought desperately and felt the sudden danger of his situation. With a much bigger build and years of strength behind him, he correctly predicted this would be over in seconds, but not who would win.

He staggered back to his door, confusion adding to the shock produced by his muscles after being repeatedly struck by blunt edged weapons. On shaking legs and with arms barely able to lift the bat he staggered drunkenly.

The first knife came from a boy barely into his 'teens. A thin blade shoved deep into his side and quickly pulled out as the boy danced back laughing wildly at the first blood being spilled. The man stumbled from the agonising pain in his side.

Another knife plunged in and whipped away. As the man dropped to his knee's screaming in pain the pack descended, knives lunging, bats striking and chains whipping his skin. Within seconds he was dead. A bloodied mess of cuts, bruises and livid welts, flowering spots of blood spreading across his light coloured t shirt from the knife wounds.

'Yeah we fucked you up blood,' one youth danced over the corpse, spitting on the dead man's face.

'I'm gonna t-bag him,' another one shouted and crouched down to rub his groin over the deceased's face, 'this is where it's at mofo,' he laughs with high pitched childish delight as his mates bend double at the sight.

'Get the stuff,' Maddox calls out with a firm tone. The youths burst into the man's house, smashing the inside up with screams of joy. Bats and sticks creating havoc as they rampage through the rooms, destroying everything in sight.

'Ryker,' Maddox called to the youth and nodded his head for him to come over. Ryker stared back with defiance and then slowly walked over, dropping one leg down to limp in full gangster style.

'Where you at bruv?' Maddox asked him.

'I is right here innit,' Ryker stared back.

'Why you dissin' me in front of the crew Ryker?'

'It's all good Maddox,' Ryker replied, 'I didn't mean nuffin.'

'We's the feds here Ryker, get it? We make the rules now and they's got to see I'm in charge,' Maddox points towards the house, clearly indicating the youths inside, 'I'm in charge out here so don't fuck wiv me bruv, you get me?'

'Yeah it's all good,' Ryker repeated dropping his eyes from Maddox and shuffling from foot to foot, showing submission. Maddox held his hand up which Ryker took in a quick firm grip, leaning in to bump chests before moving off with a swagger back towards the house.

Maddox watched as the youths start carrying supplies out, using bin liners and supermarket carrier bags loaded with tinned food, cans, bottles and packets.

'Alright Maddox,' a young girl walked up to him, her hair pulled back in a harsh ponytail, large hooped earrings dangling from her adolescent ears.

'Alyssa what's up,' Maddox greeted the girl with a nod.

'Nuffin, you?'

'Nuffin.'

'That old man was buggin'' she smiled with a row of crooked teeth covered in railtrack braces.

Maddox stared down at the girl wearing an open pink hooded top, her push up bra trying to force a cleavage where nature had yet to develop. Spotty pale skin and chewing gum with loud squelches she stood there shuffling while shaking her head, 'he got proper fucked,' she added. *Just like you every-night you dirty sket* Maddox thought to himself, nodded back he wondered if the

Bossman would be pissed off that they had to kill another one for refusing to pay up. Maddox, at eighteen and being just that bit older than the other youths, and having already served sentences in Young offenders Institutes had been the natural choice for the Bossman to use as his number two, and it was a position Maddox intended on keeping.

'It's well hot,' Alyssa said with a whine.

'Take your top off then,' Maddox replied, instantly regretting it as Alyssa took the words as an invitation.

'Why, you wanna see my tits then?' She asked with a stupid grin.

'No,' Maddox replied bluntly. Alyssa's face fell at the re-buff.

'Just coz they ain't as big as Skyla's,' she whined again.

With a brief smile Maddox walked off leaving the girl staring after him with a hungry look on her face. Maddox waited for the crew to come out and told them to start heading back, knowing the stuff should be taken back before anything else happened.

Carrying the spoils the youths slinked away from the house. Already the conversation had shifted from the life of the human they had just ended to the party to be held tonight, promised by the Bossman for all their hard work in cleaning the area of the *dirty infected* as he called them.

Survival in the urban sprawl at the best of times relies on wits, being quick and able to go through long periods of suffering. Skills the youths gathered around Maddox had long perfected. Each one of them born and raised on the huge council estates built along the south coast, thousands of people from low income backgrounds forced to live in cheaply built low rise blocks of flats and terraced houses. The estates were really several housing projects added to and developed over the last forty years, a sprawling mess of long residential streets, light industrial units servicing the population, twisting alleys, shops with barred windows, supermarkets, pubs and cheap clothing chains. Whole communities struggled to survive and get by. Crime was rife and the police view, along with many other authorities was to leave them to suffer. With the council only paying the bare minimum for repair the estates festered into graffiti covered walls, houses with boarded doors and windows, front gardens full of broken appliances and furniture.

The youths knew no different, living in social housing with parents and families struggling with their own vices too much to raise their children with any sense of responsibility. Fathers and mothers in prison, brothers and sisters in young offenders or with foster carers, struggling to make ends meet on benefits and turning to petty crime as a way to boost their income. Drugs use and small scale supply, taking stolen goods, bent gear, dodgy rip offs, everything was fair game. Good food was rare and these youths grew accustomed to getting by on what they could find. Frozen snack food bought cheap from the local supermarket value range. Nutritional value low. Sugar and salt content high. Bodies became lean and under developed from the poor diets and regular exercise of running from the home owners they burgled, the shop keepers they shoplifted from and the police that didn't stand a chance of catching them.

Young bodies consuming quick fixes that send them wild with energy. Rejection from family life meant they grew into gangs roaming the streets with their own hierarchy and rules. Self-governing and over time any sense of boundaries broke down as they became wilder and more feral. Alcohol and drug use were common, under-age sex the normal way of life, stealing and petty crime the standard rules of behaviour.

Education systems failed as hard pressed teachers learnt they could either invest a disproportionate time into these youths and stand very little chance of making a difference, or concentrate on the ones that wanted to learn and develop. Abandoned by society and left to run riot on estates that learned either to tolerate them or move out; they grew hardy and tough. So when the event happened and everyone else froze with the shock, unable to think, act quickly or defend themselves, these youths carried on life as normal. Their pack instinct kept them safe. Fleet of foot and cunning meant they could run and hide faster than the mostly obese population. The foraging skills honed over years of stealing meant they found food and sustenance. The normal morale code of society was already separated from them by many degrees. So to them, life carried on as normal.

The Bossman, having lived amongst this kind for many a year and profiting from the misery all around him, saw a chance of sustaining a way of life. Deep within the largest council estate the Bossman had been growing an empire by taking over disused industrial units. When the former owners were hounded out by the recession and the sharp rise of petty crime the Bossman moved in and planted his fortunes.

These units were taken over and adapted into hydroponic factories. Rows and rows of high yield skunk cannabis plants growing under a systematic set up of Very High Output lamps. The VHO lights set on timer to achieve the highest potency by giving the plants the strongest light source for the greatest length of time. The heat meant the plants emitted a strong distinct odour which was sucked away by fans forcing the warm pungent air through long ducts and filters, breaking the scent down before pumping it out harmlessly into the undergrowth outside.

As each unit was taken over they were knocked through with makeshift doors holed into the adjoining walls. Each section was used for a specific purpose. The nursery where the baby plants were covered by plastic covers and protected during their infancy. The second growth stage where the plants stood a few inches high. The third growth stage of sturdy but immature plants. Through to the final growth of giant bushy plants, ripe with sticky buds and each one standing six feet in height. A forest of Marijuana, a wooded copse of cannabis leaf, high heat and humidity and the plants were cared for with the same attention as the average tropical garden centre.

The drying area where the plants were cropped and left in a strictly controlled dry environment. The weighing and bagging section where the plants were cut down and bagged into their sale bags, bought in bulk from the internet and delivered to an address on the estate. The Bossman was shrewd and maintained a kindly uncle type figure to the youths. Everyone on this and the surrounding estates owed him in one way or another. Either on tick for weed they had taken but not paid for, or on money loaned out by him. When re-payment became too hard they simply started work for the Bossman. Dealing in a set area or holding large amounts of pre-wrapped cannabis ready to be collected and dealt. This way they took the risk and no one *ever* snitched on the Bossman. Fear of the repercussion, of being alienated and seriously hurt and more because of the constant supply of drugs they relied on.

Nearly every youth ended up running directly for the Bossman, he knew they would easily outrun the police and the penalties would be far less for a juvenile than for an adult and in return they were well rewarded. Sell more, get more. Sell a lot and get a lot. Sales prospered and despite the recession and lack of career options the youths flourished under the Bossman's watchful gaze.

Always ready to listen to their problems and enforcing discipline through the bigger lads he rarely had to use force himself, but his reputation was well known enough to ensure he was never crossed.

As the world fell, the Bossman moved quickly. Gathering his youths and moving them into the industrial units he quickly set about fortifying the land. Stealing flatbed Lorries and raiding garden centres and builder's merchants he erected high fencing covered with coils of razor wire. The Bossman already had a small arsenal of weapons, mainly shotguns and rifles but a few pistols too, and his arsenal was quickly enhanced as he led a well-armed raid on the local gunsmiths, looting the place empty. By late afternoon on the second day of the event, the Bossman had used the newly gained weapons and the flatbed Lorries to raid the local shops and supermarket. Stripping the shelves and stock rooms bare, stockpiling everything from tinned goods to clothing in the many cupboards and store rooms of the compound. Now, nine days into the event and the compound was the safest and best stocked place for miles.

Knowing the power supply would end soon, he set about securing solar panels and wiring, setting the panels on the roofs of the units and running the cables down to feed the lights that fed the plants. The plants that he still used as payment for the youths sent out to rid the immediate area of the dirty infected. House by house, street by street, section by section the youths swept through, killing everything that got in their way. At night they hunkered down and prepared to defend their territory but by day they advanced and slowly gained the streets.

As reports of survivors drifted back to the Bossman he realised there was an avenue of earning to be tapped into. His crews were taking the risk in dealing with the dirty infected and that meant everyone was safer. If they wanted to live in his area they had to pay so the Bossman introduced the *Street Security Taxing Operation* and got Maddox to brief the crews to only take half initially and only to take it all if it was obvious the survivor would refuse to pay or if they tried to attack the crews.

Not wanting to take the constant risk of being out on the street himself, the Bossman promoted Maddox as his number two in overall charge. Then in turn Maddox established crews working in set areas. Each crew had a crew chief and that crew chief could run their crew as he or she saw fit.

Eight crews each with between ten to a dozen youths and the compound was full, but the method worked better than he ever expected with each crew becoming a tight unit.

Food and water was plentiful, and these youths had already survived years of going without so they didn't need much. And by allowing them to get stoned every night meant they were mostly peaceful, apart from the few cases of acute paranoia that caused fights. Quickly dealt with by the crew chiefs and a punishment decided by Maddox. The crews worked well alongside each other and were quick to back each other up, moving between areas and sections as the need arose.

Some of the adults that survived the carnage sweeping through the close knit streets tried to barter their way into the compound. Some, younger and prettier women were taken in on the basis they would tend to the plants, feed the youths and keep the compound clean. The others were sent away. If they refused they were removed. If they resisted they were killed.

It was brutal but it worked.

Maddox led his and Rykers crew back through the estate towards the compound. Listening with interest as the boys and girls talked about the music they were going to listen to during the party tonight. Maddox had spoken with the Bossman in his office, suggesting they hold a weekend party to give the youths a chance to blow of some steam. The Bossman readily agreed, telling Maddox he could sort it out as he saw fit but telling him to keep a few of the bigger lads sober and clear headed to act as bouncers in case of problems.

It was also Maddox that decided who was to provide security within the compound each day. At first he selected the bigger lads himself but then he put the job down to the crew chiefs to nominate three from each crew to stay back each day. Those youths were armed with shotguns and given easy sentry jobs on the walls, fences and main gate. A few more were sent out to stand sentry on the junctions of the road leading into the compound. Short wave radios sourced from a local electrical outlet were used as a way of keeping constant contact. The sentry jobs inside the compound were seen as a cushy number and gave the youths a chance to look cool and hard with guns. The sentry roles out on the junctions were hated as the youths were left isolated and under strict orders not to piss about or go anywhere.

Despite the strange set up, some rules were enforced with instant punishment if breached. Racism was outlawed and faced severe consequences if used by any youth, no matter what the circumstance. The strong ethnic mix of the youths meant there was no predominant race in higher numbers. Religion was as outlawed as Racism and despite many of the youths coming from various religious backgrounds they were told they could worship in their heads but not to anyone else. Sexist attitudes were gone with nearly as many girls being crew chiefs as boys. One of the crews, headed by Sierra, consisted solely of girls and had one of the highest kill rates of the dirty infected.

Maddox had worked with all the crews and made sure he got on with all of them. Everyone had respect for Maddox. He was fair and easy going; ready to teach the younger kids but renowned for his hard streak and had a reputation for having never been beaten in a street fight. Well-developed for his age, the Afro-Caribbean lad was stacked with muscle on his lean frame, hours spent in the prison gym, enhanced by high protein and surprisingly, he never smoked weed or took pills. He was happy to deal it and made good money working for the Bossman, introducing good contacts and steadily working his way up the chain of command even before the event happened.

Upstarts like Ryker were dealt with quickly and Maddox, like any good manager, was quick to spot dissenters and trouble makers. Taking them aside and addressing the offending behaviour, preventing the issues from developing. Ryker would be watched from now on. As a crew chief he was given extra weed and more food, but the last day or so he'd been coming back with more tax than was right. Telling Maddox that the residents were refusing to pay up so they had to be dealt with and killed. Maddox suspected Ryker was killing them out of fun, which went against what they were trying to achieve. Knowing that a family of survivors would keep paying up with whatever they sourced and foraged themselves would be a better future prospect than just taking everything they had now. A few kills here and there helped spread the word and made the others take notice, but too many would see the residents left on the estates trying to flee and run away.

Today though, Maddox could see they didn't have any choice. He had tagged along with Rykers crew himself, to see how they operated. The big bald man had to be dealt with though, he was the type that would always cause problems for the crews so it was better he was sorted now.

Maddox was irritated that Ryker wasn't given a chance to show his bartering skills though as he wanted to see how Ryker would deal with a family of survivors willing to pay

Nearing the compound, Maddox, out front and watching intently, looked round for the sentry that should be on this junction. The chair and table dragged out onto the street for the sentry to use was empty. Frowning, Maddox held the others up and started walking over to the empty chair as a youth ran out of the nearest building doing the zipper up on his baggy jeans, shotgun wedged under his arm.

'Ah fuck Maddox...' the youth said in a panicking voice, 'I needed a piss.' The fear was heightened by Maddox remaining silent as he strode quickly at the lad and stopped inches from his nose. The lad cowered back, clearly terrified and grimacing from the expected punch. Maddox held his hard gaze for long seconds before turning to face the gathered crew watching with unsuppressed glee at the prospect of a beating.

'Go on,' Maddox told them bluntly. They did as ordered and moved off down the street towards the compound, laughing and looking back at Maddox towering over the child.

'Zayden yeah?' Maddox asked not needing the confirmation. He knew every youth in the compound, knew who their families were, knew what background they had and who they were mates with. Knowledge was power. Power got you off the street.

'You're with Darius's crew,' statement not a question but the terrified youth nodded back anyway.

'You need a piss Zayden, you piss here. If you gotta take a dump, you shit here...you get me?'

'Yeah Maddox,' Zayden whimpered full of remorse and fear.

'Don't be leavin' your post again, what if the dirty infected got past here? What then Zayden? You'd get fucked over is what.'

'I know,' Zayden nodded quickly, fumbling to bring his shotgun from under his arm but not having the room to swing it out with Maddox standing so close, and not daring to brush the gun against Maddox either, so he held it clumsily between his arm and his free hand stretched over.

'Darius will sort you out,' Maddox sighed and saw the relief rise Zayden's eyes as he realised a beating wouldn't be happening. Maddox used violence as a tool and despite what many thought, he did not get the sadistic pleasure most of them got from unabated violence. He grew up hard and with a good skill at fighting, learning to think coldly and not allowing his temper to draw him into making mistakes. Knowing that with every fight, there was a winner and always a loser.

'Stay on your post,' Maddox added before walking off and leaving the youth breathing a long sigh. 'Also,' Maddox turned to smile at Zayden, 'we got the party tonight innit, and I see that Lauren givin' you the eye,' Maddox laughed, his features changing dramatically as he flashed his bright white teeth, 'don't be fuckin' up and missin' the chance to get it on wiv her eh bruv?'

'No…I swear down Maddox…' Zayden beamed back almost floating off the floor with the thought that Maddox had seen him and Lauren smiling at each other for the past couple of days.

'And make sure you bag it up,' Maddox pulled a cardboard box of condoms from his pocket, launching them at Zayden as he walked off grinning. Maddox took a few steps, left it a few more seconds and quickly glanced round. Zayden was stood firm and upright on the junction with the shotgun clasped between his skinny arms. Giving Zayden a beating would have kept him alert through fear, but ruling through fear alone brought issues. Issues him and the Bossman didn't need. Instead he took the lads fear and made it positive instead. Letting him know that Lauren fancied him was a finishing touch that put the kid on cloud nine and Maddox knew he'd stand there alert and watchful for the rest of the day.

Striding with confidence Maddox thought ahead to the many tasks that needed sorting. Prioritising them in his mind as he approached the high solid metal gates topped with coils of razor wire. Already opened up for Ryker and his crew to enter, the youth allocated the gate guard role for the day waited as Maddox walked in.

'Alright Maddox,' the youth nodded, his sweating face peering out from underneath his hood.

'You's sweatin' bruv,' Maddox stared at the lad and glanced round to see if the boy had thought to drink during the hot day. 'Where's your bottle Liam?'

'Bottle?' Liam asked in a surly tone then instantly regretted it on getting a glare from Maddox.

'I told you to make sure you had water, where's your bottle?'

'Don't like water Maddox,' Liam answered.

'What did I say happens when you don't drink?'

'You said I'd get de-hydrolated.'

'De-hydrated,' Maddox corrected him, 'you get de-hydrated. Your piss stinks and your cock will shrivel up. D'you want your cock to shrivel up?'

'That's fuckin' gross,' Liam spat.

'Then drink some water innit.' Maddox helped him pull the gate closed and told him to go fetch two bottles from the storeroom while he took watch. Liam handed him the shotgun before running off through the compound. Staring round him Maddox took in the view. The long low rise units stretched off into the distance, open ground all around a mixture of concrete and grass. The Bossman had secured a good area. The high fencing stretched round one side with natural high walls bordering the other. On this side there was the barest signs of living. A few chairs, sofa's and odd furniture scattered about for use of the sentry guards. A wooden shed literally picked up and carried in from a nearby garden served as a sentry hut as the youths rotated on the patrol patterns set by Maddox. Staring at the land Maddox thought ahead to how he would get the concrete ripped up and seeds planted for food, sustaining their stocks and ensuring survival after the easy months of summer have passed.

To his eye there was a future here, the nearby houses could be converted and taken over, the boundary fence extended and more accommodation gained. Watching Liam come jogging back with two full bottles of water Maddox thought of how they'd need a clean water supply once the bottles were gone and if the taps ran dry. The plants consumed huge amounts of water every day and that would need to be sustained too.

Liam handed him the bottle and stood there, unsure of himself as Maddox stared back expectantly.

'Drink,' Maddox said the word simply and watched as Liam sulkily screwed the top off and started glugging the clear liquid down. Within the first few gulps Liam realised how thirsty he was and how refreshing the water felt in his parched mouth. Greedily slurping it down, some of the water splashing from the bottle from his chin and down the front of his hoody. Leaning his head back to upend the bottle, Liam drank the contents down in one go, giving a gasp and then a big belch as he pulled the now empty bottle away.

'Alright?' Maddox asked with humour

'Yeah it's good innit,' Liam answered with a grin that made him look like the young boy he really way.

'You don't have to wear that all day,' Maddox said, pointing at the dark top worn by Liam. The boy looked pale and sickly. Too much weed, too many late nights and not enough decent food and this was another problem faced by Maddox. The kids had a certain amount of freedom within the compound as long as they followed the rules. Outside they had their sections to cover but smoking cannabis all evening, eating crap munchies and drinking alcohol would waste them away. Maddox knew they had to sustain their energy in order to survive, and he needed them to survive so they all survived.

'I'll be back in an hour,' Maddox handed him the second bottle of water, 'make sure that one is drunk too, you get me?'

'Yeah sweet,' Liam nodded already feeling better for the liquid purging through his system. Walking off, Maddox headed across the concrete, squinting his eyes against the glare of the sun he crossed the end of the first unit, glancing in through the wide metal double doors slid back to reveal the occupants inside. The first unit had been hastily converted into a day room with sofas, easy chairs, tables and rugs laid out. The young women taken in to run the compound worked from the day room, running further into the unit to tend the plants and controlling the stores held behind locked doors. On seeing Maddox cross the doors the few women inside the unit, sheltering from the heat of the plantations and the heat from outside waved and smiled.

Nodding back Maddox walked across the doors and stopped at the corner, facing the wide grounds at the back of the buildings. Big canvas tents taken from the looted shops covered most of the ground. At first they had been stuck up in any old fashion, with no thought given to layout. As the crews were decided, Maddox re-designed the layout so each crew chief had their own tent with the rest of the crew split into smaller ones. Each crew had a large day tent where they could meet, chill out or do what they wanted when not on duty.

Strangely, after years of rejecting anything to do with home or family, the youths took to the system with eagerness. The crews worked themselves out, making minor adjustments here and there, keeping the walkway lanes clear and making sure there was a clear and distinct gap between each section.

There was still plenty of open land here, Maddox thought as his eyes swept across the grounds, a huge open bonfire was lit everynight, known as the pit and it gave the youths somewhere to gather round and crash out smoking joints.

Walking alongside the long wall of the units, Maddox made his way across the camp towards the pit, his mind still making mental checklists. Halfway along he entered the units through a single door propped open. The pungent smell of cannabis filling his nostrils instantly and the humidity from the watered plants prickling his already hot skin. Walking through the units he briefly checked each growth stage, looking for any plants wilting or hanging low from lack of water. The women working their way from plant to plant with hoses nodded, smiled and waved as he walked through.

After several minutes of walking he reached the last unit, this one set aside solely for the Bossman's use. Knocking on the door he waited for the invitation to enter.

'Enter,' a deep voice boomed out. Maddox grinned to himself and pushed the door open to see the Bossman sat behind a desk staring at sheets of paper laid out in front of him.

'Boss,' Maddox nodded respectfully.

'Maddox, how you doin' son? Everything alright is it?' The Bossman looked up, his voice friendly in genuine warmth at the sight of his deputy.

'All good,' Maddox replied. He walked over and sat down in a big comfy chair opposite the desk, noticing the heavy smoke of a recent joint hanging in the air.

'So how was Ryker?' The Bossman asked with an interested but obviously stoned gaze. A medium built man with close cropped hair just starting to grey at the temples. Dressed in a suit he could be a high class lawyer, dressed in overalls he could be a reliable mechanic. The Bossman suited anything he wore and with his easy smile and laughing eyes he got on with just about everyone he met. People liked him, people wanted to like him, but more importantly, people wanted him to like them.

'Good,' Maddox nodded, 'we found one man in his house but he refused to pay so we had to resolve the situation,' Maddox explained. The street language dropped now as he spoke in calm measured tones.

'Who did the talking?' The Bossman asked.

'Ryker started but I took over at the end, he clearly wasn't going to pay so we had to sort it. He came out with a bat and started taking swings at the crew.'

'Who was it?'

'A bald man in a semi-detached house on Sycamore Avenue,' Maddox replied.

'What old Naylor?' The Bossman looked surprised for a second, 'he always was a bloody idiot, good builder though I'll give him that. Christ so he survived it did he?'

'He did,' Maddox answered, 'but not now.'

'Oh well, serves him right. You had to do what you had to do,' the Bossman nodded deeply with a knowing look. 'So everything else alright is it?'

'Zayden left his post out on the junction to go for a piss, sorted him out though.'

'What that little lad out there on his own?'

'He's on Darius' crew; Darius said he's a good lad.'

'How did you sort it?'

'I gave him a hard stare till he shit himself then gave him a bollocking, told him I knew Lauren fancied him so he didn't want to miss the party by being in the shit.'

'Good lad,' the Bossman laughed appreciatively, 'good work, never use a slap unless you have no other choice. Win 'em over and they'll work their bollocks off for you.'

'I know,' Maddox nodded listening intently. He always listened when the Bossman explained things. It was the Bossman that got him out of talking *street* as he called it, when they were together, telling Maddox that a king had to be able to talk with all his men. It was also the Bossman that taught Maddox getting people to love you gave them more loyalty than fear will ever give. But fear, used at the right time and the right place, will do the work of a thousand requests.

'Liam was on the gate sweating in his hoody, he hadn't drank any water for hours,' Maddox continued.

Shaking his head and tutting, the Bossman looked worried as he rolled another joint, 'we need to sort that out Maddox, this heat will have them dropping like flies if we ain't careful. Are they washing? If they don't drink and don't wash they'll get sick. Ever heard of dysentery?' Maddox shook his head, 'It's what the soldiers used to get when they went days without clean water, shit food and not cleaning themselves. If we get that here we'll all be down with it, gives you the chronic shits and makes you weak.'

'Okay boss,' Maddox nodded, 'so we need to get them washed and drinking clean water. I was getting worried about the shit they're eating too, and smoking weed all night.'

'Here's what you do,' the Bossman leant in speaking quickly and using his hands with quick movements, 'get the crew chiefs to be responsible for making sure they're washed, but make sure the girls to do the girls I don't want any perving going on mind, get some exercise equipment outside and get the kids seeing you and some of the other fit lads training, they'll want to join in and be like you but then you tell 'em that unless they start eating decent they can't train. Give 'em an incentive, as for the weed. Well it keeps 'em settled. That Darius is a fit lad, get him and that Ryland in on it.'

'We got stacks of those multi-vitamins here boss, can we start giving them out in the mornings?'

'Bloody good idea Maddox,' the Bossman smiled encouragingly, 'yeah do that, anything else?'

'The party. I got some televisions taken from the houses near here and I got the Xboxes all rigged up, you still alright if we switch the power over for a few hours, we got a DJ booth rigged up too.'

'Maddox, you do what needs doing son. I told you, you're in charge on the ground so you make the decision. I'm here for the bigger things, to oversee it all and make sure we got enough of everything.' The Bossman replied lighting the joint.

'Yeah sweet boss...'

'Maddox! What have I told you about your language?'

'Sorry boss, I meant thank you.'

'That's better. You speak to them how they understand it but you got to know how to speak with everyone.'

'I understand.'

'Do you? Well I am not sure I fully understand the last statement of confirmation you made, and I would ask that you kindly elaborate for me?' The Bossman switched to a cultured tone; sounding intelligent and refined he looked as expectantly at Maddox, just as Maddox looked expectantly at Liam just a few minutes ago.

'Do I have to?' Maddox groaned with a sheepish smile.

'I would rather that indeed you do have to.'

Sighing, Maddox sat up straight and rolled his eyes as the Bossman smiled in good humour, 'well in reply to your previous comment concerning my assent of confirmation I would hereby state, for the record, that my confirmation of understanding was given in a truthful manner and one which I can barely see any reason for doubting. Therewithal I challenge any doubt on my words and seek clarity should there be any further confusion on the subject.'

'Maddox! That was brilliant!' The Bossman beamed and leant over to shake his hand, pumping it greatly, 'it's getting better all the time!'

'Thanks boss,' Maddox answered.

'Look I know the world is fucked beyond repair and those fucking things are stomping about eating everyone, but you never know when you might need to speak properly. A king needs to talk with all his men. There is a world beyond this estate Maddox. Other survivors that will come here and want to trade. We heard that explosion a few days ago so we know there is shit going down in other places. Now anything else?' Maddox nods in response. They had all heard the explosion of the housing estate detonated by Dave and Jamie, and they all felt the tremor in the ground as window panes rattled in their frames followed by a huge mushroom cloud boiling up high into the sky. It was early morning, barely dawn and it brought every youth out into the open grounds of the compound and staring off into the distance and it served to remind them all of the things that must be going on in other places.

'The planting of crops I mentioned...'

'Maddox, it's only been a few days. Slow down son,' the Bossman sat back in his chair and puffed on the joint, 'let's get tonight out of the way, give the lads some chill out time, we'll get together over the next couple of days and work out exactly where you want to do it. Okay?'

'Yeah okay boss,' Maddox relented with an easy smile.

'Good now piss off; I got plant feed and yields to calculate.'

'Okay,' Maddox got to his feet and crossed the rug covered floor.

'How's it going with Skyla?' the Bossman asked quickly.

'Skyla? Yeah she's alright,' Maddox replied aloof as always when the bossman asked him about women.

'Just alright is she? She looks more than alright to me son.' He said lighting the joint and inhaling deeply.

'We'll see,' Maddox grinned before letting himself out and slowly closing the door. The grin faded as the door shut with a click. Maddox liked the Bossman and was genuinely pleased that he had given him the top job, but he also knew he had earned it. Sorting through a thousand tasks every day that came through him instead of the boss. As the days went on, his reputation grew as did his sense of responsibility. Even the women in the units saw him as the go-to-man. The Bossman was friendly enough but after the initial mad rush of the first few days, getting the compound secure, stocking food and getting weapons he spent more and more time in his office, worrying and fretting about plant food, what yields he would get from the plants, smoking joints and leaving everything to Maddox. The bossman had always smoked weed, but never this much and it worried Maddox.

As he left, Maddox thought back to that first night. He'd been with the Bossman driving through the estate in the big Mercedes as Maddox counted out the nights takings.

'You done well tonight then Maddox?'

'Yeah very well,' Maddox replied quietly as he leafed through the thick bundle of twenty pound notes.

'Any trouble?'

'Nah, couple of those jumped up college kids again trying to give it large.'

'Be careful with them,' the Bossman warned, 'don't deal to them yourself. Get one of the kids to do it, if they get nicked they'll bubble you up quicker than anything.'

'I did,' Maddox replied.

'Good lad...what the fuck is that?' The Bossman leant forward, looking through the windscreen at the figure stood in the middle of the road.

'He must be pissed,' Maddox chuckled.

'What round here?' The Bossman replied looking round at the quiet residential street.

'Is he bleeding? Look he's hurt,' Maddox peered at the man covered in blood and staggering around on unsteady feet.

'Who is it?' The Bossman asked, 'is he one of ours?'

'I fucking hope not,' Maddox answered knowing that anyone touching one of their kids would be dealt with very harshly.

'Nah that's a man that is, not a kid,' the Bossman brought the car to a gradual stop a few metres from the figure.

'I'll go and see,' Maddox replied.

'I'll come with you,' the Bossman said. They climbed out of the vehicle and moved towards the figure, both of them staring hard and trying to see who the man was. Thick wet blood coated his face and a large open wound was flapping on his neck.

'Alright mate?' The Bossman called out, 'what happened?' The figure turned and stared towards the Bossman, a low growl coming from his throat.

'Boss,' Maddox shouted the warning as the figure burst to life and ran at the Bossman. Maddox met the man just feet before he reached the Bossman and powered him to the ground. The injured man writhed and bucked, howling loudly as it tried to lunge and bite out.

'Fucker's trying to bite me,' Maddox yelled and slammed his fist into the side of the man's head. The blow had little effect as the man kept thrashing his head and gnashing at Maddox.

'Hold up son,' the Bossman ran in and kicked the downed man in the ribs. Still no effect and the thing raged and fought furiously.

'Fuck me he must be on crack,' the Bossman shouted, 'have him Maddox.' Maddox responded with a flurry of hard powerful blows aimed down at the side of the man's head, purposefully avoiding the already bloodied face and not wanting to get blood on his hands.

'He ain't stopping,' Maddox shouted in alarm.

'Shit...' the Bossman leapt back as another howling figure lunged at him. The fight stepped up a notch as both men realised the danger of their situation. Two crazy men trying to attack them on their own turf. This must be serious. Maddox jumped up and slammed his foot down onto the man's face and heard the snapping of bone. Without further delay he turned round to see the Bossman flick the blade out on his switchblade and stick the sharpened point repeatedly into the chest of the attacking figure. Maddox ran over and grabbed the man from behind, pulling him away as the Bossman plunged the knife into the throat.

Dropping the body to the floor they both stood in shock, staring at the bodies then at each other.

'What the fuck was all that about?' The Bossman asked quietly.

'We gotta go boss, the fed's will be all over this.'

'Yeah right, fuck is that another one?' They both turned to see another figure running at them. A middle aged woman dressed in a paisley dressing gown and pink fluffy bunny slippers. A ragged wound on her face and blood coating the front of her night clothes.

'You are fucking joking...' the Bossman shook his head.

'Boss, give me that,' Maddox took the knife from the older man and walked at the figure charging towards them. Side stepping at the last second as the woman lunged forward with her lips pulled back. Maddox punched her hard to the side of her head and she went down thudding her head into the side of the Mercedes.

'Watch the bleedin' car!' The Bossman shouted.

'Sorry boss,' Maddox replied. The woman showed no reaction and clambered quickly to her feet, turning to lunge at Maddox. He danced backwards trying to fend the woman off with his free hand. Feeling the side of a car behind him and knowing the woman was going to bite him he lashed out and swept the blade across her throat. A crimson spray of blood spurting out and soaking Maddox's clothes.

'You'll have to burn them now,' the Bossman tutted, 'you'll be covered in her DNA.'

'Boss, what is going on?' Maddox shouted, 'they're trying to bite us.'

'Fuck me...more?' the Bossman shouted as more figure appeared further down the street running towards them in that same jerky manner.

The powerful headlights of the Mercedes illuminated the throng of night clothes wearing attackers as they poured up the road. The Bossman watched them intently, taking in the injuries, the blood soaked clothes, the jerky motion of their running and finally....the red bloodshot eyes.

'Maddox, get in the car son...quick.' They both climbed in and slammed the doors closed. Without hesitation the Bossman put the vehicle into gear and pressed his foot down hard. The car shot forward, accelerating quickly and heading straight towards the oncoming group.

'They ain't moving,' Maddox shouted as the first ones impacted on the bonnet and went flying over the top of the vehicle. More thuds as the vehicle ploughed them down and sped off.

Each street they went through more bodies were out in the road. Groups of people were fighting each other, more on the ground being bitten and savaged. Screams and shouts pierced the air as they drove quickly through the estate.

'Get to the units,' Maddox shouted through the window at a group of youths running down the street. They swept through shouting the same thing to any youth they recognised as one of theirs, telling them to pass the message on.

By the time they got back, there were already crowds of youths standing about and looking either pumped up or terrified.

That's when the Bossman showed why he was in charge. Within minutes he had the units open and the youths safely inside and watchers out guiding more kids in.

He was a good leader and despite the now constant weed smoking, Maddox felt a deep sense of loyalty to him.

Re-entering the drying area he quickly inspected the drying crops, counting the bundles and checking the correct amounts were there. No one would dare steal from the Bossman or Maddox but it didn't hurt to check everything once in a while.

'Lenski,' Maddox called out to the high cheek boned woman walking past the door with a clipboard in hand. Lenski had been one of the young adult women accepted into the compound as society outside the gates crumbled. Quickly proving herself to be intelligent and capable she effectively "ran" the inside of the units when Maddox wasn't present, holding the keys to the food and alcohol stores.

'Maddox, you are back then,' the Polish woman replied, her English good but still retaining a strong Eastern European edge.

'Yeah, everything okay here?' Maddox forgot to re-introduce his street talk, sticking to his preferred normal voice while talking to the beautiful but very hard faced woman.

'Is good Maddox, all is good here yes?' She nodded back giving a brief smile.

'The sentries aren't drinking enough in the heat and they don't have the brains to come and get something. Can you make sure someone takes water out to them every couple of hours and make sure they've got food too.'

'Sure, I do this,' Lenski nodded again, making a quick note on her own ever growing list of things to do.

'Also, can you get the packs of multi-vitamins out and make sure there's a bottle in every tent...'

'Multi-vitamins,' Lenski added it to her list.

'And we need to make sure they're washing properly, are they using the baby wipes you gave them?'

'I do not think they use these,' Lenski replied in her husky voice, 'the packets they are still full no?'

'I'll speak to the crew chiefs and get them on it but we might need your help with the girls, yeah I'll get you and Sierra to talk to the girls and Darius and me can talk to the lads.' Sierra and Darius were both crew chiefs and also an established couple. At seventeen years old they were also older than most of the youths and looked up to as figures of authority.

'Sure, I do this too…I do more every day,' Lenski replied with a pursed mouth.

'I can send someone else in to help you. I'll sort it out tonight.'

'That is a good thing, the plants they need the water, the food it needs to be done, the washing clothes is many…in here we only have a few but you have many.'

'I got it Lenski,' Maddox could see she was being genuine. Initially the older girls had been quiet and sullen and after a couple of days he could tell they were thinking they were being held captive and forced into slave labour. Maddox could see the problems this would cause and took them all out into the streets, showed them what was out there and said they could come or go as they pleased. Admittedly, he did take them to the roughest area where the most kills had been made and they quickly chose to remain in the safety of the compound. Since then Maddox had made it clear they could leave anytime they wished. None of them did. Lenski had taken the role seriously and guarded the food with a hawk eye, making sure her girls washed the clothes, cleaned the base and tended the plants. Maddox greatly admired the beautiful woman and despite the comments being made now, he knew she cared for the youths.

'Is okay with me now,' she added with a smile then looked at him thoughtfully, 'you okay Maddox? You look tired. Many late nights no? Come and sit I make you drink.' He followed the woman as she turned and walked through the plantation.

'Have the crews brought much in today?' He asked instead of eyeing up her shapely backside.

'We get some yes, many more tins of food now. More today than yesterday. Did you ask about the garden for the crops?'

'He said we'll talk about it after the party.'

'But this is July, we late for planting already. Plant now quickly. Or we do the idea I said.'

'Lenski, the Bossman isn't going to give up a unit for growing food.'

'But we eat or we die. The food they bring it good but it not last many weeks. The young people they eat many times. We have the lights the water the heat….'

'Okay I know. Let's get tonight done then I can ask him tomorrow.'

'Poor Maddox, so busy.' She turned with a smile. Not being able to tell if she was genuine or being sarcastic Maddox stayed quiet. 'You are just Eighteen no? A child. But you are a man Maddox; you are a great man the way you do this,' she added.

'Someone has to,' Maddox replied quietly, uncomfortable with the compliment.

'You lead here, you tell everyone what they do. All the day I hear Maddox say this, Maddox say that, Maddox the great,' she laughed, a pleasing sound full of delight which made him smile.

'All I hear is Lenski said no, Lenski said get out, Lenski said piss off,' Maddox replied quickly. She laughed harder, whacking him on the arm with her clipboard.

'I rule with fear you with love,' she smiled again.

The afternoon stretched on. Another day passing slowly with crews returning to the compound, bags filled with taxed goods taken from the survivors found living on the sprawling estates. Reports of clusters of the *dirty infected* roaming certain streets. Crews despatched to find and eliminate them. Listening to the reports given by the chiefs, giving instructions, arranging the party for the evening and everything done with the compound going through Maddox. No signs of flustering or irritation at the constant interruptions.

The muscular teenager evolved into his role as natural leader and with each passing hour of each passing day, his aura grows. He learns quickly, developing his own easy style. Giving orders that aren't questioned, advice that isn't rebuked. Lenski finds she is equally busy as Maddox learns that he can't take everything on himself and fielding more and more of the questions and requests for help to the Polish woman. A natural hierarchy developed from necessity. Capable people doing the things needed to be done. As with Maddox, Lenski develops her own style. Not as friendly or approachable as Maddox but she listens to each youth in turn and jots down on her ever growing list or sends them packing with a few words of caustic advice

It seems that every few minutes something else happens. Someone else has a question. Never more than a few steps taken in any given direction before one of the youths calls out in street language, some of them confident and coming straight to the point, others shy and shuffling nervously as they're prompted and probed to find the problem.

Late afternoon Maddox found himself alone in his quarters. Two small adjoining offices, separated by stud walls. One of them his room, the other initially empty but then given over to Lenski as Maddox watched her develop. Knowing that by giving her a private room she would be seen as a higher up, and also serving to give her some privacy which she would value and then make sure she worked hard enough to keep. Other than the bossman, theirs were the only fully private rooms. The crew chiefs had their own tents but nothing beat having solid walls round you and a fully functioning door that could be closed. As it was, because of the sheer volume of work needed to be done within the compound, neither of them used the rooms apart from a few hours of exhausted sleep. Standing there enjoying the quiet for a few minutes, away from the hustle of the compound now full after nearly all the crews had returned he allowed his mind to settle and again started going through mental checklists of what was still to be done. Sighing he turned at the door being knocked and pushed open.

'People at the gate,' Lenski said simply.

'What people?'

'I not know this,' she shrugged.

'Come on,' Maddox walked past.

'I come with you?' She asked to clarify but already walking next to him.

'Yeah,' he nodded; staring ahead at the armed youths running towards the front of the compound.

The gathered youth's parted as Maddox waded through them, reaching the front and staring through the central section giving a view of the street ahead. Several adults were gathered on the junction where Zayden should be, looking back down at the compound.

'Where Zayden at?' Maddox asked.

'Here,' Darius pushed the youth forward.

'Zayden, who are they?' Maddox questioned the lad.

'I dunno swear down, they said they wanted to talk to the Bossman.'

'They armed?'

'I didn't see nuffin, no guns.'

'Do you know them?' Maddox asked peering through the gap and thinking they need a scaffold tower built high so they can see over the top of the gate.

'Nah Maddox,' Zayden answered.

'Darius, you and me bruv, get a shotgun.'

'I got your back Maddox,' Darius said quickly.

'Sierra,' Maddox looked over to the girl, 'you too.'

'Open up,' Maddox gave the order as one gate was swung open with enough room for them to step through. 'Stay behind me,' he told the crew chiefs. They dropped back a few steps, staying quiet and keeping their faces blank as Maddox and Lenski walked ahead.

Striding down the straight road Maddox took in the details of the adults; three men and two women all looking filthy and gaunt. Maddox recognised three of the faces from the estate and clocked that they're not customers of the Bossman, just some of the many background people that made up the life here.

Watching the approaching foursome the group started moving towards them. Holding his hand up to warn them to stay back, Maddox asserted control of the encounter by being the one to walk to them. Already sending a clear signal.

'Are you the Bossman?' One of the men asked as Maddox came to a stop several metres away.

'Nah bruv,' Maddox answered, 'he's busy innit.'

'We want to talk to him,' the man said.

'I said he's busy innit, what you want?' Maddox kept his tone blunt but his face passive.

'Your boys are taking too much, we got nothing left,' one of the women said, her face and hair looking filthy and bedraggled.

'Have you seen the infected?' Maddox asked, 'no you don't see them, we sorted them so you got to pay up innit.'

'I got kids,' the woman blurted out, 'they ain't getting enough to eat with your tax taking everything.'

'You's all from the Oak estate innit. How old are your kids?'

'We want to talk with the Bossman not some bloody kid,' the first man to speak said angrily.

'Who are you?' Maddox glared at the man, 'the Bossman busy so you got me, how old are your kids?'

'Twelve and Thirteen,' the woman replied wiping a strand of greasy hair from her face.

'They can come here, live with us, we got plenty of food for them.'

'Yeah 'cos you got all our bloody food,' the first man strode forward, his face red and flustered. Maddox sensed Darius and Sierra shifting behind him and waved his hand at his side, signalling them to stand down.

'You got all the kids here and all the food, we need to eat too, we want our food back.'

'Nah bruv, you get me?'

'Get what? We want our fucking food back.'

'Go find some,' Maddox replied watching the man intently, his face still passive, 'we found our food, you find yours. You pay up and we keep it safe innit.'

'No innit,' the man shouted, his anger exploding at the impudence of the hard faced youth staring back, 'you're just fucking kids playing at grownups, if we had those guns we'd be in charge.'

'But you ain't bruv, you stayed at home shittin' your pants while we got this rigged up, we took the risks and got the prize… go home.'

'You're fucking lucky you got them shotguns behind you,' the man raged from a few feet away, pointing and thrusting his finger at Maddox.

'Or what?' Maddox answered.

'Or I'd kick your fucking head in,' the man bellowed.

'Go home,' Maddox dismissed the man with a sneer, 'tell your kids they can come and live with us. We got weed you can have but no food.'

'Weed?' The woman asked with a sudden interest. You ain't that hungry then are you, Maddox mused to himself.

'We don't want any fucking drugs, we want food,' the man stepped forward again. Maddox stared ahead, avoiding looking at the man but sensing his proximity.

'Back up bruv,' Maddox warned him.

'Why you gonna shoot me?' He sneered, dangerously over stepping the mark.

'Why can't we live here too?' The second woman asked her voice strained and weak.

'No,' Maddox replied, 'go home. You come here again and we'll fuck you up, swear down.'

'Right I want to speak with the Bossman right now,' the man exploded in fury.

'Jeff...' one of the women said with a warning tone.

'No, I'm not going to be told what to do by a bunch of fucking retarded chavvy gangsta kids...' Maddox reacted quickly, crossing the distance and punching the man once in the face; dropping him instantly. No anger, but using violence and fear to enforce the message he'd already given them several times. He also knew that they were being watched by every youth in the compound.

'Go home,' Maddox stared at each of them in turn, his voice still low and calm.

'We're going,' one of the other men darted forward to start dragging the unconscious form away.

'What about the weed?' The woman asked.

'We'll drop some round tomorrow,' Maddox replied. Turning he indicated to the others and started walking back towards the compound. Going ahead with Lenski while Sierra and Darius drop back and cover the rear.

'Why we not give them food?' Lenski asked quietly. Maddox paused before answering, quickly trying to figure if her question was challenging his authority.

'We got plenty of food now, but we also got plenty of hungry mouths to feed and you said it, that food will run out soon if we don't keep it coming in.'

'But the people, they will leave no?'

'Not yet, there's still loads of infected out there and they don't feel safe enough yet. We keep pushing them and take what we can for now. When the time is right we can back off and give a little.'

'This is…how you say…er…the planning?'

'Strategy,' Maddox answered as she nodded in understanding. 'We give in now and they'll want more and more, it's human nature. We stay hard now, take everything and get them scared. We'll know when it's time to change.'

'But you kill the people when they don't pay.' She asked in the same open tone, a look of genuine puzzlement on her face bringing Maddox to a stop. He stared into her eyes, seeing no sign of challenge but a proud woman wanting to know why.

'This wasn't out fault. We didn't cause this. The Bossman reacted quick enough to make the compound and fill it with food. He was already doing the job of the parents to these kids. It was him they came to when they needed help, him they turned to…'

'Not just him no? I think it was you too.'

'Yeah maybe, but *we* got this secured and built. *We* got the food. *We* killed the infected while they hid. They saw us out there fighting and they could have come out and helped. They didn't. If we let them in they'll try and rule it and fuck it up. Yeah we kill when they don't pay. We killed a man today...' He watches her face closely but she shows no reaction 'he didn't pay, I warned him but he came out fighting so we killed him. He had plenty of food that will feed this lot for a while. He was old and had a choice. And his death will tell the others who we are. You get me?'

'You talk in different ways, you are like onion with the layers no?'

'Onion? I ain't no fuckin' onion blood, swear down bruv innit,' he replied quickly with an easy wry smile. Lenski watched his passive face and the deeply intelligent eyes. This youth was a natural leader and she observed that he chose his clothes carefully too. Going for black but not-too-baggy jeans and a plain white t shirt that accentuated his powerful shoulders. No hooded top either, his hair short but not shaved, no baseball cap or head covering. Features open and watchful, never letting his face betray his mind.

Walking back in the gate to an excited buzz of cheering and youths gathering flooding round Maddox, yelling he was the man, and that punch was bad. Maddox took the compliments well, smiling and taking high fives before starting to stride out a few steps and waving his arms to motion them to be silent.

'Listen up,' his voice barely raised quieted the last of the chattering youths, 'this is our base for us. Ain't no mofo's comin' in here and takin' our shit. We the feds now bruv, you get me?' His simple words spoken in a language they understood keyed them up into a frenzy as they cheered loudly.

Waving his arms for silence he saw Darius smiling at him, nodding in compliment.

'Right, we havin' a party here innit, we got tunes, food, liquor and some nice smoke from the Bossman's own private collection,' another cheer sounding out as the children bounce up and down, 'but...listen up, listen up,' Maddox raised his voice slightly and the intense look on his face made them fall silent within seconds, 'I need you to do somethin' for me. If we gonna run this shit we need to be clean innit, some of you's stink worse than the pigs,' some laughs sound out as they soak his words up, 'I want my crews clean you get me? You get clean before you get to party. Darius, you get the crew chiefs wiv me blood, Lenski too. The rest of you do one and get some water.'

As they crowd dispersed Maddox knew he timed it perfectly. The youths, after seeing him lay that man out would have stripped off there and let him hose them down if he'd asked. Hero worship in their eyes, young faces looking up and adoring him.

'What's up Maddox?' Darius asked as they stepped aside to speak quietly. Sierra and Lenski both watching him as the crew chiefs gathered round.

'Nuffin', you?' Maddox gave the instant reply.

'Nuffin,' Darius replied.

'The Bossman said we got to clean them up innit, they get Dysentery and we're fucked,' Maddox explained and stopped as he saw the puzzled looks on more than a few faces, 'It's a disease innit, soldiers get it when they don't wash properly, you get the proper shits and die,' Maddox exaggerated what he'd been told, but knowing he needed to get the seriousness across. 'Sierra, you and Lenski get the girls done. Make sure they're washed proper innit, you get me?'

'Yeah,' Sierra nodded, 'we got shower gel and shampoo innit. Where we doin' this Maddox?'

'Here,' Lenski pointed to the side of unit, 'we got some...er...'

'Screens,' Maddox helped her find the word.

'We got screens no? Stop the boys looking at the boobs,' she smiled, 'the water it cold but the sun it is hot no?'

'Boys round the other side then by the drains, we get screens up too, this ain't no PE lesson for piss taking you get me?' Maddox stared round the male faces, lingering on Ryker for a few seconds.

'It's all good bruv,' Ryker shrugged and nodded.

'Swear down,' Maddox warned them, 'some of them boys is young innit, we ain't no fuckin' teachers bein' all pervy, let them get clean in private.'

'Girls too,' Lenski matched Maddox's glare, 'you keep boys away or I take the gun and shoot them in the balls,' her hard tone taken with her fierce glare caused a few sniggers but the point was made.

'Tonight,' Maddox continued, 'they can chill out and get caned, but we stay on it. Darius, Jagger, Ryland, Mohammed, Sierra, Skyla, Lenski you all wiv me, no booze, no weed. The rest of you chill out but stay sharp.'

'Who you puttin' on the gate?' Mohammed asked, a thickset youth of sixteen with a serious face.

'We doin it, take it in turns innit, you get me?' Maddox replies. He was going to pick Ryker for sentry duty too and make him stay straight, but after the last few days Maddox wanted the lad to feel safe enough to unwind and see how he would react. Maybe provide an opportunity to sort him out properly.

'Questions?' Maddox asked and instantly regretted it. With the crews being so young he forgot the crew chiefs were only slightly older and still youths themselves. Trying to find their feet and learn as they went along. Questions were thrown at Maddox and he did his best to answer all of them, Lenski stepping in and taking a few off him, notes made on her clipboard and telling many of them she would sort it out.

Several minutes later the chiefs were filing away talking amongst themselves, leaving Maddox and Lenski alone.

'Skyla she like you no?' Lenski asked, straight to the point as usual.

'Yeah I guess,' Maddox replied.

'You like her? She very pretty, she make the eyes at you all the time.'

'I saw that,' Maddox grimaced remembering how Sierra pulled the zip lower and lower on her hooded top to show her over developed cleavage thrusting out from her low cut top. The sixteen year old girl was beautiful but that was it. She was sixteen and although Maddox was but two years older, somehow it felt wrong.

'And the boobs, I thought maybe she take them out,' Lenski stayed straight faced making Maddox laugh.

'I think she young for you, you need the real woman,' she winked before turning away with a swish of hair, exaggerating a sexy hip swing and looking back to make sure he was watching, laughing at his evident surprise.

The youths were separated. Boys being taken to the far side by the large drains built into the ground and the girls led away to the front. Screens taken from the cannabis plantation and previously used to block the view from the grimy windows are taken outside and erected as large makeshift shower cubicles. Hoses, used to water the plants are dragged out and fixed to the side of the screen.

Grumbling, moaning, whining and making excuse after excuse the boys lined up as Maddox made the crew chiefs go first. Telling them quietly to show they're enjoying it. Taking it to the next level, the chiefs stripped off one by one and sang their way through the quick shower. Rap songs to start off with quickly change into any tune remembered and within minutes a competition was started with points awarded by the crowd for the song belted out.

The water was freezing, but as Lenski said, the sun was hot and before long the ground was foaming from the liberal amounts of shower gel and shampoo scrubbed and sluiced off. With not enough towels to go round, Maddox ordered them to dry off quickly before getting dressed and stretch the towels out on the hot ground. Darius, showing as good initiative quickly inspects the clothes left by the showering youths and orders the filthiest to be set aside for washing. Those without new clothes were taken aside by Mohammed and Ryland to be supplied with new garments taken from the looted shops.

Round the other side of the units, the girls fared much better. Naturally inclined to be cleaner than teenage boys the girls relished the chance to wash and each one took several minutes to scrub and wash their hair. A second hose was dragged out and some of the more confident girls showered two at a time. Chattering and laughing about the boys, who fancies who and badgering Lenski for new clothes and make-up.

Within an hour the youths were clean for the first time in days and Maddox stared glumly at the pile of filthy garments left over, then shaking his head as the girls filter back round followed by Lenski and Sierra carrying armfuls of dirty clothes, quickly dumped onto the already huge mound.

'So I will be cleaning these too?' Lenski asked with a challenging look. Maddox stared back and shrugged, suddenly feeling out of his depth for the first time since it began.

Picking up on the subtle change in his eyes, Lenski quickly smiled, 'it's not big problem, we clean them.'

'Okay,' Maddox smiled back. The resilient lad was used to looking after himself, using laundries to get his own clothing washed and taking care over his appearance. But suddenly having to sort out the laundry for so many filthy kids clothes was too much.

'They need burning,' Sierra added with a grimace.

'Punishment detail,' Maddox said quietly then looked to the two women, 'we use it as punishment when they fuck up.'

'Might work,' Sierra nodded.

'Is better than my girls doing it,' Lenski agreed.

'Maddox, is Lenski a crew chief?' Sierra suddenly asked an innocent question that showed her young age. Being unable to just accept the situation fluidly and needing the rank structure laid out clearly.

'No, Lenski is in charge of the base when I'm not here,' Maddox replied in a tone that did not invite further conversation.

'So does that mean she's number three then?' Sierra asked, clearly showing she missed the tone that didn't invite further conversation.

'I am not number,' Lenski interrupted, annoyed at being spoken about like she wasn't there.

'The Bossman is one, Maddox is number two so you must be three innit?' Sierra said as if it made the most perfect sense.

'Yes.' Maddox said with a glance at Lenski.

'Yay,' Sierra quickly hugged the startled Polish woman and walked off beaming, telling Darius that Lenski was number three now.

'Nice one,' Darius shouted over and set about telling more people, who in turn told more people who then stared back at Lenski smiling.

'I am not number,' Lenski grumbled to Maddox.

'You are now,' Maddox replied, 'you just got promoted.'

'Do I get the pay rise too?' Lenski nodded at the grinning youths as the latest gossip that Lenski was number three whipped through the camp.

'Yeah, you get more weed,' Maddox joked, knowing Lenski, like him, didn't smoke it.

'I never try it,' she replied.

'Never?'

'I never do the drugs. Is it nice?'

'They like it,' Maddox shrugged.

'Do you like it?'

'No, I like being in control,' Maddox replied.

'Yes. I see that.'

'They'll want to know who is number four next, then five and down to the last one.'

'Three is enough?'

'For now,' Maddox said, his mind already working ahead and seeing the power struggles that could break out as the youths clambered for authority over the rest, 'they'll want deputy crew chiefs, assistant crew chiefs and someone in charge of the toilet.'

'You remind me now, we need more toilets, there is only a few here.'

'I know,' Maddox replied, 'add it to the list.'

'I did that already.' They stand in silence, two young people drawn together and watching a new society form right in front of them. One, a hardened black youth takes everything in, watching the subtle behaviours that shape the culture already developing. The other, a young woman from a different country, clutching a clipboard and blowing a stray strand of hair from her eyes, seeing tasks that need to be done, making lists and nodding to herself as she mentally ticks them off.

'Rats and cockroaches,' Maddox says quietly.

'Where?' Lenski looked at the ground in alarm.

'Us, we're rats and cockroaches. There was something the Bossman told me that the only things that would survive a nuclear war would be rats and cockroaches,' he shrugged, 'that's us.'

'I am not rat!' Lenski exclaimed.

'Cockroach then?' Maddox smiled.

'I give you the cockroach, I put them in your bed,' she said laughing before walking away with another disdainful look at the mound of stinking clothes.

Food is prepared by the girls in the units, helped out here and there by the younger youths drawn to the older women by a sense of being near someone maternal and caring. The power is taken from the lighting units set up above the plants and diverted to the games station and monitors. Music decks and speakers are dragged out near the pit, wires stretching back inside the units. Youths gather and congregate as a sense of excitement grows. Play lists are formulated and arguments break out over who is going first on the decks. With many budding DJ's all wanting to display their skills Darius and Mohammed are forced to step in and resolve the disagreements by pushing the youths back and organising a list.

The prepared food is given out one crew at a time as they withdraw to their tents to eat together, a rule enforced by Maddox to prevent squabbling and all out carnage. Peace descends for a short time, giving the older youths and crew chiefs a chance to get the final touches ready. Some old disco lights are stretched round the pit, some of the plant UV lights stacked here and there. Then into the units to gather up the pre-wrapped lumps of weed. Taken round to the tents by Maddox and Darius, each youth given enough to see them through the night.

Maddox, never before feeling any sense of guilt about supplying the weed and taking the cash for it, feels a deepening sense of shame and worry. Young kids, some of them barely ten years old, reach out to take the cannabis in their small hands. Smiling with red tired looking eyes. Children given a drug to keep them passive and quiet. He understands the thought process, that having so many young people ripped away from whatever fucked up family life they had and shoving them into an area with no real care or love is a recipe for disaster, but giving them drugs to keep them docile? Is this the right thing to do?

Confused at the new thoughts creeping into his mind, Maddox moved from tent to tent. Seeing the way the young look up to him, eager for a few words or something said by Maddox that would mean he's noticed them. He takes his time and mentions each youth by name, telling them they're doing a good job, mentioning a joke heard about them, or a boy or girl he saw watching them. He takes it easy with the shy ones, speaking quieter and with a softer tone. Hardening his jokes and banter with the more rough and ready lads. The girls make eyes at him, zips get pulled down and cleavages pushed out. He pretends not to notice and keeps eye contact, smiling, joking, sharing stories and listening to their tales.

As he steps out of the last tent his eyes move back to the end of the units, where the Bossman's office is. Knowing the great man will be sat inside smoking a joint and jotting down his yields, power output, water usage and leaving everything to Maddox. Wondering if the Bossman will make an appearance tonight, Maddox heads back towards the pit and the final touches being put to the decks. The Bossman got all this set up; he moved quickly while everyone else stood with their mouths hanging open and hid under their beds but for the last few days he's stayed in his rooms.

The afternoon draws into evening. A palpable dual sense of nervous excitement spreads through the compound. Worry, that the night will draw the infected out, if they will hear the howls tonight, if any of them will charge at the gates or fence. But looking forward to dancing, drinking, smoking weed and getting caned.

As the night started to fall Maddox stood at the top of the compound, on the corner of the building line, maintaining a view of the tents, the building and the front gate as the sun dropped below the line of council houses. The crew chiefs, spotting him looking into the sky signal for their crews to be silent, faces go taught and look up. Youths moved out from the tents to stand in silence.

Maddox swiftly checked the gate nodding to Darius stood there holding an old rifle. Lenski and the girls, on hearing the sudden drop in noise emerged from the open door and stand in silence. Worried expressions etched onto their tired faces. Lenski holds her clipboard to her chest. Maddox knows the area has been swept clean, and nearly every house in the nearby vicinity has been checked but the worry that they could have shuffled back into the streets and now, with the daylight fading they could turn and come after the smell of fresh tender young meat.

Long minutes ticked away. In the built up urban and without a view of the natural horizon it was impossible to tell when the sun was down and the night was properly upon them. But still they waited as the sky grew darker with each passing second. No howls sounded out, ripping the air apart. Silence everywhere. With a pre-arranged signal Maddox nodded at Mohammed on the decks. He flicked a switch, lights flashed on and the solid bass beat stormed out from the speakers. The youths, still looking up at the sky jump and twitch, spinning round to look at the grinning Mohammed and the multi coloured lights. Ryland, on seeing the signal drops a match into the pit and steps back as the long flames shoot up from the petrol soaked logs already stacked in place.

Cheering erupts and the youths surge forward. The now clean and scrubbed faces bursting with relief in the absolute belief that if Maddox says it's safe then it must be. Seconds later the young boys and girls are jumping round releasing the anxiety. The older ones hold back and saunter in casually, trying to look cool and show a sense of not being bothered.

Hearing laughing Maddox turns to see Lenski and the girls all smiling and pointing at the dancing youths. She smiles a huge grin at Maddox, offering a little wave. He nods back and turns to see Darius intently staring out through the gap, peering down the street.

'So you gonna get wiv Skyla then bruv?' Darius asked his friend as they stood by the main gate a few minutes later.

'Nah mate,' Maddox shook his head.

'She's fit innit.' Darius observed.

'Yeah but not my style,' Maddox said.

'Lenski?' Darius asked watching closely for a reaction, knowing his friends ability to stay completely straight faced.

'Nah bruv, too busy innit. Swear down we got too much going on here,' Maddox replied.

'You see the Bossman?' Darius changed subject, being reminded of how busy Maddox was. He, almost as much as the Bossman, knew how capable Maddox was and how much the compound now relied on him.

'Earlier,' Maddox shrugged.

'He still sat inside with his toke?'

'Yeah innit,' Maddox smiled.

'He comin' out tonight or what?' Darius asked, wondering along with everyone else why the Bossman was keeping to his office so much.

'He won't,' Maddox said.

'Is he alright then?'

'Dunno, he seemed alright but just sits inside smoking weed and workin' out the yields and crops.' Maddox replied. Darius inhaled sharply as though it was a bad thing Maddox had said.

'He's leavin' it all to you bruv.'

'We need him,' Maddox said quickly, wanting to dispel any stupid idea that might be forming in his friends mind. 'He knows more than us, he got this place sorted and he said about the Dysentery, we don't know stuff like that.'

'Fact,' Darius quickly sided with Maddox, picking up on his quick reply and wanting to show he didn't mean anything.

'You hungry bruv? Go get some food and I'll stay here.'

'Sure?' Darius checked before starting to stroll off.

'Watch Ryker,' Maddox called out, 'I don't like that kid, he's trouble innit.'

'I'm all over it,' Darius raised an arm and was soon lost in the deep shadows. Alone, Maddox leant against the gate and thought once more about the scaffold tower they need to be able to see over the gate instead of peering through the gap. One of the garden centres nearby should have something they could use. Then he thought to the local shops and the scaffolding rigged up round one of them while work was being carried out. Just take that, he mused quietly. Get the crews to carry it back. Need some lights out here, too dark now the street lamps are gone. Spotlights or something on the top of the scaffold tower like the guard towers have in the movies.

The beat of the music drifted round to him and Maddox found himself humming along with the tune being played. The estate was huge, covering miles of social housing and run down streets. Bordered on two sides by fields and open countryside that was rarely ventured into and cut off by strong high metal fencing. An agreement worked out by the farmers before the project was started. The north side was cut off by the motorway and the south by the shore. Those houses on the shore were nice and kept by for the families that proved they could look after their properties.

Thoughts poured through his mind, working out ways to maximise the area. He could use the school playing fields to plant crops, and maybe get some of the crews down on the shore catching fish. He knew there were still hordes of the infected gathered about, but eventually they would be killed off, more might come but they would be dealt with too. Thinking back to the conversation he had with Lenski earlier he wondered how he knew what he knew. The Bossman had taught him many things but most of it was down to Maddox growing up on the streets and learning quickly. Striving to drag himself out of the benefit dependant life that everyone else seemed to cling too. He knew the risks of dealing but took those risks knowing it was the quickest way to get money, status and then get out and be somewhere else. He wasn't drawn to the world of gangsta. He wanted out and that was the way to do it. But now, now it was all gone and out of necessity he was left holding the baby.

There was no reason why some of these houses couldn't be converted to house the cannabis plants. Put solar panels on the roof and then use the space in the units for living in when the weather got bad. He thought the Bossman wouldn't like that idea, being away from his babies.

But if they extended the compound out to take in the houses then they would be safe, and maybe use a few of them to live in too. In time, they could keep extended the fence and barricade out and create a big compound but then the adults would want in. More adults meant more problems and it would mean having to make more deputies, more helpers, more guards, more guns then it was back to the shit community that was here before.

'The great leader should be with the people no?' Lenski said, interrupting his thoughts and holding out a mug of steaming black coffee. Not sure if she meant him or the Bossman he simply took the coffee and smiled.

'Are you hungry?' She asked.

'Nah, I had something before.'

'We take out the crisps and snacks you said, they go mad and eat them like pigs, everywhere it smell of the weed and they drinking the beer too.'

'A mess then,' Maddox asked imagining the chaos that would reigning on the other side of the units.'

'But they enjoy it,' she added, 'the little ones are dropping off.'

'Ryker?' Maddox looked at the woman, his meaning clear.

'Ah, he is loud,' Lenski nodded, 'he shouting and making noise and I heard him shouting with Mohammed.'

'What about?'

'I not know this, the music it is too loud no? But Darius he speak and make him calm.'

'Okay.'

'So what you do here alone?' She asked quietly.

'Thinking, we could move the fence out and take in those houses,' Maddox nodded to the nearby buildings, 'be better when the weather gets colder.'

'It is good plan,' she nodded.

'Maddox!' Mohammed sprinted round the corner shouting in alarm. 'Ryker's going fuckin' nuts innit, he's got a blade out.'

'Take this and stay here,' Maddox thrust the shotgun at a startled Lenski who held the foreign object at arm's length.

'What I do?'

'Point and pull the trigger,' Maddox shouted already running after Mohammed. He expected Ryker to do something stupid, in fact he was banking on it so he could sort the lad out properly, but pulling a blade is serious. A thin layer of smoke rests gently on the warm air above the open ground, caused by the fire burning from the pit and the joints being puffed continually. The constant bass beat of the music abruptly ceases as he charges past Mohammed towards the crowd gathered round the far side of the pit, all turned away and watching something blocked from Maddox's view.

Pushing his way through Maddox breaks out from the crowd and Ryker stood holding a long knife, fresh blood dripping from the blade and soaking his hand. His eyes look wild, feral. Darius stood in front of him pointing his rifle at Ryker and shouting for the youths behind him to move. Sierra edging in closer also with her weapon pointing at the frenzied looking lad.

'DROP THE BLADE,' Darius's voice booms out, the pitch higher and showing his young age.

'FUCK YOU, I SWEAR DOWN I'LL SHANK YOU UP,' Ryker screamed back, spittle flying from his lips as he backed away, eyes darting left and right.

Maddox stepped round Darius and spotted Zayden lying on the ground, his small hands clutching the bleeding wound in his stomach and crying quietly, whimpering for help.

'Pull him away,' Maddox shouted at the closest youths, pointing at Zayden, 'get him inside and get something on him to stop him bleeding.' Maddox, unarmed and glaring with wide eyes pushed past Darius to step in front of Ryker, 'WHAT DID YOU DO?' He roars.

Ryker fixed his eyes on Maddox, fear flitted across his face and he raised the knife higher, pointing it at Maddox.

'He fuckin' dissed me innit,' Ryker shouted defensively.

'He's a fucking kid,' Maddox bellowed back.

'New rules blood, I ain't getting dissed by no one,' Ryker sneered waving the blade at Maddox. His drug and alcohol fuelled brain buzzes with adrenalin. The sudden ending of his medication for severe hyper-activity sending him steadily spiralling. Boundaries blurring as the position of crew chief boosts his self-image, propelling his behaviour to plummet as desperately tries to show his crew how ruthless and hard he is. Zayden, the small terrified lad sat near him smoking weed and drinking Vodka, trying to show Lauren he can hang with the bigger boys. As the banter got worse he tried to keep up, using swear words he'd never normally use until he crossed the line and laughingly called Ryker a twat. He over-stepped the mark and he had to be dealt with. Ryker, desperate not to lose face confronted him with a violent outburst of temper. Demanding he say sorry. Zayden laughed for a couple of minutes before realising the other youths were backing away in fear and leaving him isolated in front of the raging crew chief. He did apologise, despite feeling the shame in front of the terrified Lauren. But the damage was done and nothing Zayden could have said or done would change the outcome. Ryker needed to prove himself so he pulled the blade from his waistband and shoved the pointed end deep into Zayden's soft stomach. Screams erupted as Ryker pulled the knife out and held the trembling child by one hand before shoving him to the ground with a look of disgust. Expecting a cheer for his actions Ryker was confused when he was suddenly surrounded with everyone yelling at him and Darius pointing his rifle.

'You is a scrawny little prick,' Maddox said through gritted teeth. The silence became profound as the youths flicked their eyes between the stand-off. 'You hear me Ryker? I said you is a scrawny little prick. I'm dissin' you Ryker, calling you out bruv innit.'

'Fuck you Maddox,' Ryker screamed back, feeling a sense of fear creeping up inside.

'Scrawny,' Maddox drew the words out, dragging the sound so everyone could hear, 'little prick innit, shank a little kid? You a pussy bruv.' Maddox stepped forward, his arms down at his sides. Ryker backed up waving the blade at the advancing figure.

'You ain't a crew chief no more, you cleaning the toilets now innit, you got to clean everyone shit up. I'll make you wear a dress and call you Nancy.'

'FUCK OFF,' Ryker screamed his face contorting with rage.

'Nancy,' Maddox goaded him.

'FUCKOFF...'

'Nancy.'

'JUSFUCKOFF,' Ryker's words flew from his mouth as he lunged forward and swiped the blade at Maddox who simply blocked the swing and gripped Ryker by the wrist, twisting viciously and causing the blade to drop from his paralysed hand. Maddox pulled his fist back and repeatedly slammed the hard knuckles into Ryker's screaming face. Writhing and trying to break free, Ryker desperately twisted and turned. Maddox stepping round with him and sending punch after punch into his face. The hard blows splitting his lips open, cracking teeth, breaking his nose, fracturing eye sockets and still he didn't stop. As Ryker dropped down Maddox went with him using two hands to rein blow after blow into his head. Ryker slipped into unconsciousness as Maddox grasped him by his collar and started dragging him over towards the big drains. Ditching the twitching form on the ground he turned and pulled the shotgun from Sierra, opening the weapon and checking each barrel before slamming it shut. Without a break in stride he walked back, pointed the weapon at Ryker's head and pulled the trigger. The booming retort rolled round the enclosed camp as Ryker's head eviscerated, leaving a bloody stump and a pink mist hanging in the air.

A single piercing scream erupted from deep within the crowded youths. Young faces squeezing eyes closed, tears streaming down soft cheeks. No one spoke. No one moved.

Maddox turned round and stood facing the crowd as he quickly opened the breech and ejected the spent cartridge, instinctively pulling a new one from his pocket, ramming it home and snapping the weapon closed. Handing the gun back to Sierra he addressed the youths.

'He had it coming,' Maddox's voice carried loud and clear, 'but he was right about one thing, these are new rules. We don't have the feds now, no courts and no trials. If anyone does shit like that they can expect the same,' his street language slipped but not one youth noticed as they stared at their leader, hanging from his awful words. 'I will take care of you, we will all take care of each other, we are family, but that...' he pointed at the bloodied corpse, 'is bad shit. We don't use weapons on each other, if we have an issue we sort it out. You all watched Ryker shank Zayden. You should have stopped him but you was all too stoned.' Maddox shook his head knowing they would have been too terrified to confront the crazed Ryker but using the time to ram a point home, 'too much weed will fuck you up,' he continued, 'and we don't mix weed with booze, parties over. Get this cleaned up and no weed for the next few nights.' Maddox knew the Bossman wouldn't like the ban, but he did say he was in charge.

The crew chiefs moved in swiftly, breaking the crowd apart and ushering them away. Muted chatter filled the air; the shock of the event was palpable. Maddox swept his eyes across the crowd, coming to rest on the soft orange glow coming from the open door to the units. The Bossman stood in silhouette watching the proceedings while puffing away on his joint. Maddox stared back as the orange glow came back again, then the Bossman was gone, moving back to his quarters and leaving Maddox to deal with everything again.

Lenski appeared coming round the building, her hands free from the clipboard for the first time in days. She walked straight at Maddox and stopped when she saw the bloodied headless cadaver on the ground. Taking the sight in with a glance she betrayed no reaction, simply staring at Maddox with an intense gaze.

'Zayden got stabbed in the stomach,' Maddox said quietly.

'Where is he?' Lenski asked with sudden concern.

'They took him inside.' Maddox replied to the already running form of Lenski sprinting for the door. She pushed her way through the youths and disappeared inside.

'I got this bruv,' Darius said from nearby and motioning his head towards the dead body, 'do what you gotta do, we'll get it cleared up.'

Maddox nodded and walked quickly after Lenski, the crowd parting as the poker faced man walked through and entered the gloom of the units.

Inside, he made his way through the building to the lights in the rear section with the adult plants. Zayden laid out on blankets. The tiny body looking more like the child he was than ever before. His top pulled up to show the bright red blood making his skin look pale and white. The body inert, the chest not rising or falling. Maddox stops inches from his head and looks down to the pale face and the eyes staring lifelessly up at him. From this angle it looks like Zayden is staring straight into Maddox's eyes. He survived the apocalypse only to die on the filthy floor of a drugs factory, stabbed to death by a teenager high on drugs and booze. Streaks of tears mark the child's face forming clean lines through the dirt. The blood on his hands is red and wet, glistening from the lights shining on the plants.

Thoughts burn through Maddox's mind, spiralling and plummeting but still his face remains expressionless. Not one kid had been lost since this began. There had been injuries, sprains, cuts but not one of them had been bitten, but right here and now, staring down at the lifeless form of a child bled out from a needless single stab to the stomach makes him feel dirty.

'What we do now?' Lenski stood up wiping the blood from her hands on a rag.

'We bury him,' Maddox replied.

'Where?'

'Here.'

'No. We need the ground for crops, not here.'

'Where then?'

'Somewhere else, is there a church here?'

'Yeah, and a synagogue and a mosque, but no ground on any of them. Just buildings.'

'Somewhere, do you know his house?'

'Yeah.'

'It has garden?'

'No, he lived in a council flat.'

'At the school then?'

'We need the field for crops too...and he hated school, they all did.'

'I not know,' Lenski sighed dropping her head.

'Wrap the bodies in refuse bags and sheets; put them in the sentry hut.'

'Okay, I do this. Where are you going?'

'To see the Bossman.'

Maddox walked away, shoulders brushing against the leaves of the plants stretching out to absorb the light shining down. Sweat on his head shining from the heat and humidity. He walked through the units, reaching the door of the Bossman's room, walking straight in without pause. The lights off and the room reeked of cannabis, heavy smoke hung in the air stinging his eyes and catching in his throat. The soft orange glow ignites from the chair behind the desk as the Bossman inhaled another drag of his joint. Maddox stands feet from the desk, his anger and hurt suddenly abating from the shock of finding the Bossman sat alone in the dark. His eyes slowly adjust to the gloom as the light from the still open door permeates the room. The silhouette of the Bossman forms gradually. Sat back in his chair and staring straight at Maddox. Waiting in silence.

'Is he dead?' The Bossman asked his voice low and hoarse from the harsh smoke.

'Yes,' Maddox replied.

Silence descended again. Oppressive and charged, the end of the joint flares as another drag is taken. The Bossman exhaled slowly, smoke spiralling from his mouth.

'Ryker stabbed him,' Maddox added.

'So you shot Ryker,' the Bossman's reply is instant and challenging.

'He stabbed Zayden,' Maddox replied equally as quickly.

'So that makes you jury judge and executioner does it?'

'What?'

'You're a killer,' the statement is tinged with a very slight slur but the tone is dangerously low.

'We've all killed,' Maddox said.

'The infected don't count,' the Bossman said.

'So what should I have done?' Maddox asked after a long pause.

'I've been watching you Maddox, watching how they come running to you. They didn't come to me when Ryker stabbed Zayden, they ran to you.'

'You put me in charge, I been on the ground with them for the last few days...'

'So that makes you number one now does it?'

'What? No!'

'Seems like it to me, Maddox the great. Doesn't smoke weed, doesn't drink. Holier than fucking thou ain't ya...

'Boss...'

'...You sold this shit and made money but you never touched it, never liked being out of control did you Maddox. Now look at you, got a whole camp running at your every whim, shooting little kids in the face...'

'Boss!'

'Go and wash my boys and girls...Go and eat vegetables my boys and girls, don't smoke drugs my little children...I am Maddox. I am fucking better...'

'Boss please,' Maddox asked his tone low and still unable to see the Bossman clearly in the dark shadows.

'What?' The Bossman suddenly asked, 'what do you want from me?'

'Ryker was bad, we talked about it earlier. You told me to watch him...he fucking stabbed Zayden. He had to go.'

'Go?'

'What...'

'Go where Maddox, where did you send him?'

'Boss, you know what I meant. We couldn't kick him out. He's too dangerous and could have whipped up support from the survivors on the estate. We had to sort him...'

'We Maddox, we did that did we? We decided to shoot him did we?'

'You were watching, you could have said something.'

'Say something to the mighty Maddox...you might have decided to shoot me with the other barrel.'

'I wouldn't do that,' Maddox said softly. The Bossman was stoned out of his mind, slurring but his voice was hard. Maddox had never seen him like this. Never seen him showing the effects of cannabis and never drunk.

'Coming after me next are ya?'

'No Boss.'

'Wanna be number one eh my lad?'

'No.'

'Numero uno...Maddox the numero uno,' the Bossman giggled suddenly. The wheezing of his chest clearly audible.

'Boss I'll come back later.'

'No!' The Bossman snapped, stopping Maddox as he turned to the door, 'you overstepped the mark boy...who are you to tell them not to smoke weed?' The slur of his tone ends as he spit the words out.

'They needed a break...'

'Don't speak back to me,' the Bossman growled, 'I'm the boss here Maddox. I make the rules. It seems you've gotten a bit too big for your boots my lad.' The Bossman rose from the chair, stubbing the joint out and easing himself round the desk. Pausing briefly to gain his balance from wobbling on unsteady feet he walked round to stand directly in front of Maddox. Closer now Maddox can see his eyes are vacant from the weed and his face looks drawn. Standing face to face the Bossman slapped Maddox round the face. Once. Hard. The sound ringing out and causing Maddox to flare his eyes. With gritted determination he stands his ground and shows no reaction.

'Come on Maddox,' the Bossman reeked of tobacco, alcohol and weed, breathing foul breath into Maddox's face. 'Come on then boy,' he goaded again, pushing Maddox in the chest.

Feeling a rare surge of anger Maddox squeezes his hands into fists at the side of his body, tensing his muscles and staring straight ahead.

'You know what you are Maddox...' The Bossman leant in, millimetres from the youth's face, purposefully breathing a low blast of fetid air into eyes. Maddox held his rage in check, hard lessons learnt from a hard life and every ounce of strength pitted against showing a reaction.

'You know what you are...boy...' the Bossman poked Maddox in the chest with the end of one finger, prodding his pectoral muscle and forcing him back a step. Seeing the reaction, the Bossman repeated it, prodding harder and forcing Maddox back again.

'I'm gonna tell you what you are....' He poked his digit hard into the muscle forcing Maddox to half turn as he stumbled back, quickly regaining his balance and breathing deeply.

'You...are a jumped up street nigger,' the atmosphere changed instantly as Maddox whipped his head round to glare straight into the eyes of the suddenly frightened Bossman. His fists clenched and he exhaled once. The rage driven into cold fury and he lashed out hard. Driving those already bloodied knuckles into the Bossman's face.

The Bossman reeled back, slamming into the desk and crying out in a strangled yell. Scrabbling furiously on the desk the Bossman brought his knee up hard into Maddox's groin. He flinched back enough for the Bossman to roll away, falling with a thump to the floor and crashing into the chair he was using just seconds before.

Recovering quickly, Maddox knew this had to end. The Bossman won't stop now, his pride, his power, his survival hinges on beating Maddox. Both men knew the prize at hand and the forfeit if they lost. Maddox launched himself over the top of the wide desk intent on landing on the older man and finishing the job. The Bossman, suddenly alert and realising the danger grabbed at the pistol grip poking out of the open drawer. Maddox slammed into him, driving him down into the ground and forcing the air from his lungs. The Bossman, in reaction tensed his hands and pulled the trigger of the pistol not seen by Maddox. The gunshot deafened them both in the enclosed room, the ricochet pinging off followed instantly by the sound of splintering wood. Maddox reacted quickly, now knowing his employer and mentor was holding a gun he drove the back of his elbow into the Bossman's skull. His face slammed against the hard floor, nose breaking as the Bossman screamed with agony pulling the trigger again and desperately trying to buck the youth off.

Maddox slammed his elbow down again and went for the gun, reaching out with both hands to grip the pistol and twisting round to drive his feet repeatedly into the Bossman's head and neck. The gun fired again as the Bossman tried to desperately empty the magazine before Maddox gained control of the weapon. Gunshot after gunshot rang out as they fought, kicking, writhing and screaming with terrified rage. Maddox lifted his foot and slammed the heel down on the side of the Bossman's face breaking the cheekbone. The grip on the pistol loosened enough for Maddox to twist it free from his hand.

Losing the gun and screaming in terror the Bossman rolled away as Maddox fumbled with the weapon, got his hand on the grip and his finger on the trigger and fired point blank range into the solid mass of the Bossman. Two shots ripped through his upper body and the third made a small neat entry into his cheek and took the back of his head off. Skull, brains and blood sprayed out in a wide arc coating the wall.

Maddox stayed in position, breathing hard and hardly believing what had just happened. His ears were ringing from the gunshots, the stench of cordite and cannabis made his eyes water. The Bossman lay dead just a few feet from him. The back of his head gone.

Slowly he lowered the pistol and gave a silent thanks for the lessons the Bossman had given him, showing him how to load, clean and fire the different guns available on the black market. Using the desk he levered himself up and stared down at the third person killed in the compound within the last few minutes. Two of them from his own hands.

'Maddox...' Lenski whispered. Leaning on the desk he dropped his head and looked back at the door and Darius, Sierra and Lenski stood there.

'He went for me...' Maddox straightened up and turned towards them, the pistol held down at his side.

'We saw,' Darius said quietly.

'Is he dead?' Sierra asked their view of the Bossman blocked by the desk and the gloom.

'Yeah,' Maddox replied looking back at the corpse. Lenski entered first, carrying a large torch and shining it down onto the body. The other two filtered in behind her and stared down. After nine days of constant killing neither of them flinched at the corpse but they both reeled from the implication.

'I shouldn't have come in here,' Maddox shook his head, 'I knew he'd be stoned...but not that much.'

'Bruv, after what happened you had to see him innit,' Darius said, 'he fucked up.'

'Maddox, this not your fault. He called you nigger and he hitting you. He try to shoot you.'

'I know,' Maddox breathed out deeply, 'how's everyone out there?'

'You not worry, they good now.'

'Did anyone else see it?' Maddox asked worrying if the news had yet spread. On seeing the nods he groaned, knowing the camp would be buzzing and terrified from the killings and what it meant.

'Come on,' he nodded as he moved towards the door.

'What you do?' Lenski reached out pulling his arm back to turn Maddox round.

'We need to speak to everyone.'

'Now?' Darius cut in.

'Yeah now,' Maddox stared at Lenski, not wanting to pull his arm away by force. She dropped her hand and nodded, knowing it was the right thing to do.

The four of them filed out of the room as the full weight of the consequences hit Maddox. This was his. His compound. These were his people. Ending it like this was wrong. But it had happened and Maddox knew there was a secure compound of feral youths, drugs, booze and guns and if he didn't act quickly it would fall within hours.

Lenski picked up on a similar train of thought herself. At first she thought her and the other older girls had been allowed in to give sexual favours or services to the older lads and the Bossman. But despite some clumsy flirty comments from a few youths, not one of them had tried anything. Even the Bossman had acted properly and he could have taken what he wanted with impunity. Lenski had watched Maddox transform over the last few days. At first he followed the Bossman at every step, but now he made his own decisions with confidence.

They walked through the units and past the blood stains on the ground where Zayden had bled out before his body was removed. Youths were all through the units staring quietly as Maddox and the others walked through. They ran ahead and out the doors, alerting the others that Maddox was coming out.

As they stepped out of the units and into the cooler night air Maddox saw the fire in the pit was still burning and the music decks were being slowly dismantled. The atmosphere was electric as terrified faces stared at him. Eyes wide with the shock of seeing Ryker kill Zayden. Then Maddox kill Ryker and now hearing that the Bossman had attacked Maddox.

Maddox, leading Lenski, Darius and Sierra moved over to the pit so the flames would illuminate him, making him visible to everyone. He stood silent for a few seconds breathing deeply and staring down at the dancing flames. The smell of wood smoke was a blessed change from the reek of cannabis and pistol fire.

'The Bossman, he attacked Maddox,' Lenski spoke out in a clear loud voice surprising Maddox. 'I see this, Darius and Sierra they see this too. He attack Maddox and call him the street nigger,' gasps sweep round as air is sucked in quickly. It wasn't the word used that made them gasp. The word was familiar to them in everyday language, as well as a thousand other insulting and extreme words. What made them prick up was that Maddox had been called it. And by the Bossman.

'The Bossman tried to shoot Maddox with the pistol,' Lenski said. 'Maddox defend and he kill the Bossman.' Audible gasps, mouths drop open and eyes go wide as the rumour so freshly circulated and hardly believed, despite the gunshots, was so quickly and bluntly confirmed.

'Listen up,' Maddox's deep voice boomed out. 'This happened but it doesn't change anything for us. We still the same and we carry on like we were. You still get food and clothes, we still run this estate and this is still our base. The Bossman was a good man, but the weed fucked him up. It made him paranoid and sick, same with Ryker. It fucks you up good and proper if you take it all the time. We got a lot of work to do now...'

'Are you in charge now Maddox?' One of the youths called out.

'You the Bossman now?' Another voice added.

'I am in charge now,' Maddox nodded, 'but I'm not the Bossman, he's dead. I'm still Maddox.'

'Do we still call you Maddox?' The first voice called out again. Maddox smiled to himself at the thought that the youths need that authority to cling on to, who is in charge? Who is boss?

'Nah you's got to call me Mr Maddox Sir now innit bruv,' the youths laughed at the quick joke and Maddox smiling. He looked normal to them. The same man they'd come to accept as their leader over the last days. The Bossman was always spoken about but it was Maddox who did all the work and they all knew it.

'It's Maddox,' Maddox added quickly before anyone could think it was his real name from now on.

'Get some rest, we'll sort this out and everything will be okay. Crew chiefs come over here for a minute...well what you's looking at? Go on, get some rest.' The youths shuffled away as the crowd broke up. The same Maddox as every other night telling them to go to sleep and rest. Reassured that things seemed okay they formed groups and talked quietly. Most of them still coming down from the weed smoked through the evening.

Maddox waited until the crew chiefs were assembled round him, nodding at some of the youths hanging around too close, motioning them to move away with a warning smile.

'That was bang out of order he calling you that,' Skyla said, moving to stand close by Maddox and already pulling the zip down to show her heaving cleavage.

'That's fuckin' sweet that you're in charge now Maddox,' Ryland said with a grin.

'Yeah,' Maddox nodded back, 'listen, when the survivors on the estate find out the Bossman is dead they'll think we're weak,' He explained watching their faces, 'so they might come and try it on here, try and get in or take over. I want double guards on here which means the crews will be smaller, so I want each crew to pair up with another one. The chiefs share the responsibility and also I want one crew chief awake all the time and overseeing the guards.' The chiefs listened intently as Maddox outlined the immediate changes. Drawing up a list of watches starting from then and telling the chiefs he wanted them checking the gate and walking the compound too.

As he spoke, more idea's started forming. More plans and the realisation that he could implement what he wanted now without having to check first. He held himself back from going through more, seeing the chiefs yawning and fidgeting.

Eventually he sent them off, reminding them to stick to the watch list and report directly to him or Lenski if anything happened.

Maddox took Ryland and Darius into the Bossman's room and wrapped the heavy body in black bin bags before rolling him and the bits of him splattered about, into a sheet and carrying him outside to join the other two bodies in the sentry hut.

Finally at some point during the early hours he entered his room and collapsed exhausted on the bed. Staring up at the low ceiling, his mind a blur with the future and how things can be different. How he can make them different. Less drugs. Better food. Safer.

Something about the deaths he caused and the emotions he felt sparked a thought process and awakened a sense of remorse about the survivors killed on the estate. They had to be dealt with, that much was for sure but now after this night he realises that death was easy to give. If there is to be a future then it should be a decent one, otherwise what's the point? Why go through all this just so they can kill more people?

The sudden realisation that what they've been doing is wrong burns through his soul. This isn't the way; he knows this but the thoughts become muddled and slip into visceral images spinning through his head as he drifts into the first layer of sleep, images of Zayden stood out on the junction holding his bleeding stomach while laughing about the box of condoms.

The eighteen year old hardened criminal sleeps fitfully as he becomes the new leader of a community of drug addicted kids, and one with a sudden conscious.

Three

Day Ten.

Sunday.

Maddox wakes instantly from the loud knocking at his door, still dressed and flat on his back in the same position that he flaked out in just a few hours ago.

'Yeah?' His voice sounds deep and ragged, unrecognised by his own ears. The door opens to show Lenski stood there smiling and holding two steaming mugs. She's dressed in different clothes, jeans and a simple top. She looks clean and fresh.

'Everything okay?' He asks quickly.

'Sure sure,' she waves her free hand gently, motioning him to stay put, 'I knew you want to be awake before the youths yes? So I bring you coffee.'

'Coffee,' Maddox repeats the word dumbly before collapsing back down. He stretches his arms and legs out groaning noisily.

'Ssshh,' Lenski laughs, 'they will think we are doing the sex.' She stands at the end of the bed staring down as Maddox looks up quickly from the mention of the word sex from a beautiful woman stood in his room, 'ha! That got you awake,' she laughs again.

'Not funny,' Maddox groans sitting up and extending his hand for the coffee. She steps in and passes the cup. Fingers brushing as his hands fumble to grip the hot ceramic mug. 'Thanks,' he murmurs. She sits down next to him on the bed as he takes the first sip and rubs his face with his free hand. Suddenly aware of her close proximity and the downward pressure of her weight on the mattress.

'Last night it was crazy no?' She says quietly.

'Nuts,' he replies, 'anything happen overnight?'

'Nothing, I took coffee out to the gate. Skyla she was there, she does not like me I think.'

'Why not?' Maddox asked and instantly regretted it, knowing the reason why.

'She like you,' Lenski shrugs lightly, 'you spend the time so much with me, she not like this.'

'She's young,' Maddox mused, 'they all are.'

'But not you? I am only twenty one. That make me old though to the children.'

'Ancient,' Maddox answered quickly with a quick smile.

'You! I not ancient,' she slaps his shoulder affectionately. Leaving her hand there she squeezes his hard muscle, 'are you okay?' she asks with a worried expression.

'About last night?' Maddox answers feeling her hand rubbing and enjoying the pleasurable feeling. Normally he'd flinch away from unwarranted contact from another person but her manner makes him relax and he doesn't sense anything other than care from the woman. No threat or clumsy flirting like with Skyla and the other girls.

'Of course last night,' she says continuing the rub and staring across at him.

'Yeah it's okay I think, nothing we can do now is there? Just got to roll with it.' Lenski picks up on him saying *we* and not *I*.

'No, nothing we can do. It done now but I worry you feel bad for killing the Bossman and...'

'He would have killed me; as soon as he said what he did I knew it was on. There's no going back from something like that. He could have backed down, or I could have but it would have happened today or tomorrow. Getting fucked up on weed and sat on his own would have made him worse.'

'And Ryker?' Lenski gently pushed the question, needing to know how Maddox was thinking about it now a night had passed.

'It's done,' he says quietly, 'we can't lock people up here and if we sent him away he could have caused problems. He had to die after what he did. Zayden didn't deserve that.'

'Maddox?' She asks in a quiet voice. He turns to look into her eyes, her face looking soft instead of the normal hard stare, 'maybe many they didn't deserve the killing, maybe we not kill so many people now.'

'I was thinking the same last night,' they stare at each other, her hand still gently rubbing his back. 'We'll stop killing the survivors but we've got to do it carefully...'

'Why?'

'Like I said, they might see losing the bossman as a sign of weakness. If we just suddenly stop killing and become nice, they'll be in here and taking us over. It needs to be done carefully, we still got a shit load of kids here that need protecting and there's so much we don't know too. The Bossman knew about the Dysentery, none of us would know that.'

'Not the word maybe we do not know, but being clean is obvious no?'

'There could be a hundred things like that we don't know about...'

'Then we will find them no? We make it work.' Lenski says softly, her hand still gently massaging his back.

'Yeah,' Maddox whispers staring at her, the atmosphere suddenly becoming charged. Eyes locked on each other they gently lean in, closing the gap. Two hearts hammering in two chests. Two young minds drawn together. The youths, the chiefs they all have Maddox and Lenski to take care of them. Maddox and Lenski have but each other and the weight they feel is suddenly shared. Two people that moved in different circles never associated and never knew the other existed. They may have crossed each other in the street with barely an appreciative glance at the others attractive form, but that would have been it.

After what seems an eternity their lips brush and gentle kissing continues for long minutes as the heat between them builds, still clutching their coffee mugs they move to embrace and laugh when the contents slosh over the rims of the mugs. The brief diversion does nothing to end the moment as the cups are lowered and they fall back onto the bed. Kissing passionately, touching, caressing. The need for contact, for that thing of closeness that every human strives for. Not drunk, not stoned, not some random act taking place after a nightclub. Two people taking the lives of many in their hands and needing an escape. The constant state of extreme emotion, surrounded by death and suffering vents as the pressure between them explodes into an urgent loving ecstasy.

Maddox, for an eighteen year old male is tender, loving and caressing. Knowing his hands are strong he restrains himself which sends shivers down Lenski's body. Her slim athletic frame grips the hard muscles in his arms, feeling the ridges of his abdominal muscles. Sensing his power, his aura. Feeling safe and protected. He, in turn feels nurtured and loved and in a strange way he also feels protected. The hardened young man knows his physical prowess and has worked hard to become strong and healthy, but with Lenski he feels protected from the psychological draw of going back to what it was. With her understanding him, even for this short time, he feels empowered to try and change.

Tenderness builds gradually until it becomes an urgent need and they make love. Desire wants and needs, emotions so powerful they cannot be expressed by words pour from them. Instinct moves them, propels them to action. The intrinsic need to progress the species tempered by the one thing that marks humanity apart from all else. Love.

It's over in minutes but it's enough for both of them. Enough to forge that contact and make that connection. A contract drawn between them of mutual respect, desire and genuine care.

The suns golden rays penetrate the once grimy window, wiped and scrubbed by Maddox so he could always have a sight of the world outside. Dust particles glint and dance as the warm air settles over the naked forms lying with entwined arms upon the small bed. The contrast between them is stark. The pale, slender curves of Lenski snuggling in close against the dark, defined frame of Maddox. They kiss more, stroking and smiling in the early morning light. Faint noises caused by the rustle of bed clothes, exhaling and the soft sound of skin against skin. Delight in both their faces. Eyes bright and searching, staring, gazes being held. They shuffle up to a seated position; Lenski reaches down with her slender arms to bring both their mugs up. The coffee, still warm is sipped quietly as they manoeuvre to maintain the closeness. Neither one wanting to break the spell.

To the south, across an expanse of deep blue water, at the end of a long wooden pier Howie and Lani clasp hands as they lay down to sleep, exhausted from battle and in need of that same contact, that same connection. Fingers as entwined as the limbs of Maddox and Lenski.

Humanity rolls on. Awakening inside young hearts as love builds.

'LISTEN UP!' Maddox's voice booms out across the compound. Young tired faces stare back, sipping the bottles of water handed out with the order to get them finished. Maddox stands tall and erect next to the pit, one foot raised on a log used for seating. Lenski nearby, holding her clipboard close to her chest and watching with pride as her lover commands every face within the base.

'No patrols today, maybe later but not now. We are going to extend the base. The houses either side of the road leading away from the base will be taken in and the fence will be pushed to the end of the junction. Then we're going to put the fence into the gardens at the end of the junction. They've got high walls all round them so we still get the protection but we get more space. We will knock the garden walls down between here and the junction so we make the ground open all the way to the end. That gives us more space for planting food to grow and it gives us more privacy. The two houses on the end will be used as sentry points with guard rooms, that means we can use height to look down and see further.' Maddox pauses briefly, drawing breath and making sure they're still watching him. The faces remain fixed, hanging off every word he says.

'Every crew will be given a job and the chief will make sure that job is done properly. It's gonna be a hard day and we'll need one crew keeping guard, make sure your weapons are close all the time. Anyone caught without their weapon nearby will be washing all the shit smeared pants, you get me? That means you Liam.' The youths burst out laughing as Liam takes a deep bow grinning happily at being named.

'Darius is moving up too, so that means we need two more crew chiefs. Work hard and we'll see who stands out today,' that got their attention with the prospect of moving up to one of the coveted jobs. Maddox turns and nods the pre-arranged signal at Lenski who steps forward examining her clipboard.

'Sierra will take first guard out on the junction,' Lenski looks up to see Sierra nodding back. She already knew parts of the plan and had been warned her crew would be first up for guarding.

'Darius will take his crew and Ryker's to the shops down the road and bringing back the scaffold please yes? Skyla, can you take your crew and start knocking down the walls into the gardens on the right side and Mohammed the left side. Aaliyah you will be taking crew with Jagger and Ryland and help with the moving the fence yes? Questions?'

'Are we gonna live in the houses?' Liam shouts. A good question noticed by Maddox and Darius and already a contender emerges for one of the crew chief slots. More questions get thrown up once Liam got his answer, which was that they didn't know yet. Maddox and Lenski field most of the questions, with Darius stepping up to take one or two and asserting his role at the top of the table. Not one youth picks up on Maddox's change in manner, his use of normal speech instead of the usual street talk; even Darius drops some of the slang in favour of trying to be like Maddox, noticed with a wry smile by Sierra.

The crews move about getting into their groups as the serious work of the day begins. Confusion descends for the first few minutes as each chief is bombarded with more questions, they in turn seek out the new leaders to find out exactly how they're going to do what they're tasked with.

The fence is the first thing once Sierra has moved out to the junction and staggered her crew out across the roads. The crews gather round and slowly figure out what tools are needed to detach the gates from the high fencing and the drilled bolts in the ground, and then half dragging, half carrying the heavy loads down to the junction. Once they're sure the fence can be erected safely, only then does Maddox give the order for Skyla and Mohammed to start bashing the high brick walls down. Making sure they understand to only make enough room for two or three people to walk through and no bigger.

As the sun rises so does the volume of the young voices, shouting out and calling to each other, all the time working like demons with a sense of urgency and purpose. Darius leads his two crews out from the compound, a quiet word already spoken with Liam, telling him to keep an eye on the younger ones and be ready to help. That was all it needed and the young lad is transformed with his chest puffed out and a serious look in his eye.

Throughout the hot morning they work hard. Walls are knocked through as the children get coated in brick dust and filth. A few cuts and bruises here and there quickly tended to by the ever watchful Lenski and her girls. The plants forgotten for the day as everyone comes out of the units to get stuck in. Maddox works hard, moving between the crews and helping lift, carry, move and graft shoulder to shoulder with everyone else. He takes the time to comment and praise the hard working youths.

As the last section of fence is moved up and stacked at the junction Darius returns with a long line of children carrying scaffolding poles and wooden boards, he ditches them down and sends Liam back with Ryker's crew to bring the rest.

'Alright Maddox, what's up?' he takes the bottle of water held out by the leader.

'Nuffin', you?'

'Nuffin.' They both grin at the long standing greeting shared by them for years. 'That Liam, he doin' well bruv.'

'Good, he's up for crew chief then?'

'Yeah I think so,' Darius replies, trying to remember not to use so much slang now.

'Did you see any infected?' Maddox asks.

'None, not one,' Darius replies with a shrug.

'We need to move quickly and get those fences up, we're undefended now,' Maddox says looking back down the road and straight into the compound.

'Where do you want me?' Darius asks.

'Everywhere,' Maddox says with a big grin making Darius laugh at seeing his best friend so animated instead of the usual deadpan poker face.

Four

The infection is everywhere. In every village, every town, every city and every country and it targets those that cause the most damage. Knowing that in order to survive those killers must be stopped.

All across the world, the undead gather in great numbers headed by a host body of enhanced powers, and of ever changing and evolving abilities. The infection works quickly to understand the human brain and the processes it can achieve.

Telepathy has been accomplished by the infection manipulating the blood cells passed from the enhanced host into the bodies of the infected. The few remaining survivors spread across the planet are outnumbered so vastly but still they fight back and inflict huge losses to the hosts.

For every human taken, many hosts fall and the infection knows it cannot withstand this rate of attrition. Without conscious thought the infection cannot simply choose to disengage and withdraw. Survival means being finding new hosts and preventing the loss of the ones already taken.

In the south of England. Past the northern edge of a vast and sprawling council estate a lone zombie stands staring on the motorway which forms the border of the huge urban jungle. Skin a sickly pallor, dried blood round his mouth, clothes filthy, torn and hanging from his gaunt frame.

Losses have been taken here, far too many. Inflicted by young host bodies fighting with an alarming and ferocious savagery.

The zombie stands erect and with intelligence within the red bloodshot eyes. An adult male employed as a taxi driver before he was blessedly taken into this new state of being and for the last day he has been busy. Busy finding hosts, drawing blood and building resources. Summoning every host for miles and drawing them here.

Past the motorway, over the crash barrier and above the slight incline hordes of undead gather in the rolling fields. The drooling decaying fetid undead shuffle and groan quietly. Sensing the need to stay in this place despite the urge to move and find food. The undead shuffle in from every direction, massing in great numbers.

Still wearing his blood splattered photo identity badge from his previous life, the super zombie stares into the estate. Patiently waiting as more bodies shuffle into view, stumbling across the sun baked tarmac to join the legion.

This enhanced host has learnt, as Darren did, that moving too fast during the day weakens the bodies. So it conserves that energy. The only thing it doesn't know is if it can resist the urge until night fall, or whether he will succumb to the depraved hunger and charge earlier.

Five

Maddox stands back from the junction, looking down towards the compound, now out of sight behind the high fence and gates erected across the road. Panels fixed to the sides of the houses, using the tools the Bossman sourced during the first couple of days, and copying how he drilled into the ground and bolted the thick metal posts into place and attaching the panels to the posts. The walls of the houses on either side form a solid line down to their garden walls, and more high fencing topped with coiled razor wire has been fixed against the walls, providing a solid unbroken line, securing the base within.

'Check the gates,' he yells out and watches as Darius pushes both the solid metal gates out. Wide enough to drive a lorry through they push out to a ninety degree angle. Satisfied Maddox shouts to close them back up.

The next decision is where to put the guard tower. They can use the upstairs windows of the houses to view down the opposite street but not the full length of the street opposite. He wants the tower outside of the gates, in the middle of the junction but that would mean whoever was inside it could get isolated or trapped. Maybe something could be rigged up from the top of the tower to the window of the closest house, an escape route. But the gap is too big; if he moved the tower closer to the building they would lose the view.

'Where you puttin' it?' Darius asks as Maddox walks back through the gate into the now extended compound.

'We'll try behind the gate first, we'll get a bit of a view of the side streets but a full view of that one,' he points to the road leading away opposite them, 'we'll have people in those windows too.'

'So we got to cover the front, the sides and the back too?' Darius questions with a serious look, 'if we're all at the front or in the units it leaves the back open. Why not just use a crew each night, you know, make them in charge of the security for that night and they can rest the next day.'

'I like it Darius,' Maddox nods with respect, 'fuckin' good idea, yeah you get that sorted then.'

'I'm on it!' Darius grins broadly at having his suggestion taken on board.

Leaving Darius to oversee the scaffold tower, Maddox makes his way down the short road, admiring the greater stretch of ground they have gained, looking at the front of the houses on either side and wondering how to make best use of them. As he nears the old fence point Lenski walks out from the end of the unit clutching her clipboard and drinking from a bottle of water.

'The fence it look good yes?' She asks, handing him bottle. He takes the water and takes a long plug from the top, feeling the refreshing liquid cascade down his parched throat.

'Yeah, we got it all fixed in, Darius just doing the tower now.' They fall into step side by side, walking towards the sounds of banging, shouts and clouds of dust as the kids happily smash walls down. Stepping over the fallen bricks and debris they look through to the end; a clear line of sight through the small gardens to the high end wall and the even higher fencing fixed against it. The youths working here, smashing up the big lumps of concrete and wall to make them easier to move look up and smile as Maddox and Lenski walk through.

'We should use the houses for the crews no? Ten houses we have gained here, the five on each side so with eight crews is good yes?' Lenski asks, watching Maddox finish the water off, he lowers the bottle and grins apologetically.

'Sorry, I was thirsty.'

'This I see,' Lenski says with one raised eyebrow, 'you like idea, we put crews here yes?'

'Yeah I think so,' Maddox agrees and outlines the details of Darius's plan to keep one crew up everynight and tasked with security. They stroll through to the end, and then back out and up the other side.

'Maybe we give the crews the food for the week and they do as they want with it?' Lenski suggested.

'Nah,' Maddox laughed, 'they'll eat the best stuff the first night and sell the rest for drugs.'

'Oh the drugs, what we do with them?'

'I know what I want to do,' Maddox drops his voice, and Lenski notices the hard edge to his tone, 'I'd fuckin' burn the lot of 'em.'

'We do this yes?' Lenski urged.

'Not yet, one step at a time. Remember where these kids have come from. They've grown up on this shit so we need to tread carefully. And there will be plenty of people out there that will still want it.'

'For what? Why they need this drug now?' Lenski demanded with a scowl.

'Look what's happened, the worlds fucked up overnight. Maybe that shit might make it easier for them or something. The point is there are people that will want it, so we can use it for trade.'

'Okay,' she shrugs clearly not convinced but willing to let the point go for now. 'What you do next?'

He sucks in a breath and lets rip, 'get the scaffold up and work out where to put the tower, then gotta look at the houses and make sure they all the same size otherwise it'll spark the crews off if one gets something the others don't, then we need beds and bedding and while we're moving all the stuff from the tents we need to check to make sure they're clean. We also got to work out a way to divide the rooms up and give everyone equal space, now do we give the crew chiefs their own room or not because these houses ain't that big really....'

'Okay okay,' she waves her clipboard to slow him down, 'I take the point.'

'Yeah...lots to do,' he cocks his head to one side staring at the freckles on her nose.

'You very busy.'

'We both are,' he nods. She nods back.

'See you in your room in two minutes?' She asks quietly.

'Definitely,' he replies. They walk separate directions as Lenski jogs back toward the unit and Maddox finds Darius to tell him to hold the fort.

'Why where you going bruv?' Darius asks in confusion while trying to organise the scaffold tower being erected.

'Er…I got something to do.'

'Where ?'

'Inside,' Maddox stares at the distracted lad trying to convey a message to stop asking.

'Inside?' Darius asks while hefting a long pole, 'what you doing inside?'

'I need to speak to Lenski…'

'Lenski?' Darius repeats. He catches the glare from Maddox and stares back dumbly for a second before finally catching on, 'oh Lenski!' He laughs with delight, 'yeah of course bruv, you go have that private chat and I'll stay here.'

'Yeah thanks,' Maddox growls softly and walks off leaving Darius smiling and shaking his head. He makes himself walk at a normal pace towards the unit, checking about him, nodding and waving at the youths and girls coming and going. Once inside he checks about, making sure he's out of sight and starts running to his room. Bursting in and finding Lenski already undressed and laying naked on his bed.

'I think Darius knows,' Maddox says as he quickly strips off.

'About us? Is that good?' Lenski asks with a grin.

'Right now...I don't care.' He dives onto the bed provoking a squeal from Lenski that's quickly cut off as their mouths find one another. Furious but fun work takes place both inside his room and all across the compound as slowly a new community is forged.

Six

'I'm telling you they're just little kids, the little shits we'd see running around here on their bikes,' Jeff yells, wincing at the pain from his black eye and swollen nose.

'Jeff, we agree,' the man opposite him implores, 'but they're tough little bastards and they got guns. Look in the bloody mirror if you don't believe what they can do.'

'This?' Jeff points at his own bruised face and moves round in a circle to take in the faces of the crowd gathered together, 'this was a lucky shot done by some little wanker, I would've stopped him but he had two little bastards with shotguns stood right behind him.' The two women with him yesterday raise their eyebrows knowingly. Jeff didn't have time to react, that youth moved so fast none of them saw it coming until it was too late.

'Now listen,' Jeff softens his tone and looks round at the survivors all brought together in the main library of the council estate. This being the least likely place the kids would go to. Surprisingly, not one survivor had seen a zombie or a youth so far today.

'Now come on, listen,' Jeff repeats, 'they've taken all our food, our supplies and for what?'

'Well we all got here without being eaten.' A voice shouts from the back, 'they've got rid of the dead things.'

'Yes well,' Jeff bridles at the quick answer, 'be that as it may but we have all seen how slow those things are during the day. Any of us could have killed them off.'

'But we didn't,' the same voice shouts, 'they did and I ain't seen one of them since late yesterday afternoon.'

'But the fact is we could have done if we wanted, but we couldn't because we were too scared of those bloody kids. Did you see what they did to old Naylor?'

'He was a bloody idiot,' that same blasted voice shouts out again, irritating Jeff and making him wince more than the pain on his face. 'He was always getting nicked for knocking people about, thought he was a proper hard bastard he did. Ha! Sod him, bloody kids did a good job if you ask me.'

'But those bloody kids didn't know he was like that did they, and they done it before and they'll do it again.'

'Has anyone seen them out today?' that same bloody voice from the back asks.

'Who is that?' Jeff cranes his head over the tops trying to see. Bodies shuffle out of the way as a bespectacled older man comes into view, smiling round at everyone.

'Watcha,' the man nods in greeting, repeated the word a few times as he stares round.

'So has any of you seen the kids or what?' the old man asks.

'They were carrying some scaffolding poles from the shops earlier.' Someone answers

'Where to? Jeff asks.

'Dunno, maybe that base they got.'

'Yeah that base that's got all our food and all the guns, that base with the big safe fences round it...'

'What's your point nipper?' the old man asks.

'My point,' Jeff sighs, 'is that they've got everything and we've got nothing and it ain't bloody right. They're just sodding kids!'

'Kids eh?' The old man asks.

'Yes, kids!' Jeff repeats as if that proved everything.

'So you're complaining because the children are safe and protected with lots of food behind big fences and lots of guns...the children that is...the small ones that...'

'Well yes of course the children should be there,' Jeff quickly cut across him fearing he was losing the point already, 'but why should the rest of us suffer and go without.'

'You got the whole estate, you can come and go as you want, take what house you want...' the old man started counting the advantages off.

'Well we can't come and go as we want with those things out there.'

'But we ain't seen those things have we, those kids have killed 'em all, those kids you're complaining about...behind those big fences with the guns.'

'YES ALRIGHT...thank you for that,' Jeff rubbed his face and whimpered from the pain shooting through his nose, 'all I'm saying is that we should all be behind the fences with the guns and the food, we should all be safe, then we'd have the guns and could kill those things.'

'Oh them kids didn't use guns on them things,' the old man pulled his glasses off and started wiping the lenses with the corner of his filthy cardigan, 'they did it with sticks, stones, bats, knives and their bare hands too,' he added as he slid the glasses back onto his nose, 'but not guns.'

'But they had all the food,' Jeff argued, 'so they had the energy and the…the…well the energy.'

'You said energy already,' the old man smiled graciously, 'and they we're out by the next day killing 'em before they got all the food.'

'Have they taxed you old man?' Jeff asked with an exasperated tone.

'Me?' the old man looked surprised, 'of course they have. Damn polite they were too, I said I was happy to give my half seeing as they got all them young mouths to feed and they was out killing the zombo's and all that…some black kid, Madsticks or something, anyway damn polite he was and said if I had any grief I just had to tell him and he'd make sure it was sorted.'

'Said the same to me,' an older woman interjected.

'His lot bloody killed my neighbour though, and in front of his wife. She ain't said a word since then.' That's what he wanted and Jeff seized on it quickly, turning to the man and shouting;

'So your neighbour was an innocent man just trying to feed his family and these little shits killed him in cold blood.'

'Well I wouldn't quite say that,' the man replied rubbing his chin, 'see the bloke did go at 'em with one of them samurai swords, you know…the ones you get from the Sunday newspapers…' murmurs and nods rumble quietly round the room, 'yeah so he kind of did provoke them.'

'Sounds like he was just trying to defend his property if you ask me, and right in front of his wife too you said…'

'Yeah, right in front of her it was…after they took the other two swords of her that is. But still,' the man's voice trails off, unsure of what his original point was.

'Right well I just don't think we should be living a life of servitude under a communist regime designed to disinherit us of our hard earned possessions,' Jeff said, remembering some of the course he was sent on by the trade union, he looked round to a sea of blank grimy faces and one old bespectacled man sniggering with mirth.

'Thems words a bit much for us stupid council house folk I reckon,' the old man smirked.

'Why should we get robbed in our own homes, we need food too,' Jess translated and got a few nods of encouragement now they understood what he meant.

'They're all drug addicts, high on crack and meth and speed, they'll be selling our babies to the highest bidder before long and forcing us into the sex trade…' Jeff spun round sensing that he might just be getting somewhere, 'and when this is over...when the government get control back, which they will, and when the army come rolling through here, which they will,' Jeff's voice rose in volume as he moved between the nodding faces. Most of them unsure of why they were nodding but happy to be nodding all the same because they were scared and starting to get hungry and this man was saying things in a loud voice and he looked quite tough with those bruises, 'they're going to want to know why we didn't stand up to a bunch of kids who were probably trained by terrorist camps, oh yes, they were probably trained by terrorist camps who want to end your way of life and make you slowly starve,' Jeff spun round dramatically, seeing the startled faces watching him, 'where do you think this started from eh? We've all heard of germ warfare haven't we? We all know about dirty bombs don't we? That's what they're doing here, dropping dirty bombs full of germs and turning people into flesh eaters while they steal our children and turn them into terrorists....well we won't stand for it....no we won't! They are dropping bombs and germs on us and taking our children, making us into sex slaves and forcing us to take crack up our veins! Well it stops now! It stops tonight! We will take out children back and give them the discipline they need. Brain washed they are, and we need to de-brainwash them, so who will join me tonight in protecting our country and stopping those evil terrorists from injecting Heroin into our babies eyes?'

Every hand in the library rises, apart from one belonging to an old man with spectacles who tuts and shuffles his way through the idiotic and pumped up crowd to stand for a few minutes in the nice warm sunlight. He quite liked the young lad called Madsocks or whatever it was; he was very polite and had a good firm handshake. You can tell a lot about a man from the look in his eye and the hand he gives to shake. The estate was probably the safest now that it ever has been so whoever that Bossman was, well he was doing a good job.

The old man sighed and wondered why people had to go and keep changing things. It was quieter now, well now those bloody zombo things were gone and if it stays like this then the estate will be a very nice place to live again.

The old man looked up the street and contemplated going to that compound he'd been told about, just to warn them a little bit about some of these idiots coming to make complaints tonight. Give 'em a chance to get a few excuses ready, or even switch the lights off and pretend no one's home. But it is far away and the sun is very hot, so thinking maybe he would prefer a bottle of beer from the crate that nice young man left him to drink and those kids were sure to be round at some point today, he could tip them off then and save his tired old legs.

So, with a sigh, the old man slowly started making his way back along the debris littered, blood stained, corpse strewn street, back to his boarded up house to wait for the pack of feral kids to come back round.

Seven

'Using a car battery would be hard as it would need to remain connected to the engine while it's running otherwise it will drain too quickly. But we could use that,' Nick points to the long sleek vessel tied on to the end of the pier. I look over at the big white catamaran used for carrying passengers between the Island and mainland. With one main interior level for passengers and a small outside area on the top, it looks low and fast.

'They have power sources running from the engine, all we'd need to do is start it up and they've probably got a facility on board to heat water too,' Nick adds with a look of yearning in his eyes.

'Hot water?' I ask.

'Yeah for the hot water taps in the toilets, can I have a go?' Having brought me outside to show me his idea he stands waiting, itching to be given the nod to go and play on the big ship.

'Do you think you could drive it?' I ask him.

'Drive it?' He replies puzzled, 'what for going back in? In that?'

'Yeah why not?'

'Bloody hell, yeah definitely,' Nick laughs at the idea, nudging Tom and nodding towards it.

'We'll come on with you and make sure it's clear then leave you to it; I'll let the others know while you figure out a way of getting on it.' Walking away I leave Nick and Tom talking excitedly about getting to drive the ship. The end of the pier is huge, a vast open car park shaped like a hammer on the end of the long thin approach road. Blowers and Cookey have sat on the reverse side, happily fishing away while maintaining a constant view of the land and the pier. The catamaran is on the outside edge. The only problem is that these waters are tidal which is why the pier was built in the first place. Even this far out from the shore the tide still comes in and out which means it was tied securely to the pier when the tide was in. And then left there while the end of world began. When the tide went out, the boat sank and ripped out all the ropes and mooring posts from the vast weight slowly sinking. All but one rope must have snapped or torn free, leaving just one tied onto the front. With the motion of the tide the ship has swung out and is facing the pier. Later, when the direction of the tide changes the boat will come back and nudge against the structure. Something it's already done a few times judging by the dents alongside one side and the thick black scuff marks on the front. Luckily, the weather has been exceptionally mild without high winds otherwise I've no doubt it would now be floating away to France or have smashed the pier up.

Walking back into the café I see Lani bending over in the large storeroom behind the counter, going through the shelves and sorting food out. Again, and fortunately for us the café serves a mostly transient customer and with ferries coming and going every half hour during the summer it meant the waiting time was very limited, which also meant the café served mainly pre-packaged snack food. Good for us as most of it was in the cooler store room and either still in date or just gone. Mostly muffins, cakes, biscuits and the like, and boxes of crisps and chocolate bars. But it will have to do for now. She catches me walking past and smiles sweetly, which I return without blushing for once.

At the back, Clarence sits dozing in a chair while Dave is seated off to one side, his knives all laid out on the table and a sharpening stone in his hand, running back and forth along the already lethal blade.

'We're going to try and board that big ship tied up, Nick thinks it will have power and maybe hot water if he can get it going,' I explain. Blowers and Cookey both twist round to listen and Clarence holds his hands over his eyes to shield them from the sun while squinting up at me.

'Hasn't it swung out?' Clarence asks.

'Yeah, we need to figure a way of getting on board and clearing it,' as soon as the words are said they're on their feet. The rods get reeled in and put to one side as they gather axes and knives up.

'You caught anything yet? I ask the lads.

'We got a crab but it was as ugly as Blowers with massive pincers so we put it back,' Cookey replies. Lani joins us seeing the weapons being taken up and I quickly relay the plan while she grabs her meat cleaver.

Outside we walk to the outer edge and stand there staring at the vessel gently bobbing a few metres away. I turn round and check our position, making sure we can still see the pier stretching out behind us down to the shore.

'Well unless Clarence can pull it back in I reckon the easiest way is going to be along that rope,' I nod at the thick taught rope stretched between the pier and the vessel.

'There's no movement on board,' Clarence stares out with his eyes shielded from the sun again, 'should be safe enough to get a couple on board and check it through.'

'I'll do it,' Lani says, eyeing the rope.

'Hang on,' Clarence walks over to the rope secured to the mooring post and looks down at the length wrapped round the thick post, 'there's enough rope left to pull it back in, come on.' He starts unwinding the rope from the post and feeds it out behind him as we run up and each take a double handed grip.

'Ready,' Clarence releases the last coil from the post and immediately the ship starts pulling us towards the edge. The big man runs round to the back, grasping the rope and taking an anchor position as we start straining to pull it back in.

'Shit,' I grunt as the receding tide pulls the boat away from the shore. The sheer weight of it outmatches even our combined pulling strength. We dig in cursing and grunting but getting pulled gently towards the edge of the pier.

'You didn't think that one through Clarence,' I shout through gritted teeth.

'Sorry boss,' he yells from the back.

The ship drifts away and we cling onto the rope refusing to give in, hoping we can prevent the motion and start dragging it back in. The edge looms closer and closer with Lani at the front, followed by Dave and the rest of us stretched out in a line. Clarence curses loudly as he slips on a patch of oil, without his strength we're suddenly yanked forward. With a yelp Lani sails over the edge of the pier followed by a yelling Dave. As they release their grip, the boat gains more momentum and anyone left holding the rope is jerked towards the edge. Everyone one of us sailing over the and into the blue waters with yells and shouts.

Plunging in and luckily the tide is still quite high so the drop isn't too bad. I push back up to the surface spitting water from my mouth. A braying donkey sounds from somewhere and I turn round to look up at Clarence bent double and clutching his stomach as he laughs uncontrollably at the sight of the rest of us all bobbing in the water.

'I want hot water,' Lani yells out and swims after the rope. Reacting quickly I swim after her with Nick right behind me. We each gain a length of rope between our hands and start pulling ourselves hand over hand through the water with Lani in front moving swiftly along the rope.

She climbs nimbly clear of the water and scales the thick rope, using her feet against the side of the vessel and within a few seconds she reaches the top and pulls herself onto the front of the ship. I go next gritting my teeth I start lifting myself out of the water. If this had been two weeks ago I don't think I would have stood much of a chance, but now with most of the fat burnt from my body and after constantly swinging the heavy axe I surprise myself with my strength and grin stupidly as I clamber up the side, copying Lani and using my feet to help me up. Reaching the top I grab the side and lever myself in, falling down into a wet puddle. Coughing and spluttering I go to stand up and watch as Nick's grinning face reaches the lip, Lani and I help him over until we're stood there dripping and smiling like idiots.

'I bloody hope you can drive this thing,' I nod towards the retreating pier and lift my arms high above my head to wave, showing the others that we made it.

'Have either of you got a weapon?' They both shake their hands after patting sodden pockets down.

'Don't worry, I'll protect you both,' Lani smiles and moves off down the side. Nick and I shrug and walk along the narrow gangway towards the big sliding door.

'Oh dear,' Lani calls back after peering in through the glass. Joining her we peer through the darkened glass at the group of undead all stood swaying in the middle of the floor.

'Well its day so they're slow,' Nick muses, his breath misting the glass in front of his mouth.

'Yeah but hand to hand?' I answer, 'only takes a bite mate.'

'Open the door and lure them outside,' Lani suggests.

'Okay, grab those fire extinguishers as soon we get in, ready?' They both nod and I pull the door back. We rush into the cool interior and quickly yank the heavy metal cylinders free from their fixings.

The main level is the width of the vessel and fitted with rows of seats with two wide aisles running down either side.

We grab at the fire extinguishers and pull the covers off. I get a big heavy red water filled one while the others get smaller chemical filled extinguishers. The undead react and slowly shuffle round, giving groans as they see their lunch waiting for them.

'Fuck is that the captain?' Nick asks at the sight of the uniformed zombie with a dark blue suit with golden stripes on the cuffs and wearing a flat cap on the back of his head.

'Guess so,' I reply quietly as we back away towards the open door. I pull the plastic strip from my handle and aim the hose at the approaching horde. A jet of water sprays out as I squeeze the handle, soaking the zombies faces and having no effect other than washing some of the dried blood away.

'Let me try,' Nick says and pulls the strip out. He steps in squirts foam into them from a few feet away. Thick creamy foam that covers their faces. They groan and moan at the abuse but other than that they keep coming.

'My turn,' Lani darts in and opens up with her chemical powder extinguisher. The noise is really loud and makes Nick and I jump. She holds the aim on one poor sod who gets blasted back by the high powered jet of powder. He staggers into the others as the powder gets into his mouth. He staggers back and tries shuffling again but then starts coughing and spluttering as he chokes on the power in his throat. We watch in fascinated horror as the thing shuffles and flaps his arms about whacking the others and knocking the captain's hat off. Eventually he falls down and stays writhing on the ground.

'Get another one,' Nick urges. Lani obliges by darting forward and squeezing the handle. A thick jet flies out then ends abruptly.

'Shit,' she pumps the handle then steps in and swing the solid metal tube into the side of the zombies head, smashing it down onto the ground as she retreats back to the door. We slowly move backwards and out onto the side of the ship. The zombies follow with their awkward shuffle, reaching the threshold and getting bunched up as they all try and turn onto the narrow walkway running down the side. Two of them simply fall off the side, unable to navigate the ground and stepping out into thin air.

Two left who amazingly keep on the narrow walkway, shuffling and swaying their way along. I edge forward and jab the end of the tube into the face of the closest one. He reels back a step and teeters of the edge before recovering and coming forward again. I step in and jab out harder, forcing him to knock the other one of the side and down into the water. With a smashed in nose he again recovers and starts shuffling towards us.

'Hang on,' Nick shouts and leans over me to fire his thick foam into its face and covering the eyes. Blinded, the zombie groans loudly and keeps coming as I step in and swing my heavy water filled tube in a massive uppercut. The impact reels the thing backwards onto its arse, it flails about for a couple of seconds before gently sliding off the edge and splashing into the water.

'He's extinguished,' Nick says.

'Ha nice one mate,' I reply.

After throwing the bodies out the side door and into the sea, we quickly squelch down the aisles and clear the big room within a couple of minutes. A door set into a large central column leads to a steep narrow staircase. Going first I climb up and reach the bridge. Expecting a bank of modern equipment I'm surprised at how minimalist the bridge is. Just a central desk area with a few monitors but lots of switches, dials and levers. Nick follows me and immediately goes to the unit. His actions are the same as at Tower Bridge and he stares at the many instruments, running his fingers over them and murmuring to himself quietly.

'There'll be an engine room downstairs Mr Howie, could you clear that while I figure this out?'

'Okay mate,' I nod to Lani. We go back down the stairs and start searching round for a way into the bottom of the boat. More doors at the rear lead out onto a small platform with metal stairs leading up onto the top outside deck. A solid metal door set into the rear of the vessel, painted white and with a thick metal bar handle locking it in place. I pull the lever back; the door opens on soundless hinges presenting a wide staircase going down. We step over the high ledge and descend into the engine room.

Gaining the bottom we peer down the dark length of the ship, the only light coming from the open door at the top of the stairs. Standing still and breathing quietly we listen for any other noise. Nothing, just the creak of the vessel.

'Stay here,' I whisper to Lani, she nods once and I move off down into the gloom. My eyes adjusting as I gradually make my way down. A large central engine block takes up most of the room, shiny with things poking out and tubes, wires and leads feeding off it. Wide metal tubing snakes round the sides of the ceiling and the floor is bevelled stainless steel, offering good grip. I keep my steps slow and steady, breathing gently and holding the fire extinguisher up high, ready to slam down onto any zombie faces that lunge in. Nooks and crannies everywhere, deep recesses hidden in shadows, slowly I make my way down towards the rear, or would it be the front, yes it's the front of the ship I'm heading towards but the back of the engine room. Bloody military and bloody ships with different bloody words for everything. We never had this problem at Tesco you know.

A loud clunk startles me from my internal moaning, followed by lights blinking on and the sound of things humming, whirring and other machine noises. I tense up expecting there be someone stood there with a hand on the light switch while leaning back in a big black chair and stroking a white cat, *ah Mr Howie...we've been expecting you...*

Instead there's just an empty room, well it's empty of people, or undead anyway but filled with machines and the giant engine in the middle. An old fashioned phone fixed to the wall chirps loudly, a bright red light fixed to the top flashes brightly. Lani steps in with a puzzled smile and picks the phone up.

'Hello, this is the engine room,' she says with a very polite tone and listens for a few seconds, 'please hold captain while I pass that message onto the chief engineer...it's Nick' she shouts to me, 'he's got an override system up there and said there should be a button or switch down here that you can use that will give him full control from the bridge.'

'Hang on, any idea what it looks like?' I stare round at the confusing mass of instruments and dials.

'He said it's probably either red or green colour, so that it's easy to spot...his words not mine,' she adds with a smile when I pass an eyebrow raised look. I move over to a desk and start examining the display.

'Captain...I don't have the power...' Lani speaks loudly into the handset with a mock Scottish accent making me laugh.

'Got it,' I shout over, switching the green button marked simply with control – engine – bridge. I select bridge and stand back feeling rather pleased with myself.

'Mr Howie said he found it…uh huh…yep okay captain.' She replaces the handset, 'he said he'll figure it out from here.'

'You know I can't believe we just bloody did that,' I remark, 'separating the group and putting ourselves in danger like that, no weapons and not really sure if we can get the thing going or not…that was a bad shout.'

'We reacted with instinct Howie, it's a good prize and worth a little risk and if it didn't work then the others would figure out a way of getting to us.'

'Yeah but what if something happened while we were separated?'

'Howie, you can't control everything and they know what they're doing.'

'No I didn't mean they wouldn't be able to function without us, bloody hell Dave and Clarence could do the work of twenty normal men. I mean just being split up, I don't like it.' With a loud clunk the engine splutters into life. A low grumble that slowly builds with a whine into a loud roaring that makes the floor vibrate. We both smile hugs grins as the engine settles back down to a low steady rumble.

'There you go,' she smiles as I walk back towards her and the stairs. The engine increases in pitch as the boat starts moving. Down here with no windows we can't tell how fast or what direction. As I get closer to Lani the boat lurches round as Nick steers it over sending me flying into Lani stood only a few feet away. We collide and grab out to steady ourselves, coming to rest face to face with Lani pressed up against the wall. Our bodies touching, faces just inches apart. I can feel the warmth of her body radiating through her wet clothes. She stares up at me, her dark eyes and golden skin, beautiful lips parting slightly. The temptation to lean in and kiss her overwhelms me. My head drops as she watches me closely, her eyes close and she moves forward a fraction. My heart is pounding more than in any battle so far, adrenalin surges through me and I can feel the blood roaring past my ears. It's warm here. The noise of the engine blocking all other sounds out. Her body so close. I can feel her breath on my skin, soft, warm, inviting.

The boat spins round in another harsh turn causing us to break apart and I stagger away trying to maintain my feet. The spell is broken and I stand still for a second breathing heavily, she remains wedged into the same position. Her feet braced, preventing her from getting rolled about. A look of disappointment briefly flashes across her features, instantly replaced as she opens her eyes and smiles at me.

'We'd better go up,' I have to shout over the engine to make myself heard. She hesitates for a second before pushing herself off the wall and nodding back to me. Leading the way we go back up the stairs and into the passenger lounge. Having a view of the landscape now and I can see the waters are gently rolling by as Nick brings the power down to a more steady pace. Taking care in case Nick tries another hairpin turn we reach the narrow staircase and climb onto the bridge. Nick is at the central desk moving his gaze between the dials in front of him and the view outside.

'Well done mate,' the engines are now a distant thrum and we can speak at nearly normal volume.

'It's bloody complicated,' he turns round grinning, 'they've got side thrusters and things. I reckon it's so they can push the ship into the side of the pier or maybe keep the thruster things on and hold it there while people are getting on and off. There's alarms flashes at me too so I don't think I've gone through the right sequence to get the thing going…but…' his voice trails off as he looks down at a flashing red light, shrugging he continues, 'but at least we got it running. Sorry about the hard turns but it's more sensitive than it looks.

'No problem,' I reply finding a pair of binoculars hanging from a strap I lift them up and turn round to view the end of the approaching pier. The figures are clear through the magnified lenses, especially the size difference between Clarence and Dave.

'Getting it alongside is going to be hard Mr Howie,' Nick says quickly, 'I can line it up but I don't know enough to keep it still.'

'Have a go mate, what's the fuel like?'

'Nearly full, I reckon they would have filled up overnight ready for the weekend.'

'That's lucky then.'

'Lucky day so far.'

'Touch wood it stays that way,' I tap the side of my head, 'if we get it tied up we can get everyone on board, take whatever we need from here and anchor up in the sea…it's got to be the safest place.'

'I'll have a go Sir,' his voice sounds focussed, his face a picture of concentration as he navigates the multi million pound ship towards the ancient solid wooden structure. Lani leans by an open sliding window, the wind blowing her hair and drying her wet clothes. Her eyes are closed with a content serene look and I kick myself for not taking the chance to kiss her. Bloody fumbling idiot. Shaking my head I turn back to the now fast approaching pier.

'They always go off to the side and turn in so they can drive alongside it,' Lani says in her strong voice.

'Which side?' Nick asks.

'To the right, I think it's deeper there.'

'Okay,' he replies quietly and gently steers the ship away from the pier. The ship goes past the end and Nick starts the turn, bringing the front sweeping round in a long arc. Eventually the vessel is lined up facing the end of the pier. Nick powers forward gently, sweat dripping from his forehead as his eyes flick between the pier and the front of the ship. Using the binoculars I watch Clarence striding towards the end nearest us. He watches the approach then quickly lifts his arm motioning to pull away.

'Move to the left mate,' I relay to Nick. At the dead slow speed the ship takes a few seconds before the end swings out, Clarence watches a few seconds and then motions to pull back in. I relay the instructions as Lani watches from the side window. Poor Nick does his best, making minor adjustments before smashing the side of the ship into the end of the pier with a hard jolt.

'Sorry,' he yells with a look of horror.

'Forget it mate, it's not our boat,' I shrug as he lines up and drags the side of the ship along the hard edge of the pier. Loud screeches of metal against wood rip through the air. The rest of the group come into view as I stride over to the window and lean out.

'Get everything ready and get on, we'll stay on this for a bit.' They nod back and quickly move off towards the buildings. Lani and I descend down to the passenger level and out through the still open sliding passenger door.

'NICK?' I shout out, 'CAN YOU HEAR ME?'

'YES,' His voice drifts out of the open window on the bridge.

'GO A BIT MORE FORWARD…KEEP GOING…MORE…ALMOST…YES! THAT'S IT, HOLD IT THERE.' The pier's access point, a lower level accessed by steps leading down and allowing vessels to berth with the lower tide, draws level as

Nick lines it up perfectly, then goes gently sliding past as we overshoot. 'TOO FAR…NEEDS TO GO BACK.'

'TRYING,' Nick's voice sails from the window. The engine changes in pitch as Nick reverses the boat. Too much power and we slam back into the side of the pier.

'USE THOSE SIDE THRUSTER THINGS,' Lani shouts up.

'I'M TRYING!' Nick's harassed voice comes from the window.

'I'll go up Howie,' Lani says before darting back in and jogging over to the staircase. I wait patiently for a few seconds before I hear their muted voices drifting down. The engine changes in pitch again as the vessel suddenly surges sideways and slams into the pier once more with a loud bang.

'DON'T YOU LIKE THIS PIER NICK?' Cookey shouts out as he jogs back carrying several of our kit bags, the shotgun butts all sticking out.

'PISS OFF COOKEY,' Nick retorts loudly. Cookey smirks before carefully dropping down the steps. A fluctuating gap between the vessel and the pier forms between Cookey and I.

'Chuck them over mate,' I say. Cookey drops them down and starts launching them into the open passenger doorway. As he leaves I move back in and stack them up to one side. Tom and Blowers arrive next, more bags and also carrying boxes of muffins, crisps and cases of water bottles. Everything gets chucked over as they run back and forth, effectively stripping the café of anything usable. Clarence must be directing them, getting them to take everything that might be of use. Fishing rods, the heavy winter coats we slept on, a cardboard box full of black, hand held radios with stubby aerials. Then Tom and Blowers appear carrying the heavy coffee machine between them, the lead dangling from Tom's teeth.

'Bloody hell,' I exclaim, 'good idea though,' I add with a nod. They perch dangerously on the edge trying to work out how to pass it over.

'Put it down and one of you jump in,' I can see them both falling down the gap and getting crushed by the ship and as much as we all like coffee I judge that maybe losing two of our group is a price too much for it.

They lower the coffee machine as Clarence appears carrying armfuls of axes. Dave just behind him. They work themselves out with Clarence taking the coffee machine while Blowers takes a running jump and launches himself into the ship. Tom goes next, leaving Clarence stood there holding the shiny coffee maker.

'NICK PUSH IT IN AGAIN AS GENTLY AS YOU CAN,' I shout up, Lani's head appears through the window, looking down she sees the stupid task we're attempting and nods down to us. A couple of seconds later she shouts "HANG ON" as the ship pushes against the side of the pier.

As the vessel connects, I shout "NOW" and Clarence steps forward holding the coffee machine out as Blowers and Tom take it from him. Between us, we manage to grapple the machine on board and give a cheer when we get it inside. The small victory bringing a sense of accomplishment.

Within a couple of minutes we're all loaded, our small group re-united. The kit gets left on the floor as we all go up onto the bridge, the lads all grouping round Nick and Lani. Clarence strides up to the grinning lad and pats him heavily on the shoulder, almost sending him sprawling into the desk.

'Brilliant Nick,' he rumbles with a grin and I can see Nick is pretty much floating off the ground with the compliment.

'Lani worked out the side thruster things,' he replies. Clarence and the others turn to the woman and re-start the compliments while she smiles graciously.

Turning round I see Dave looking as expressionless as Lani, but something in his eyes tells me he's not happy.

'Sorry Dave, we shouldn't have gone after it like that,' I say quietly.

'We split the group Mr Howie,' Dave answers with a straight look. My stomach drops at the implication and disappointment clearly evident to me in his otherwise unchanged tone.

'It was instinct Dave; we saw the rope and went for it. I know what you're saying and I thought the same just after we got on board.' He stays looking at me silently. 'Lesson learnt,' I add in a quiet voice.

'It's good though,' he adds thoughtfully, 'and safer than being on land.'

'I thought you didn't like boats.'

'I don't.'

'But this is alright?'

'It's safer for the group, keeps us together so yes it's alright.'

'Okay Dave, point taken.'

'There is one problem Mr Howie.'

'What?'

'We're on the water which is flat, and we're on a big white boat that everyone for miles will be able to see moving.'

'So it's a good thing having this boat but also a bad thing having this boat?'

'Yes,' he answers, 'good and bad with everything Mr Howie.'

'Dave, if you had a full cup and drank half of the contents how would you refer to the remaining contents of the cup?

'It depends.'

'On what?'

'What the contents were, for instance if its water then I would refer to the content as water, if it was soup then I would...'

'No I mean not the actual content as in the substance...okay so you have a cup of water and you drink half of the water. How would you refer to the water still in the cup?'

'I would say it was the water in the cup?'

'Okay, no I mean like you've had half of the water, so...?'

He stares back at me, hardly moving, 'I'd drink the rest not knowing when the next drink is coming.'

'Yeah good idea, but how would you say the cup is left.'

'Empty. I finished it.'

'No before you drank it.'

'Full.'

'No, when you've had half of it...'

'Soon to be empty because I know I'll drink it.'

'Aha but it was full.'

'Yes it was...but I drank it.'

'So the cup is empty?'

'After I drunk it, but it was full before.'

'Right so at the point of it being half filled, would you say half full...'

'...Yes...'

'...Or half empty?'

'...Yes.'

'Which one?'

'It's both.'

'It can't be both.'

'It is both.'

'If you had to choose one...which would it be?'

'Neither, I'd drink it.'

'If you couldn't drink it...'

'Why can't I drink it?'

'Er...it's poisoned.' Stupid thing to say.

'I drank poisoned water? Why would I do that?'

'You didn't know it was poisoned.'

'Who poisoned it?'

'Doesn't matter, look you just can't drink it okay? You've had half and it's not poisoned but you just cannot drink the other half.'

'Okay.'

'So what would you call it?'

'Useless.'

'Useless?'

'I can't drink it. It's useless.'

'Shall we get that coffee machine plugged in?'

'Okay Mr Howie.'

Nick and the lads piss about on the bridge, laughing at each other taking turns to drive the boat. The rest of us try and sort through the kit loaded on board and find a plug socket for the coffee machine. I say try because the lad's hard turns as they egg each other on send us flying about all over the place until Dave, already looking very unhappy at being on the boat, opens the door to the bridge and says something loud enough for them to hear. Whatever it was, it was effective as the boat immediately settled down to a more relaxed pace and in a straight line.

'Well done Dave,' Clarence rumbles appreciatively. The image of Lani pressed so close to my body in the engine room keeps flashing through my mind. Her beautiful face staring up at me, her eyes closing gently as she waited for the kiss that never happened and then the fleeting look of disappointment flashing across. Shit, this is the end of the world. I should be grabbing her hand now and pulling her to one side so I can snog her face off so we can fall to a heap on the floor.

'You okay Mr Howie, you're staring at my hand,' Lani interrupts my thoughts, bringing me back to earth with a jump.

'Eh? What? Yeah I was miles away,' I reply.

'Are you getting it on or what?' Clarence asks from a few feet away.

'What?' I feel a mild sense of panic rising in my voice.

'The coffee machine, did you get it on?'

'Yes! It's on,' I blurt back quickly as he gives me a strange stare and Lani laughs softly.

'Your face,' she whispers from the side of her mouth.

'This is your fault,' I reply with an accusing stare.

'My fault? Why because you were staring at my hand?'

'I wasn't thinking about your hand...'

'Oh, what then?'

Damn it, why does she have to ask that, 'nothing,' I shrug, busying myself with the machine and trying to figure out how it works. A row of buttons on the top plinth, small lights underneath them and images of small cups, big cups, two cups.

'Need some help?' Lani asks and steps in close. Her small but deadly hand lifts as she runs her slender fingers along the buttons, 'we need this one,' she points to a button marked with a picture of two cups. She smiles and leans past me to take two mugs from a box, her face tantalisingly close to mine again. Next she pulls a bag of coffee beans and shoves a load into a glass tube at the top of the machine. Pressing a button and the coffee is ground and pushed into a huge metal spoon, more like a mini shovel.

'How do you know how to do this?' I ask mesmerised as I watch her deftly work the controls.

'We had one in a place I worked,' she replies. I miss what she does next but suddenly the two mugs are beneath two spouts pouring the hot thick liquid into the bowls.

'We need milk really, can you start opening those portions and pour them into here,' she passes me a metal jug. My fingers fumble for the plastic lip of the small UHT milk portion. I get it open and pour the meagre contents into the jug. She stares at me, grabs one and rips the top off quickly pouring the contents in. I take another one and match her pace, she does another and we rip through them. Taking our frustrations out on the defenceless plastic pots which get mercilessly tossed onto the floor, discarded and unwanted. The white milk gets poured in, more follows as more pots fall from our hands like glistening brass shells from the GPMG. Eyes narrow and widen, mouths twitch as the portions are abused, penetrated and thrown away. The jug slowly fills and our hands work quickly. My god she is beautiful, soft lips that part to show white teeth, pink tongue darting out to moisten them. High cheek bones, the angle of her eyes, silken black raven hair cascading down her shoulders. Milk spurts on her thumb as she presses too hard on the flimsy lid, the white liquid rolls down her digit as she raises it to her lips and quickly licks the dairy juice away.

The jug gets filled, our feet covered in the wasted pots. She takes the jug and shoves the solid shaft of a metal pipe into the liquid. Turning a knob and something hisses loudly, the milk steams and froths, she watches me watching her. Bubbles form and blow on the surface as the shaft steams and rapidly heats the milk. She dials the knob back down and takes the two mugs already filled with the thick espresso coffee.

Slowly she upends the milk pot and pours the frothed thick liquid into the mugs. Gently spooning the creamy liquid out she fills the mugs and pushes them slightly towards me.

'Dave, Clarence...coffee,' I call out. The lads appear and reach over, gently removing the cups from between Lani and me.

'I'll go and see if the boys want a coffee,' she says before moving off and disappearing through the door to the bridge.

Sighing and breathing out I turn round and rub the stress from my forehead, stretching and rolling my shoulders too. Opening my eyes I see Clarence and Dave both stood a few feet away, holding frothed cups of coffee and watching me with interest. The mug looks ridiculous in Clarence's huge paw.

'What?' I ask as they both stare without speaking.

'Nothing boss,' Clarence smiles and sips at his coffee, 'very nice,' he murmurs.

'Yeah she is,' I sigh and hold my hands up exasperated, 'really bloody nice and I'm a bumbling bloody fool.'

'I meant the coffee,' Clarence says.

'Oh.'

'And she's stood behind you.'

'Oh.'

'We'll be outside, come on Dave let's have a look at the engine room.'

I turn round slowly, a look of extreme discomfort on my face as I see Lani stood there, expressionless and staring.

'I...er...' Stuttering I take a breath and get myself in order.

'You got it going then? Can I have a go?' Nick bursts out from the door and starts examining the machine, running his not so slender fingers over the buttons and murmuring to himself quietly.

'Is it working then?' Cookey comes through next, followed by Tom as they gather round the machine.

'You'll need these opened and poured in here,' I show them the boxes of milk portions and the metal jug. The frustration eases as we stand round laughing and joking as the milk portions are ripped open. The lads chucking them at each other as Clarence and Dave come back inside, the big man giving me an apologetic shrug as he watches the lads messing about. I smile back to show no hard feelings.

Coffee is made for everyone. Proper coffee with steamed milk and sugar and the strong espresso fires us all up as the laughs get louder. Gathering on the bridge we open the two side doors and let the warm air flow in. I stroll outside and sit on the public benches, enjoying a proper coffee and a smoke in a warm beautiful relaxed setting. The boxes of muffins, cakes and bread sticks get passed round. We sit there munching in the middle of the sea and watching the blue waters surrounding us.

'So what's our situation?' I ask everyone.

'We're almost out of shotgun shells,' Dave replies, 'no pistol rounds left, just axes and knives.'

'So if that had carried on last night we could have been in the shit,' Blowers says.

'But it didn't,' Clarence replies, 'don't think like that, it'll mess your head up.'

'I know we're all super hard zombie killers now, but we ain't gonna last long without proper guns and bullets,' Cookey adds, his point serious for once.

'The shotguns are good in a tight spot,' Blowers continues, 'but we need those assault rifles really.'

'We'll have to go for another base then I guess,' I say looking at Dave and Clarence, 'we could try and load up before we get back to the fort. That'll give Chris a nice surprise.'

'It certainly would, but I don't know any army bases anywhere round here,' Clarence says.

'Don't need army bases,' Dave cuts in, 'this is navy territory, we go for them.'

'A navy base?' I ask, 'seems obvious, do you know any?'

'How about navy ships?' Lani asks, 'like that one.' She points towards Portsmouth harbour in the distance. The bulk of a light blue greyish coloured navy ship anchored in amongst the backdrop of cluttered vessels and buildings.

'Aye aye, Blowers you know some navy lads can't you wave a signal flag or something' Cookey jokes, to a sputter of laughing from Tom. Great, another person that finds his jokes funny.

Blowers, too busy with a mouthful of muffin to reply simply sticks two fingers up and smiles as crumbs spill from his mouth, Tom giggles, Cookey smirks knowingly and Blowers coughs with laughter showering everyone with bits of damp muffin.

'You dirty bastard,' Nick jumps up brushing his clothes off as the rest of us giggle from the sight of Blowers trying desperately not to laugh at Cookey.

'Do navy ships have assault rifles on them?' I ask when everyone has settled down, 'or is that a really stupid question?'

'Yes they do and....'Dave stares at me with a wicked pause, 'no it's not.' Another joke from the silent killer. Things are certainly looking up. But that just makes me look round in a state of rising panic. Nothing bad has happened for the last hour, no zombies, the ship hasn't sunk, and no sign of pirates swinging cutlasses at us. Something bad always happens and generally it's every bloody half an hour.

'They have detachments of Marines on board,' Blowers explains, 'nearly all ships have them, or at least an on-board armoury so they can do vessel boarding and things, repel attacks at close quarters,' he continues.

'What about the GPMG? Do they have them too?' Cookey asks.

'Sort off,' Blowers nods, 'they have fixed guns and things on the ships, we can have a look and see what ammunition they got in the armoury.'

'Plan then,' I smile, 'we go for that navy ship and see what we can find, unless they blow us up on the way in or something...then we load up and get round to the fort with our shiny new boat.'

'Yeah because our plans always work out so straight forward,' Nicks mutters, voicing the thoughts nearly all of us are having.

'Er...who is driving the boat?' Clarence suddenly asks, looking round at everyone gathered in one place.

'Cookey you said you were doing it,' Blowers says quickly.

'Piss off,' Cookey shouts back, 'I never did, it's your turn.'

'Someone drive the bloody thing,' I shout over them and get two sorry expressions and two "sorry Mr Howie's" as they push and shove each other into the bridge.

'Nick, do you want to do it mate? You've had the most practice.'

'On it,' Nick stuffs another blueberry muffin in his mouth and heads into the bridge.

Eight

'It's good, very good,' Maddox nods in satisfaction from the top of the now erected guard tower. With a clear view down the street opposite and a decent view down the roads running off to the left and right. Darius has fastened thick planks of wood along the northern side, giving cover to anyone climbing up and down. More thick high planks on the top level giving waist high cover.

'We need a spot light up here,' Maddox says to his friend.

'I'll sort it,' Darius agrees, 'we can use some of the solar panels from the grows and rig something up, or a generator for now. What we doing with the houses then?'

'We'll use them as crew houses, let each crew have one. But we got to check 'em all first, make sure they're the same...'

'Yeah right,' Darius interrupted, 'don't give any of 'em something the others ain't got. It'll kick off bruv.'

'Fact,' Maddox nods, 'I don't like the idea of crews being in the two end houses, these ones closest to the junction. The top windows will be used for spotters anyway, so we'll stick with the other houses. Eight of them, eight crews, figures just right.'

'What about us?' Darius asks.

'We use the units, me, you, Lenski and the girls.'

'What about Sierra?'

'She gets a house with her crew, down to you innit if you want private time, you figure it out.'

'Fair one,' Darius smiles, already looking forward to some secret night time sneaking about in the dark for a fumble with his girlfriend.

'Get the crews gathered by the pit, we'll get the chiefs and the girls to go through their bedding while we check the houses and make sure they're ready.'

'You gonna get them in tonight?' Darius asks with surprise.

'Yeah why not? Liam looks about ready to take on your crew so we just need one more chief for Rykers.'

'Put Mohammed on Rykers crew,' Darius advises, 'he'll get 'em sorted out and we'll get Mohammed to choose one from his crew to step up. Liam will be fine with my crew, they're pretty good already.'

'Good idea,' Maddox looks with gratitude at Darius for his quick thinking, 'right you get the crews together and we'll give them the good news.'

Darius climbs down leaving Maddox alone and staring out over the gates. Just in one morning and a few hours of the afternoon he's drastically changed the compound. Extended it, made a bigger space and changed the mind-set of a few youths. He knew that although the youths had lived hard lives full of violence and excess, they were also young enough to adapt and maybe within a little while he could show them a better way. The survivors out there needed to know the compound was off limits, simply because the children needed a safe place and they were ready and willing to do what it took to make it safe. But maybe they could reach an agreement, one less deadly to the survivors, something that meant they could live side by side. That would take time, but Maddox knows the one thing they do have plenty of is time.

He climbs down the tower and makes his way slowly to the back of the compound, walking steadily down the street he thinks it needs a name, something personal to them all. With a smile he thinks of the perfect name instantly.

Rounding the end of the unit he walks towards the pit, rolling his eyes at the filth encrusted youths, grimy from brick dust and grease, faces blackened, hands covered in dirt. But they smile and joke with each other. Instead of looking pale and sickly the youths looked flushed with red cheeks, dressed in t shirts and vests, hoodies off. They look like children Maddox muses as he takes his place by the log.

'Good work today,' he starts off quickly, 'we got loads done and made ourselves our own street. I was thinking about a name for it,' he looks round watching them looking at him expectantly, 'Zayden Street,' smiles and nods all around, a few eyes fill with tears. 'We got ten houses in Zayden Street, five on each side. The last two next to the junction will be used by guards and for storage. The others will be crew houses, one house for each crew.' Cheers erupt from the youths. Rumour had spread that this would be the plan, and the chiefs had been asked continually all day and had to admit they didn't know either. 'One house each, but we got to sort them out before you get into them. A few things first.' Maddox waves his hands up and down, appealing for quiet. The youths respond with a few comments from chiefs and older kids. 'Liam, you are now crew chief for Darius's crew…' More cheers as Liam's face splits in half from the huge grin running ear to ear, youths surround him, patting him on the back. Maddox and Darius share a quick nod, knowing a good decision has been made. 'Mohammed, you gonna take Ryker's old crew on and we need you to choose someone to step up for crew chief, have a think bruv,' Maddox watches the serious lad nod back. Knowing he'll understand the need for Ryker's crew to be under good leadership for a while. 'Darius, Lenski and me will be in the units so we get a bit of space from you lot,' a few laughs, 'and maybe Sierra will be popping over once in a while so Sierra, make sure you choose a good deputy for when you're sneaking about to see Darius,' more laughs. 'Crew chiefs, I want the bedding checked for everyone. Nothing dirty or smelly is going in those houses and they get cleaned before they get used. We still got a lot to do. Get your tents organised and let Lenski and the girls know if you need clean bedding. We'll be checking the houses to see what they need.'

'Xbox's and weed,' a youth shouts to an outbreak of giggling.

'Xbox? Maybe…Weed…not yet.' Maddox answers quickly, letting the firm tones of authority into his voice. 'Darius,' Maddox nods at the older lad standing nearby.

'Yeah, from tonight. One crew will be in charge of security. The compound is too big for a few to be used now. One crew will stay up and do the guarding, the tower, some in the bedrooms of the end houses and patrols in the base too. That crew will be given the next morning off to sleep.'

'Questions?' Maddox shouts out.

'Do we have to use the houses? I like the tents.' A voice calls out.

'We'll see,' Maddox replies, using the universal get out reply relied on by millions of teachers, parents and guardians since time began.

The afternoon stretches on as Maddox, Darius and Lenski move from house to house, working out how many beds they will need, what rooms should be used as bedrooms, if the chiefs should have their own rooms. Bedding, pillows, lights, weapons, power supply, toilet, toilet rolls, clean water, wipes…Lenski scribbles furiously on her clipboard as the lads discuss the options and work out solutions. Crew chiefs sort through sleeping bags and blankets, helped by the girls who now have the confidence to come out of the units, seeing the children as children for the first time and not hardened gangsters swaggering about smoking drugs and showing off with weapons.

As the crew chiefs report back to Maddox, he orders them to take the bricks and debris from the walls of the knocked through back gardens and to make fall back positions where the old fence used to be. Remembering old movies where they would have s pile of sandbags and a few soldiers crouched behind, firing madly into the approaching enemy. The chiefs round youths up and start the hard work of dragging the heavy bricks over to the compound.

'I was thinking,' Maddox says quietly to Lenski, 'about the idea of using the school playing fields to plant stuff. We could speak to the survivors on the estate and get them to help, so it belongs to all of us, not just the compound.'

'Is good,' Lenski agrees quickly, 'it will show them we try to help and not kill them, is good yes? There be other places to use too. I think they move to the houses near here soon.'

'Why?' Maddox asks.

'In old days, the king live in the castle no? The people they live in the houses near the castle so the king and his knights come to rescue them if the bad thing happen. It safer to be closer, they move here soon.'

'Shit,' Maddox sighed, 'this stuff is complicated.'

'We should get a patrol out,' Darius interrupted, 'check those infected ain't getting near us innit.'

'Yeah,' Maddox thought for a second, 'get Jagger to take his out, tell 'em no taxing, just a quick walk through, or they can use bikes if they want, check about and get back here.'

'On it.' Darius ran off, jogging towards the units.

'He remind me of you,' Lenski said quietly as they watched the stocky form of Darius moving away.

'He's a good mate, we're lucky he's with us. He's always had my back. Right, where were we? Counting beds? You ready?'

'You are the dictator no? So bossy,' she laughed and held the pen ready above the paper.

Nine

'Tonight then we take back what's ours. We take that compound and we have the security and the food,' Jeff nods round at the gathered congregation all staring at him. He knew he had them ready. Just mention terrorism, babies and drugs and they'll do anything. He was ready to go for the ace up his sleeve and mention *it's what Princess Diana would have wanted.* Most of these looked old enough to remember her. But he didn't need too. They were hungry and scared, in fact they had been terrified for days but a couple of days of not seeing those zombies had given them a bit of confidence that the worst was over and now they could take the compound and live in safety. All of them imagined that the compound was stuffed to the rafters with rooms of fresh food and they could gorge for days and still have enough left to last forever.

Once the old man had left, Jeff had continued unopposed and talked them into his plan. Convincing them that those poor kids were being drugged and brainwashed by the Bossman, who was without doubt the main terrorist. They needed saving. The children needed help so they were doing this to save the babies, save the children and keep everyone safe.

Some had argued that being out at dark was dangerous, those things moved fast and were evil at night. Jeff successfully counter argued that none had been seen for a couple of days, that they were all dead and now was the time to strike. A full frontal assault, everyone was to bring a weapon, sticks, bats, knives or whatever tools they had lying about. They would charge the gates in the confusion of the night, while all the children were inside being injected with Heroin and they would take the compound. Save everyone and show them kids how it should be done.

As the congregation dispersed from the library, with Jeff making them go out a few at a time so there wasn't a mass exodus on the streets. He reminded them to meet back here at sunset. Most of them asked what time that was and had to be told it was when the sun went down.

Jeff knew the outcome already. He knew that in the confusion of the night he could slip to the back and watch this lot, whipped up by strong words, charge at the gates and take those little shits out. Then he could get in and claim the prize. He would be the leader. The Bossman. He would be in charge and get these women to do what he wanted. An image of being surrounded by tough bodyguards while beautiful council estate girls hung off his arms, a big cigar in his mouth and ordering his private army to do whatever he wanted. And that fucker that punched him, he would be the first to be killed. Not by Jeff though, unless it was dark and he could shoot him with a gun from the shadows. Jeff knew he wasn't a brave man, stupid and foolhardy but not brave. He would get these idiots to do the dirty work.

Touching his broken nose, he grimaced as he looked forward to the night and taking revenge on those little shits.

Jeff the Bossman. Yeah. That sounded good. Lord Jeff, Baron Jeff, yeah that was better. Baron Jeff of the compound.

As the last of the filthy bedraggled survivors filed out with whispered encouragement from soon-to-be Baron Jeff, he looked up at the sky wishing it was dark now and cursing these long summer days.

Ten

While Nick drives the boat towards the harbour entrance, a huge wide open mouth that stretches back deep into the city, and under order to hold a steady speed so we don't break anything. The rest of us set about sorting our kit. Energised and ready now we've got something to do and somewhere to go. Another mission. On the road and doing things again. Well on the water anyway but the meaning is the same.

Wake up; steal a boat, then plan a raid on a navy warship. What more could a supermarket manager ask for, other than a kiss from the sexiest woman I've ever seen. Maybe there'll be a dark corner on that ship we can sneak into for a few minutes.

Water bottles get re-filled, the remaining shotgun shells get handed round which amounts to four each. Four shots each before we're down to hand weapons. Bloody hell, Blowers was right, that was too close last night. Another few minutes and we could have been finished off.

Except we didn't did we. We got through by the skin of our teeth again and Darren is dead, his head detached from his body by Dave and kicked down the road just to be sure he doesn't try and staple it back on. But he's gone and about as much use as a blind fox. But that leaves that girl Marcy. Will she harbour the same vendetta as Smithy or leave us alone from now on?

My mind becomes a microclimate, a swirling vortex of suggestions, counter suggestions and ideas as I try to plan ahead. We have to get better weapons, and if I knew there weren't survivors on that bloody Island, and if Nick could figure out the missile system, which he probably could, then I'd send a load of British Navy missiles at the damned thing and be done with it. Raze the thing into the sea and Marcy along with it.

Dave find a box of batteries and with help from Lani, they slide the backs of the radios off and fit new batteries in each one. Checking each works, transmitting and listening. He attaches a radio to each kit bag and pushes fresh batteries into the side pockets.

'What's the range on those things?' I ask.

'Not far, maybe a couple of kilometres on flat open ground, less in built up areas.'

'Right, it's better than nothing though. I think now's the time for hot washes if anyone wants them.'

'I'm first,' Lani jumps up and grabbing her kit bag she runs into the ladies toilet letting the door swing closed behind her.

'There's only one male toilet on the ship, two sinks so be quick.' Tom and Blowers move off first, taking their kit bags and going into the toilets.

'So you think anyone will be on those ships?' I ask Dave and Clarence.

'Might be, there would have been some personnel on board when it happened, but it's whether they stayed there or not,' Clarence replies.

'Seems a safe place to me, they must have food, fresh water, weapons and big steep sides plus loads of big guns if anyone gets too close, like us….in a big white boat.' We stare at each other as Cookey looks between us. 'Oh well, 'I guess we'll find out in a bit,' I add cheerily and catch Cookey shrugging as he returns to re-packing his kit back.

When my turn comes, I head into the toilet with Dave to stand in front of the small stainless steel sink. We strip down to our underpants with no sense of shame or embarrassment. Taking care due to the massive puddles left by the lads messing about we fold out clothes and set about scrubbing ourselves using the ten seconds of hot water flow we get each time we press the plunger down.

'Oh that feels bloody nice,' I scrub at my face with the warm water, using soap from the dispenser to lather up and rinse off. 'So you're alright about going for the ship then Dave?'

'Yes Mr Howie.'

'Is the armoury hard to find?'

'It depends on the type of ship, if they've got a Marines detachment. Maybe Clarence or Blowers might know more than me.'

'Fair one, mate, this hot water feels lovely. Strange but I don't miss many things really. I don't miss television or movies, not the radio, I certainly don't miss work but little things like hot water, coffee and clean clothes. What about you?'

'I don't miss anything.'
'Nothing?'
'No Mr Howie.'

'How come?' I glance over to see a look of discomfort flash across his face.

'After the service everything was...well it was unstructured. Work was the only thing worth doing but it was...' I can see him struggling to find the words and the look of confusion on his normally expressionless face roots me to the spot. I want to finish his sentence for him but something tells me this is the time for listening.

'Working with you was good Mr Howie, you had order and structure but the others didn't. I couldn't cope outside of work; I didn't know what to do every day. I would sit and stare at the walls, train, exercise, sharpen my weapons. It was like I was waiting to get called back up...only they didn't call me up.' The thought of Dave not coping with something is remarkable, but then in this maelstrom of violence and upheaval his skills count for everything and he's kept us alive time after time. But I know, more than anyone, that his social skills are virtually non-existent. He lacks empathy and understanding of other's feelings and doesn't get half the jokes flying about. But he fits. My god he fits in and is revered by everyone here.

I don't want to say anything contrite or fake, and I remember my Dad telling me that sometimes the best response is to say nothing at all. So I do that, which seems to be the right thing as Dave nods at me and carries on quickly washing. He scrubs his face, neck, armpits and groin first. A squaddie wash quick and thorough, get the important bits done first and then do everywhere else. The feet are next, washed, rinsed and dried carefully between the toes. Then he does the rest of his body. I copy his actions and realise that even here, in a small toilet on-board a ferry in the middle of the sea, I'm still learning from him.

'Dave, would you mind showing the lads how you just washed, sounds stupid but it's really effective.'

'Okay Mr Howie.'

'Thanks mate.'

'I don't have to show Lani though do I?'

'No Dave, you don't.'

'Oh okay, I'll leave that to you Mr Howie,' he says bluntly picking his kit bag up and walking out of the bathroom. He pauses at the door and glances back with a quick smile and he's gone, leaving me with a mouth hanging open and shaking my head.

Excitement grows as we make final plans once everyone has washed and groomed. Gathering on the bridge and I try not to notice Lani's glistening wet hair and the tight black vest top she's now wearing and the cargo trousers taken from the fashion store we raided in the town. She looks the part, half soldier, half mercenary and all gorgeous sultry and stunning. The lads look pink faced but still stubbly and hard. At least we've all got clean tops and underwear on which, if nothing else, makes us feel cleaner.

'It's late afternoon,' I say looking at the sky, 'we get on the ship, get the gear and do one back to our fort.' I stare round at the faces nodding back,

Nick eyeing the controls and staring at the looming grey vessel ahead.

'What do we do?' Nick asks, 'go straight at it? Go round a couple of times? How we getting on board?' Looking over I see what he means. The navy ship, despite being small for a military vessel, is still much larger than us and the sides are much higher.

'Hang on,' Blowers steps to the window and lifts the binoculars to his eyes, 'yeah...that's a supply ship, it's RFA.'

'RFA?' Nick asks.

'Royal Fleet Auxiliary, it's not a warship. They use 'em to supply warships, food, fuel, medicine, ammunition...'

'Ammo? Cookey exclaims, 'there'll be shit loads then.'

'Yeah for the big guns, missiles and anti-aircraft. Maybe not for the rifles though, it depends...we might get lucky.'

We watch the vessel come fully into view as Nick slows our boat down. The ship is still way out from the harbour mouth and anchored in position by a huge thick chain extending out from the front. Closer now and I can see there are no big guns on board, the ship is squat and square shaped. More like a cargo ship or container vessel. We slowly move round it, lapping in a big circle as we stare up and examine the various windows and doors. Trying to detect movement. Dave takes the binoculars and sweeps them over and over up and down the ship.

'Any one see anything?' I ask and get a chorus of negative replies.

'Lifeboat is missing,' Blowers points to a gap on the side of the ship, from the symmetrical flow of the vessel I can see he must be right; there is a gap where a lifeboat should be. 'Someone used it and got away then?' He asks.

'Could be, certainly indicates some kind of movement,' I reply into the tense silence. 'Have we got a loud speaker or anything on here?'

'Here try this,' Nick hands me a bullhorn with a black radio mouthpiece attached by a curly cable. Taking the loudhailer outside I face towards the ship and shout into the black mouthpiece.

'CAN YOU HEAR ME? IS ANYONE ON BOARD?' Nick tries to hold the boat steady while I shout repeatedly through the hailer, eventually giving up when I see Dave staring at me. Handing it over I stand well back and get ready to flinch.

'IS ANYONE ON BOARD?' Dave's voice booms like a cannon across the water and I can imagine people in Scotland turning round to see who was gobbing off. He repeats it several times as Nick struggles to control the vessel, drifting us closer and closer to the navy ship.

'Nick watch out mate!' Blowers shouts as he tries to engage the engines and pull us away. A loud clunk sounds out, followed by a vibration and a belch of black smoke spurting out the back. Then silence as the engines cut out.

'Nick...' Cookey shouts in warning, 'the engines have stopped Nick.'

'Yeah I can see that,' Nick shouts back, pressing buttons and desperately trying to figure it out.

'Nick!' Cookey yells again, 'that ship is getting closer mate.'

'It won't start,' Nick shouts in alarm, 'someone check the engine room.'

'I'll go,' Lani runs to the back of the top deck and nimbly drops down the steps, disappearing from view as we gather round the console trying to help a very flustered Nick.

'What about this?' Blowers asks pointing at buttons flashing. A low alarm sounds from the console, steadily getting louder and faster.

'Nick, any idea's what that alarm is mate?' I keep my voice calm, trying not to get him more flustered.

'The ships on fire,' Lani's loud voice comes from the back. We all freeze staring at each other then burst off and try to get through the door at once. Thick black smoke billowing from the engine room as Lani climbs back up the stairs with her hand covering her mouth.

'It's raging in there,' she shouts.

'What happened?' Nick demands with a look of wild confusion.

'Forget it,' I shout, 'get your kit bags, Nick try and aim us for the side of that ship. We need some rope.' Everyone scatters, bursting into action. Running back down into the passenger section and grabbing kit bags and axes, passing them back up onto the bridge and out on the top open air deck.

The smoke starts to seep into the passenger section as Clarence rushes to the back and closes the door, sealing the air off and preventing the choking fumes from coming in. Blowers and Tom run outside and along the side of the ship to the front, grabbing ropes and looping them arm over arm.

'What did I say,' I mutter to Dave as he passes the kit bags out onto the deck, 'every bloody half hour.'

'I'm so sorry Mr Howie, I must have done something wrong, maybe didn't vent something or release pressure...It's really complicated and I...'

'Nick...Nick, take it easy mate,' I say softly to the lad clearly wracked with guilt, 'these things happen mate, it's not your fault.'

'But you said something happens every half hour...' Nick wails.

'Yep and it bloody does,' I reply with a grin, 'if it wasn't this it would be Cookey smashing a hole somewhere, or Blowers blocking the toilet up and making us sink... or me doing something stupid! It happens mate, forget it.'

'How we going to secure the rope to the side?' Lani asks as Blowers and Tom clamber back through the bridge carrying the long ropes.

'Tie an axe on,' Dave grabs my double headed beauty and stupidly I feel a sense of panic at the thought of it getting broken. Nick negotiates the burning catamaran towards the grey bulk of the navy vessel. The supply ship's sides are high at the front and back with a wide flat lower section in the middle and a crane positioned in the middle ready for moving heavy goods. It's the lower middle section we aim for as Nick tries his best to pilot the drifting boat. Fortunately the weather is still gloriously hot and still with no wind or high waves to cause us more difficulty.

As the ships near each other, Clarence grabs the tied on axe and stands back. With no choice as to the angle of approach the front of our vessel gets closer and closer to the rear section, knowing we'll impact as drag alongside Clarence braces his feet and starts unwinding the rope and making sure nothing will tangle.

'Almost there,' Lani shouts to Nick. Seconds of baited breath pass then a heavy jolt and screech of metal as the front of the catamaran crumples from the solid metal side of the navy ship. Clarence holds for a second, waiting as the two vessels come together side by side and with no engine noise and no wind the sound of metal against metal is ear splittingly loud.

With a grunt, Clarence launches the axe up high and over the side of the lower middle section still ten feet above our heads. As soon as the axe lands with a clang he starts winding it back in. We watch and wait for the axe to catch but it appears over the top and drops back down. With a curse Clarence quickly winds it back in and launches it again. Pulling the rope it holds taut, he tugs a few times making the muscles in his arms bulge. The rope holds tight and I tie the end onto the metal safety railing of the top deck.

'I'll go first,' Lani shouts, her pack already on her back. Hands free she climbs onto the top of railing and grabs the rope, showing her deft climbing skills as she quickly scales the rope and reaches the top of the ship, pulling herself up. She stares down into the hidden ships interior for a few seconds before straddling the side and looking back down.

'You alright?' I call up, concerned at her expression.

'We got some company,' she says, not too loud.

'Oh...how many?'

'Only a few.'

'Really? Out here, bloody hell,' nothing surprises me anymore. Dave, on hearing that there might be potential foes he can play with is up the rope like a rat down a pipe. On reaching the top he too stares down before straddling the top and looking at Lani before staring back down at us.

'There's more than a few isn't there?' I ask him. He nods once then motions towards the middle; at whatever sight we can't see. 'No Dave, you wait for us and don't kill them before we get there.' I can see he's itching to make a start. 'Lads, you go next.' They scramble up, getting pulled by Dave and Lani as they reach the top. They too look down into the middle I still can't see before glancing back down and somehow inching along to all remain straddling the edge of the side.

'Just how many are down there?' Clarence asks with concern at seeing them all perch precariously on the edge.

'We'll find out in a minute, you going next?' I ask him.

'I might break the rope,' he mutters, 'you should go.'

'Get off; you ain't that heavy are you?' I ask with a smile. He grins back and climbs up to take the rope and pull himself hand over hand to the top. His feet on the side of the ship walking up until he too gets to the top, looks down and then I see his bald head looking left, then right and finally he twists round to me with a huge grin.

'Oh you're going to love this boss.' Taking the rope I pull myself up, feeling bad at poor Nick losing the ship he struggled so hard to get. It was a pity we couldn't keep it for a bit longer and rest up though. Reaching the top Clarence leans down and decides to try and pull my arm away from my body by grabbing my wrist and lifting me up.

Reaching the top I glance down and see Dave reaching over and cutting the rope with his knife. With the tension released the white catamaran continues scraping slowly down the side of the ship, screeching metal against metal. Thick oily smoke pouring from the back.

'I hope the tide pulls it away,' I mutter quietly thinking that knowing our luck we'll probably burn down the navy too. Then I turn to look to the interior of the ship. At the faces staring up.

Drooling faces with red bloodshot eyes. Pale skin a deathly pallor, cuts and bite marks evident as limbs hang loosely down at sides. The fetid stench of decaying flesh from sailors still wearing dirty overalls and the navy blue colours of the...well the navy I guess. More than that, there are zombies in smart suits, ball gowns and dinner jackets. Waiters and chefs, chavs dressed in cheap sparkly night club outfits, bouncers in black suits. How the hell they all got onto a naval supply ship in the middle of the sea I don't know. But what I do know is there is a lot of them, hundreds in fact. The middle area is packed deep and every single undead face is staring at us. A face off and no way of getting into the ships buildings without going through them.   Dave has already drawn his knives. The lads have gripped their axes ready, Lani has her meat cleaver and Clarence is cracking his knuckles. We're all grinning now. Grinning like the bloody idiots we are.

    I'm telling you, slaying zombies is addictive. Very addictive.

'Why are they all here?' Cookey asks as we stare down at the massed horde.

'They must have been brought out in boats when it started; probably thinking it was the safest place.' I reply figuring it's the only thing that makes sense and would explain the eclectic mix of personnel on board.

'That went well then,' Lani says abruptly getting looks of surprise from the rest of us, 'what?' she shrugs, 'it's true.'

'Yeah, fair one. Right… which way we heading? It's got to be into that structure at the back surely.'

'Probably,' Clarence nods staring round like the rest of us and trying to see any other ways into the ships hold or storage areas.

'Blowers? You got any ideas?'

'No Mr Howie, aim for the big building at the back like you said.'

'Okay. Do any of them look like super zombies? Heads not lolling, not drooling, or maybe a fake zombie pretending to drool and loll it's head.' As ridiculous as the question is, they all respond seriously. Scanning the hundreds of faces and checking for any signs of one of them not being a normal daytime shuffler.

'Dave? Anything?'

'No Mr Howie, they all look the same.'

'Okay, right well I guess we should crack on then. Bagsy I go first,'

'Second,' Dave adds with a lightning fast response with everyone else shouting "third" at the same time and arguing about who got it out quickest.

'Ready Dave?'

'Yes Mr Howie,' he says and drops down to land in the middle of a batch of waiter dressed zombies. They seem almost surprise to see him there and it takes a fraction of a second for them to respond and turn into him. By which time he's grinning like a maniac back at the rest of us while I shout he's a cheating bastard and launch myself down. But it's too late; Dave has started and drawn first blood. And second. And third. Possibly fourth and maybe I got fifth by the time gravity assisted me landing and I pulled the axe back and swung out muttering that he was unsporting and a cheat and the next time we went at a horde I wouldn't warn him.

I hear Clarence laughing like a braying donkey again at the sight of Dave dropping down and beating us all to it. But then they all join in, dropping down and setting about the shufflers with unabated glee.

No precision or uniformity here. Just slaughter. My axe swings back and forth with both keen sharp edges slicing, chopping, cleaving and breaking bodies open. The shufflers don't stand a chance and we move steadily deeper into their ranks. Nick, Blowers, Cookey and Tom shouting out the numbers of their kills with a competition.

'Six...Seven....Eight,' Blowers shouts in the lead, 'Nine....Ha no ten now!'

'Twenty one, twenty two, twenty three,' Dave roars out from several metres away as he glides through the air with his blades whipping out slicing jugulars open and stabbing into chests.

'You're banned for cheating,' I shout as a zombie in a ball gown with a heaving cleavage lunges at me with barred teeth and gets an axe to the face in response.

'Twelve,' Lani shouts in triumph.

'Thirteen,' Tom roars and adds another one as he lashes out decapitating a zombie.

The numbers are shouted as the competition heats up and I notice Blowers and Cookey have instinctively teamed up as normal, fighting side by side. Tom and Nick now doing the same, Clarence off by himself crushing skulls and Dave just getting warmed up as he spins, drops, leaps and kills with every lunge and twist. Lani stays close to me, just a few steps away and I watch the savage ferocity she uses. The meat cleaver is deadly in her hands, whipping out and slicing faces, necks and shoulders. Her amazing athletic ability really shows in close quarters as she bends and flexes, taking high steps like a dancer, planting her feet and using her body weight in the thrust and slash. Her face is alive, eyes determined. She uses her free hand to clutch the hair of an undead and force it down before she hacks into the neck. Letting go and moving off to drop down and swing the blade deep into the throat of the next one. She kicks back, impacting into the stomach of a woman undead lunging for her. One full turn and she's on the still reeling body opening a hole in its stomach, intestines spilling out.

Watching Lani is like watching Dave. It's beautiful, graceful and fluid. The rest of us are progressive and we kill as well as her, but it's the way they do it. Art, beauty and grace. As the bodies drop I find a space round me and lean on my axe, watching between Lani and Dave dancing through them. Both of them warmed up now and spinning like some amazing act on a stage. Clarence glances over and catches me skiving, giving me a puzzled look. I nod towards the two in the centre of the open middle section of the ship. He quickly punches one zombie hard, breaking its neck and clearing the view as he watches what I see. He nods over at me, leaning his back against a wall and watching as mesmerised as me. The lads soon do the same as they realise Clarence and I are stood still and watching. Slowly, we shuffle back to the sides and let Lani and Dave work in a free space.

There are still good numbers of undead and we stand ready to step in, but really there is no need. They are like ballet dancers. Poetry in motion. Lithe bodies that are exactly where they need to be. Lani lacks Dave's experience and strength but the symmetry of her body, the hair flowing and waving behind her more than makes up for that. As long as I draw breath on this earth I will never tire of watching Dave do this, and now with Lani doing something similar it is simply stunning. A spectacle never seen by humanity. Utter ruthless killers, relentless in their capacity for murder, devastating in their glory but simply breathe taking in their delivery.

'Have you ever seen anything like that?' I ask softly.

'No,' Clarence replies instantly, even his deep voice is full of awe.

'Jesus, look at him,' Tom whispers as Dave spots another solid group still shuffling towards him. He runs at them, long strides and launching himself high at the very last second. His feet push down into the faces of two, sending them toppling backwards and knocking several more over. Dave lands in the middle with one arm extended and the blade buried deep into the heart of one undead while his trailing arm extends behind him, again with the blade buried deep into a spinal column. He wrenches the blades out and stands upright, like at attention before spinning round and lashing his arms out. Three more fall with bright crimson sprays of blood spurting out in high arcs as their throats are cut. As we mere mortals watch the high spray he's already gone round behind two more and drawn his blades across two more throats.

Then it's over and the ground is once again littered with the broken bodies of the undead. Blood everywhere, bits of brain, bone and tendons glisten wetly in the soon. The metallic smell of blood mixes with the odour of decaying skin. Dave drops down and wipes his blades repeatedly on the clothing of the undead. Lani standing still and checking round sees their all down and turns to see us all staring at her and Dave. She smiles with a sudden intensity and locks eyes with me, making my heart skip a beat and my face flushes red.

'Bloody hell Lani! That was fucking awesome!' Cookey shouts with genuine amazement and walks towards her. The lads rush in congratulating the girl as she nods and smiles with humble thanks and wipes the sweat from her forehead.

Drinking water and washing the blood from our hands, taking care to use the anti-bacterial wipes on our skin we make our way carefully towards the superstructure at the back, stepping over corpses.

'Here,' Dave drops down quickly and reaches down to pull something from underneath a body. Holding the object between thumb and finger he holds his hands out, showing us the shiny brass casing of the bullet.

'Someone got some rounds off then,' Clarence scans about, toeing bodies out the way and spotting more casings on the floor. We thread our way towards the structure, examining the ground.

'Here!' Tom leans his arm in between a gap at the base of the crane structure, pulling an SA80 assault rifle out. Dave strides over and takes the weapon from him, snapping the magazine off and checking the weapon through.

'Empty,' he calls out, 'emptied the magazine and I guess whoever had it ditched it and went for his sidearm instead of changing magazine.'

'This would have been packed, just one of them bitten or infected and it would have been nuts. Must have been a soldier on guard or something,' I look round imagining the scene of chaos unfolding at the infection spread from bite to bite, the screams and yells and the terror sweeping through.

'Doors open,' Clarence having taken a few steps closer to the structure spots the open door at the base and calls back. His axe gripped and ready in his hands.

'It's a big building,' I say looking up at the structure, several stories high and no doubt with further levels underneath us too, 'do we clear the lot or just go for what we need and get out.'

'Get what we need and get out,' Clarence advises, 'we'll be here for hours clearing it.'

'How do we get out?' Lani asks quickly.

'Go for the orange lifeboats, they'll have quick release mechanisms inside. They'll slide down the frame and land in the water.' Clarence explains.

'Right, if it goes bent we go for them. Let's go,' I nod at the door and walk towards it. Dave shoulders the assault rifle and keeps one knife ready while the rest of us grip axes.

The cool interior is a relief after the strong direct sun on the deck of the ship and we proceed down a long corridor, Clarence out front and the rest of us trailing behind in a long line with Dave bringing up the rear. Dried blood is smeared everywhere, on the floor, the walls and even splashed onto the ceiling. Dead bodies lie here and there, dropped from shots to the chest and head. More bullet casings lead a breadcrumb trail into the ships interior. A frantic fire fight took place here, a retreating fire and manoeuvre possibly as the undead surged towards whoever was left alive and firing.

We reach the base of a set of stairs leading up and find more bodies stacked up with the butt of an assault rifle poking out from under the entwined limbs. Blowers pulls it out and uses the shirt tails from a downed undead to wipe the blood and filth away. Another SA80, the standard issue British military assault rifle and a weapon most of us are familiar with. Blowers quickly checks the gun and like the one found by Dave, he finds it empty.

'Used as a bat,' Blowers points to the dried bits of skull and matted hair on the butt of the weapon.

'That's two, just need some bullets now,' I say quietly.

'Hang on,' Clarence shoves his foot into the pile of bodies and starts punting them aside, separating them. The few of us close enough help out, dragging the bodies apart looking for more weapons. A camouflaged soldier is at the bottom of the pile, the smell of decay mixed with shit and blood is almost too much and I notice a few of us try not to gag. Clarence bends down and grips the front of the soldiers' thick shirt, lifting him bodily up from the ground.

'Get the pistol,' he says through gritted teeth while trying to face away from the stench. Tom reaches out and unclasps the utility belt round the dead soldiers' waist, lifting the belt and the attached pistol away. Clarence drops the body and we retreat a few steps, Tom handing the belt to Dave who pulls the standard issue pistol out and finds it unused with a full magazine clip and two more full magazines on the belt.

'They the same as ours?' Cookey asks, even his normal jovial voice is quiet and restrained.

'Yes,' Dave answers. He checks the pistol through, sliding the top back and checking the moving parts before handing one magazine to Clarence and the other to me. We both pull our pistols from our belts and insert the magazines into the grips, sliding the tops back and making ready.

'Yay we're back,' Cookey smiles, still quietly.

'Not quite mate,' I reply just as quietly, 'we got one door there and stairs going up, which way?'

'Go through the door, we should check down here before we go up,' Dave replies.

'Tom and Cookey take our axes, Dave up front with Clarence at the rear, I'll go behind Dave,' they nod back as the weapons are handed over. Dave slides his knife away and holds the pistol in a double handed grip as he stalks towards the door. I copy his actions and hold mine ready, lowered to the floor.

Reaching the door he checks my position before checking the door is open with his foot. No resistance and the door starts opening, he pushes it quickly and steps through, holding the pistol high and scanning all about. I step in behind him and check about. Another corridor leads off down the width of the ship. Doors to the left and right, all of them closed.

Dave motions he's taking the left and I nod, stepping to the right and moving towards the first door. I figure he'll want them done one at a time so I pause while he kicks the first one open and steps in; he's back out within a second and nodding to me. I repeat his actions, kick the door and step in. A small office with a desk, a computer, charts and folders scattered everywhere, bloody handprints smeared about.

Gradually, one at a time, the rooms are all cleared. Left, right, left, right and we make progress. The rooms are all office space, desks and computers, charts, folders, paperwork. We find one more body in a room; a uniformed naval person slumped on the floor with a bullet wound to the head, the pistol laying just inches away from his open hand. Clear suicide and we retrieve the pistol, passing it to Blowers who clears and checks the weapon.

Reaching the end of the passageway we stop before a wide lift, doors open and prevented from closing by the body slumped half in, the face chewed off, thick crusty blood pooled under the head and flies buzzing noisily in the enclosed area.

'Stairs,' Dave points to the end and a set of stairs leading down. Taking point again he leads the way and starts heading down into the depths of the ship. No power now and we have to pause and pull torches from our bags to light the way in the gloom. Two flights down and we come to another landing, more stairs lead down. Two sets of double doors, one clearly leading towards the front of the ship and into the big middle hold area, and another leading into a passageway running the width of the ship just like the last one.

'Passageway first,' I nod at the doors and move behind Dave as we repeat the motions, kicking doors open and quickly checking rooms. Most of these are private quarters with cot beds and small cupboards. Being below the main level of the ship there are no windows, no natural light. The torches illuminate ahead of us but just accentuate the dark patches and make the shadows look deeper. The ship is inert, lifeless. Our feet echo on the floor scrapes and scuff noises sound out as we move along. The kicks to the doors bang alarmingly and we all feel the tension rising. Heavy breathing and the air is significantly cooler down here.

The corridor is cleared and we head back down to the stairs and the next double doors leading into the ships hold.

Pushing through we enter into an almost pitch black room that must be almost the width of the ship and stretching out towards the front. The only light coming from the meagre grey of the open doors. We hold at the door for a few seconds, carefully listening but hearing nothing other than the creak of the ship. Square columns are stacked throughout the room. We shine our torches into the gloom and can see they're pallets of goods wrapped in plastic, ready to be hoisted or lifted onto other vessels. With so many of them stacked throughout the room we can't see further than a few metres.

'Spread out,' I say softly and wait until a long line is formed and we start pressing into the big room. Torchlight glances about, sweeping left and right. Soft footsteps and we make our way round the sinister looking columns. The doors closed behind us and the harsh torch light is only illumination now and that just makes the shadows seem deeper. Our footsteps echo softly, breaths exhaling, the rustle of trouser legs brushing as steps are taken. The slight clink of equipment. We advance slowly, one step at a time. We pass the first columns, heading further into the darkness and now feeling oppressed from the sentry like stacks of goods behind us. Torch light dances about, sweeping the ground and the columns all around us, each one of them much taller than a man.

The smell hits me. Rancid meat left to rot. A truly awful stench of putrid foulness.

'Is that smell from the food or the zombies?' Cookey asks with a gagging sound.

'Stay quiet,' Dave whispers and I wonder if anything ever bothers that man.

A sudden low groan holds us all in place. One long single groan and our hearts race at the unmistakable sound of an undead. We freeze stock still as the noise echoes round the room, none of us able to pinpoint the direction it came from. Glancing round I can't even see the others that clearly, just bright orbs of light from the torches.

Another groan rolls round the room. Low and deep. The hairs on the back of my neck stand up but I still can't tell where it's coming from but it sounds different to the first one.

The beams of torch light sweep round quickly and I grip the pistol, raising it up to point into the darkness.

Feet shuffling on the floor, heard but unseen. Groans straight ahead, then off to the left and then the right. Groans from all around us. A feeling of being surrounded. Our torches make us instantly visible. Beacons of light being circled by an enemy unseen.

A piercing howl rips through the air as the twisted features of a zombie come running into view, drawn to my torchlight like a moth to a flame. The thing launches itself at me, moving quickly, head fixed and staring.

'Shit, no light down here...not shufflers,' I shout in warning and raise the pistol firing several times into the mass coming at me. The retort of the pistol is deafening in this enclosed space, the muzzle flash is blinding but I see the thing drop down to lie twitching on the ground. More shots ring out, single and double taps that drown any other sound out. My ears are ringing and I can't hear them shuffle or groan.

'Get into a circle,' I shout, 'on me, on me' I repeat the calls and flick my torch on and off so they can find the way to go. More howls pierce the air as zombies rush into the light, a sudden transition from dark to light, teeth barred and heads already lunging forward. Shouts of alarm and pistol shots ring out. Bodies hit the ground as the undead are shot down. We get into our basic fighting circle, backs together and facing out.

'INCOMING,' Dave bellows as undead bodies launch themselves at us. Pistols fire quickly as we expend the valuable ammunition. They click empty and we're once more back to hand weapons, fending off the savage frenzied attacks, swiping out with vicious swings and shouts of anger as the things lunge from the darkness. Holding our weapons one handed so we can grip the vital torches. Our circle spins and twists as more bodies come flying from the darkness to meet a grizzly end from heavy axe or sharp knife.

'I've lost sense of direction,' Clarence shouts out. We all have from the darkness and the spinning round. None of us are able to tell which way to go. Another zombie lunges in screeching with venomous hatred as Dave darts out and takes it down. More rush in from all sides and I grip the torch between my teeth so I can use two hands on the axe. Dave gets swallowed up in the darkness as the rest of us fight with desperation. Hand to hand combat with night-time zombies in the pitch black of an echoing ships hold. Grunts of exertion sound out as we lunge and swipe, trying to hold our circle.

'Dave?' I shout during a quick break in the fighting and removing the torch from my mouth.

'Here,' Dave shouts from the gloom.

'Doesn't really help mate,' I shout back.

'Be quiet please and let me listen,' he shouts back and we all go silent, holding position and trying to make any noise.

'Can you turn the torches off for a second,' Dave shouts.

'NO!' He gets a chorus of replies.

'Okay,' he shouts back. The sound of bodies hitting the ground reach us as Dave somehow manages to move between them.

'HERE ZOMBIES….HERE ZOMBIES,' Dave shouts into the room, flashing his torch on and off, trying to draw the things to him. They kindly respond and we hear the wet ripping sound of his knives tearing flesh open followed by the thuds of bodies dropping.

'Coming in….don't shoot,' Dave appears from behind a column and takes his place next to me.

'We don't have any bullets left Dave,' Clarence says pointedly.

'Well just in case,' Dave replies.

'How many did you get?' Tom asks.

'Eight,' Dave answers instantly.

'Oh,' Tom says quietly.

Keeping our formation we move slowly through the hold, stepping on and over bodies. Torches shining out and trying to find the way.

'Over here,' Blowers shouts, 'there's a switch to open the roof up.'

'Will it work with the engines off?' Tom asks.

'Fucking try it,' Cookey yells. We crab sideways, heading towards the side and a big red lever next to a large grey electrical box, a big white arrow points upwards with the word ROOF stencilled next to it. Reaching the side, Blowers grips the handle and pulls it down. Flashing lights and an alarm sounds out as a hydraulic whine starts up.

'INCOMING,' Lani shouts as more undead come lurching from the deep dark shadows. The sudden sight of them caught in the torchlight is terrifying. Ghostly white faces with dried blood and horrific injuries. Flesh torn open and clothes hanging off them. Clawed hands held out, and the red bloodshot eyes almost shining in the reflection from the torches.

We fight and kill as a tiny sliver of light forms in roof. More undead stagger as we hold our position and fight out. The gap in the roof widens as the blessed light starts shining down hurting even our eyes from the near pitch blackness of the hold. The light floods a small long narrow strip on the floor and I watch as a zombie runs from the darkness and crosses the light. As the daylight hits his face he slows instantly and starts to shuffle but passes back into the night and suddenly becomes animated again, howling and continuing his jerky running.

We hold our position as the gap widens. Then a heavy thud sounds out from a body falling through the widening gap to land in the strip of light.

'What the fuck is that?' Nick shouts.

'The bodies from the top, they're falling through the gap,' Blowers shouts in reply.

'EYES ON,' Dave roars and darts out to take a charging zombie down. More sickening heavy thuds as the bodies we killed on the deck fall through the doors pulling back.

'Fuck it's raining zombies,' Cookey jokes, 'shit watch out!' we burst apart as a body falls inches in front of us. With no choice but to split up we move out trying to avoid the falling zombies and the ones still running in to attack us.

'Get in the light,' I shout and move into the widening strip of daylight now stretching across the room. The rest get into line either side of me as we stand in the light dancing between the bodies sliding off the retracting roof. Zombies stagger in to attack but instantly slow as the light hits them, making our killing easier. The instant transformation is incredible. Quick moving beasts turning instantly into the drooling shufflers.

It's over within a couple of minutes. We stay within the light moving out and killing them off as they turn slow. Eventually we're in full glorious daylight and once again surrounded by hundreds of bodies.

'Now that's worth knowing,' Nick says with a full spin round, 'no light so they didn't know if it was night or day.'

'By the skin of our teeth again,' Cookey grimaces, 'what was that you said Mr Howie about every half hour?'

'Bloody fact Cookey, spread out and see what we've got here.' With the light now shining down we move through the large hold, stepping over the bodies and examining the stacks and piles of goods. Most them food and cleaning materials. Engine parts, spare machine bits. Each column has a manifesto stuck to the side.

'Tinned fruit,' Tom shouts in an excited voice and starts attacking the plastic film, ripping it away to pull the boxes down onto the deck. We gather round and scoop the plain tins up, shoving several into our kit bags for later.

'There,' Dave points to a smaller pallet, a big wooden crate with a locked lid secured by a numbered security tag. He jogs over and kicks down on the clasp, snapping it free. Wrenching the top back he delves in and starts pulling boxes out, dumping them on the ground.

Gathering round we give a low cheer at the sight of the wooden lids marked with 5.56, the standard size of ammunition for the SA80 assault rifle. Dave prizes the lids open and we find pre-loaded magazines wrapped in grease-proof paper.

'Get as many as you can,' Dave says quietly and rather needlessly as we drop down and start filling every spare inch of our kit bags with the magazines. Dave and Blowers load the two recovered assault rifles.

'This is like Christmas,' Cookey laughs, 'any pistol rounds there?'

'No,' Dave replies lifting the boxes from the pallets and checking the lid of each before stacking them to one side. At the bottom of the pile two larger boxes form the base, both locked secured with multiple security tags.

'Bingo,' Clarence clearly recognises the boxes and bends down to rip the lids off with his bare hands. Pulling the new and shiny assault rifles out.

'Oh look at them,' Nick says in awe, 'hello babies...oh we've missed you,' he takes one of the weapons, his hands moving deftly over the weapon. He strips the plastic cover off and slides the bolt back, checking down the sights, hefting the weapon to his shoulder and then starting on the strap, getting it to the length he wants.

'Have you used these before Tom?' Clarence asks.

'Not these, I fired the police weapons on the range during an assessment for the firearms teams,' Tom replies.

'Lani?' Clarence looks to the woman.

'No never,' Lani shakes her head.

'Boss, alright if I quickly run them through the basics?'

'Crack on mate, here take these,' I hand Lani and Tom a weapon each and watch as they step away with Clarence. He drops down into a crouch and starts running them through the weapons basic moving parts, naming each part separately.

'This is a good day,' I mutter to the rest of them as they strip the covers off and load their weapons, 'a very good day.'

'Apart from Nick breaking the pier and then setting our boat on fire,' Cookey adds quickly.

'Fuck you, I don't know how that fire started,' Nick retorted defensively.

'I'm joking mate,' Cookey said softly, 'just don't break this one.'

'Fuck off Cookey!' The banter starts as I think to how lucky this find was. But then it wasn't all luck. It was us, planning and working out the best way to make our luck. We got the ship; we killed the zombies and risked our lives to get the prize. With these weapons we stand a much greater chance of survival and I'm already trying to figure out how to carry more of the ammunition with us.

'Anything else down here?' I ask Dave, 'we could do with ammunition for the pistols and the GPMG.'

'Fuck it, we might find another GPMG,' Blowers adds hopefully.

'How we gonna carry it all?' Cookey asks.

'Load a lifeboat, get to shore and find a vehicle… easy,' Blowers shrugs.

'Or we take what we can now and come back later' Cookey argues.

'What's the point in that?' Nick asks, 'just take everything we can now like Blowers said.'

'Someone else could have seen us getting on here, especially with that ferry boat pissing smoke out like that, we might lose it if we leave it here,' Blowers continues.

'Okay,' Cookey nods, 'yeah fair enough then, makes sense,' the lad concedes.

'Mr Howie, I can take Blowers and start searching for the armoury while you check the other stacks here?' Dave offers.

'Okay, do that mate. Nick, Cookey you start checking the other stacks. Hang on, we've got those radios. Use them.' We all reach for the radios on our bags and switch them on, each one blaring out with a second of static before locking onto the signal.

'Shout if you get any contact,' I call out as they start moving away.

'You too Mr Howie,' Dave replies and they move off swiftly. Nick, Cookey and I start moving round the remaining stacks, checking the typed manifestos.

'Dave to Mr Howie, radio check over.'
'Howie to Dave, loud and clear over.'
'Dave to Mr Howie, likewise out.'
'Cookey to Blowers radio check over.'
'Blowers to Cookey, loud and clear over.'
'Cookey to Blowers does this take you back? Being surrounded by seamen?...over.'
'Dave to Cookey, radio discipline from now, out!'

'Sorry Dave,' Cookey replaces the radio and I have to turn away as I giggle gently and once again ponder how the lads can make the word "Dave" sound like "Sarge".

Looking over I see Clarence shaking his head at Cookey with a wry smile and trying not to laugh too before turning back to Lani and Tom.

The stacks all contain rice, pasta, flour and basic ingredients. Cleaning materials, soaps and bleaches, disinfectants and scrubbing pads. Tinned food, lots of tinned food. One pallet even contains replacement uniform and boxes of new boots. We strip that one apart and root through the boxes, but they're all high visibility stuff and big clumpy steel toe capped work boots. Before too long Clarence has got Lani and Tom dry firing and changing magazines, shouting out when they do so. He drills them over and again and I watch as the intelligence shows as they grasp the basics with ease.

'Blowers to Mr Howie over.'

'Howie to Blowers, go ahead.'

'We've got RIBS here, all ready to go for launching, we can load them up and use them over.'

'How will we get them off the ship over?'

'There's a bit hatch thing here with a winch, we can open it and lower the boats down over.'

'Roger, where are you, we'll start bringing the stuff through.'

'Go to the end, through the doors and down the corridor, I'll meet you there over.'

'Okay mate, on way,' pushing the radio back on my belt we all converge on the boxes of ammunition and try to take one each, which is easy for Clarence but the rest of us end up sharing one box between two and moving through the hold towards the end. By the time we get there, Blowers is already in the corridor, grinning widely and nodding his head for us to follow him.

Down the short passage and through another set of doors into a wide open room containing two army Landrover's, bicycles and a big powerful looking RIB with an oversized rubber skirt and a mean looking engine on the back. Four hooks; two at the front and two at the rear connect the RIB to long chains hanging from a winch and the wall next to the boat looks to be a roll up shutter. Moving quickly, all of us feeling a strange sense of oppression from the dark inert ship, we dump the ammunition crates and head back into the hold for more. Dave and Blowers head off to complete their sweep for the armoury in the hope of finding ammunition for the GPMG.

'Nick, see if you can get that door open,' I point at the rolling shutter and the complicated set of controls on the wall for using the shutter and the winch and an extended vehicle ramp used for the vehicles to be driven. Using his torch, Nick examines the controls and pulls levers up and down. Eventually he finds a manual override and starts winding a hand winch, the shutter creaks, groans and starts lifting slowly as a thin sliver of welcome daylight floods in. Taking it in turns with Tom, the two of them winch the door open as the rest of us load the boxes onto the floor of the RIB, trying to keep the weight balanced.

'Do we get in before it's winched down?' Cookey asks, looking between the RIB and the opening hatch.

'No idea mate, we'll figure something out in a minute,' I reply as I reach for the radio on my belt, *'Howie to Dave, you got anything yet?'*

'Dave to Mr Howie, not yet over.'

'Howie to Dave, okay we want to be back in our fort before dark though. I don't fancy spending the night on this ship, there could be loads of them left on here.'

'Dave to Mr Howie understood out.'

'There's a scramble net here,' Nick says, pulling a bundle of knitted ropes out from a locker in the ground, 'we just roll this down and climb down it.'

'Nice one mate, I think we're just about ready.' I walk over to the now open hatch and stand staring down at the almost perfectly flat surface of the sea. It looks so inviting and just ready to be plunged into. The sultry warm air makes it feel Mediterranean, almost tropical. Perfect holiday weather and just right for dozing on a beach reading a book and sipping a cold beer.

'Looks beautiful,' Lani says quietly from beside me. I glance over at her own sultry good looks, almost tropical in appearance with her long black hair and tanned skin.

'Definitely,' I reply and she smiles, keeping her gaze out to sea and not turning to look at me.

'I meant the view,' she says.

'Me too,' I laugh softly and turn away to see Nick lighting a smoke up, leaning against a wall and exhaling a soft cloud of smoke. He nods and offers me his packet, I nod back so he throws it over and I tap one out, taking my lighter from my pocket and igniting the end. Savouring the harshness of the smoke pulled down my throat. Cookey sits down on the edge of the RIB and rubs his face while Clarence moves round the room examining the Landrover's and bicycles.

'These take me back,' his deep voice drifts over, 'we used to use Landy's all the time. Pity we can't one with us.'

'I don't think we'll get it into the RIB mate,' I reply, 'but I'm sure Nick would have a go at driving the boat into the shore if you want.'

'No thanks boss,' Clarence appears round the front of the vehicle, grinning at Nick, 'not after the last one eh?'

'Ah, I'm really sorry about that,' Nick grumbles, 'I really don't know what happened.'

'Dave to Mr Howie,' my radio bursts to life.
'Go ahead over.'
'We found the armoury, who needs a rifle?'
'I think we all got one now from the new ones in the boxes, grab some spares though, do you need a hand?'
'No there's a trolley jack here, we'll be back in five out.'
'Okay mate.'

We chat amiably for a few minutes until we hear a steady squeak coming from the end of the room, Dave and Blowers appear pushing a low trolley with one squeaking wheel, Blowers grinning like the devil himself and Dave looking as devoid of expression as ever.

'Wot you grinning at Blowers?' Cookey asks with a laugh.

'Ta Daaa,' Blowers pulls a cover from the trolley to reveal a long machine gun, the front lifted up on a tripod.

'Very nice,' Clarence steps over and hefts the General Purpose Machine Gun from the trolley, holding it one handed and instantly looking like a bald Rambo.

'Suits you mate,' I smile at him as Dave lifts a few heavy boxes of ammunition belts from the trolley.

'You fucking beauty,' Nick calls out as he scoots over to Clarence and starts examining the weapon.

'It's huge,' Lani says with a shocked face, 'is that the GP…thing you keep mentioning?'

'GPMG, means General Purpose Machine Gun and is has proven to be one of our most effective weapons in the fight against the zombie invasion,' Clarence explains.

'So that's better than these?' Lani lifts her assault rifle and looks between the two.

'That uses 5.56 rounds, this uses 7.62, bigger rounds, more firepower, greater range, it's belt fed too which means less stoppage for magazine changes,' Clarence replies.

'They're bloody good,' Blowers adds.

'Really bloody good,' Nick grins, 'I feel better now we're tooled up properly again.'

'I know what you mean mate, right let's get out of here I don't like this ship.' We unload the trolley into the RIB, distributing the weight evenly. Dave and Blowers also found pistol magazines in the armoury and hand them round until we each equipped with a loaded pistol and spare magazines, an assault rifles and lots of spare magazines, a sawn off shotgun with hardly any shells, axes, meat cleavers and knives. Trousers tucked into boots, tight tops and we look like a nasty bunch of bastards ready to overthrow some small country.

The RIB gets winched up, swung out and lowered down the side of the vessel until it plops onto the surface of the water. The scramble net is rolled down and we start to descend, going hand over hand until we reach the boat and balance precariously on the rubber skirt and hop onto the solid base. Dave is the last one down, and once on-board we detach the hooks from the winch and push the RIB away from the ship while Nick goes to the central column and gets the engine going.

Minutes later and we're steadily cruising away from the Navy supply ship, fully loaded with weapons and enjoying the wind blowing against our faces. Nick takes it steady, not wanting to risk the valuable cargo and heads us away from the mouth of Portsmouth harbour, moving along the coast towards our fort.

Eleven

Jagger moves quickly with his patrol stretched out behind him. Sixteen years old, of mixed race background and he was a switched on kid. Coming from a heart breaking background of abuse, neglect and poverty he took to the streets from an early age and did what it took to survive and get through the day. Now, with the security of the compound and his mates at his sides he feels a sense of belonging and loyalty. As crew chief he also feels responsible and has matured tenfold just within the last few days. Respected and well-liked he intends to stay that way and is deeply pleased that Maddox is now the boss with Darius as number two. He liked the Bossman, they all did, but the Bossman was never one of them. He was a rich older white man intent on making money from the young council estate kids taking all the risks. He proved himself when the event happened and moved faster than anyone else, getting the compound secured and the kids safely inside. But still, Maddox was one of them and he knew what they'd all been through, so it was better he was in charge.

Jagger felt proud when Darius sought him out and asked him to lead a patrol out with instruction to not engage with anyone, no stopping and talking, no taxing survivors, just move round the estate and make sure nothing bad was going on anywhere and get back so they could carry on working.

As they threaded their way out of the gates, Jagger and his small company moved quietly and quickly through the streets. Stepping over and round the festering dead bodies, decomposing in the sun. He had wondered why they hadn't cleared them away but Maddox said the smell covered up the compound and made it harder for the infected to find them. That's why Maddox was in charge, cos he thought of things like that. Jagger had already decided to volunteer his crew for the night's security, wanting the honour of going first and when he mentioned it to his crew they readily accepted.

Now, in the oppressive heat of the scorching late afternoon sun the crew started their patrol. Moving down the main roads, checking the side streets and avenues and stopping to listen at every junction. The chat and banter between them was muted and quiet, his crew well-trained and experienced at staying nimble and alert. As the afternoon wore on, so Jagger felt a growing sense of discomfort.

Every street was empty. No infected anywhere, no survivors picking through the debris and litter or breaking into the houses. Nothing appeared to have changed either, it was quiet, too quiet and his crew picked up on it too. Moving quietly and examining the streets with care they found not a single infected anywhere.

'Speed up, we need to check the whole place,' Jagger whispered to his crew, afraid of speaking loud in the deafening silence of the deserted estate.

They did speed up and moved faster at a jogging pace, street by street, suburb by suburb, checking the various sets of shops and lock ups but nothing anywhere. It was eerie and profound and Jagger wanted nothing more than to head back to the compound and the laughing and joking with all his mates.

As they entered a suburb previously allocated to Jagger and his crew, he moved them down to a house he knew was occupied by survivors. Standing outside he stared hard at the house, the windows were boarded up and the door had extra planks nailed across. No sign of life. He'd been told not to engage or speak to anyone but Jagger felt something wasn't right, something was up. He hesitated for a few minutes but in the end, chose to do as told instead of trying to speak to the people in the house. Walking away he felt eyes staring at him from the house but every time he turned back there was nothing to see.

Entering the compound, the gates already open to welcome them in and proving that the tower worked by Jagger and his crew being seen way down the street, Jagger was handed a bottle of water by Darius as he crew moved off to get drinks and find shade.

'Something ain't right bruv,' Jagger took a long swig and wiped the sweat from his head, 'there's nothin' out there, you get me? Nuffin'. No infected, no survivors, the place is empty bruv.'

'You what?' Darius asked.

'I'm tellin' you bruv, there was no movement, no infected, no zombies, no survivors, nothing, the whole estate is empty. We went everywhere, all the way down to the beach and the only thing we saw was some smoke like way out to sea, like a boat on fire or something innit.'

'A boat?' Darius repeated, clearly confused.

'Yeah like miles away in the sea just some black smoke going up into the sky innit, there ain't nuffin' else out there.'

'So where they all gone?' Darius asked more to himself.

'Dunno but it freaked us all out swear down.'

'Yeah, get some rest Jagger, I'll tell Maddox.'

'Sweet bruv.'

Darius moved off to find Maddox but with a hundred plans trying to be implemented and not having felt the eeriness himself something became lost in translation. By the time he found Maddox, in the unit talking to Lenski, he simply reported that Jagger had not seen anyone and no infected either, he did mention that Jagger was freaked out a little but the conversation quickly moved on to sorting the houses out and getting clean bedding, if they should keep all of the cannabis plants or just some, if they should let the crews use their back gardens or not, and re-arranging the tents in the compound.

The emptiness of the estate, the lack of infected or survivors noted by Jagger was hardly pressed upon.

To the north, barely a few miles away and on the other side of the motorway bordering the estate. The hordes gather quietly. Hundreds and hundreds of undead, fetid, decaying, drooling and all of them hungry.

They mass in great numbers, held in place by the will of the super zombie holding his position on the unused motorway and staring with evil intent at the estate and the young tender bodies held within.

Looking up at the sky the taxi driving zombie feels the heat of the day but knows the darkness is but a few hours away.

Within the estate, survivors sharpen knives, tape blades to the end of sticks and make spears, find bats and ram nails through the ends, get bottles of white spirit and other flammable liquids and stuff rags in the necks. They quietly busy themselves, preparing for the darkness and the fun it will bring.

Some are in a state of nervous trepidation. Others are excited and a few are outright shitting themselves. But they all know that if they move together, if they fight together they will take the compound and get the prize held within it. The drugs, the alcohol, the food, the safety. Then they will be the ones living in proper comfort while those feral little shits are put back out on the streets where they belong.

Twelve

'Look at that,' Lani points over the back of RIB and out to sea, at the thick black smoke billowing from the ferry still drifting across the sea.

'That's a big smoke signal,' I mutter quietly, reminded of Dave's concerns from earlier and suddenly realising how easily we can be spotted now. We moved several miles down the coast, going away from Portsmouth and moving just a few hundred metres from the shore line, watching for the fort. None of us know exactly where it is, but we know it is this direction.

The shore line changes from beautiful sandy beaches, rocky outcrops and manicured landscapes bordered by villages, fields and seaside businesses. Small harbours dotted here and there, some of them nothing more than a couple of pontoons with fishing boats tied alongside. The whole scene looks serene and comforting. Safe even. Rural England at the seaside, whitewashed cottages, brightly coloured wooden dinghies, shoreside pubs with tables and chairs scattered about, sun umbrellas advertising beers and soft drinks.

The steady rumble of the outboard engine, the gentle breeze and the warmth of the day give me hope. Lani glancing at me every now and then, smiling and looking content. The whole thing gives me a sense of hope. Hope that there will be a future for mankind and that we can recover from this and maybe even make it better in the end.

RR Haywood

Green fields stretching away from the shore suddenly give way to houses. Lots of houses. A sprawling mess of a housing estate going back as far as the eye can see and seemingly going on for miles. Even from here the cheap shitty state of the houses are easily spotted. The rundown feel of the place. Terraced and semi-detached houses, built close together. It looks rough with items of furniture visible in front gardens. Satellite dishes hanging off walls, old paint and road poorly maintained. We all stare inland, watching as it slowly drifts by and I know I'm thanking whatever powers that rule us that I wasn't in that estate when this thing went off. It would have been hell in such a built up urban area, people living on top of each other in an already hardened state of life.

My family are working class, not posh or wealthy in any respect but thankfully we never lived on estates like that and I've heard stories about how hard they can be, and the reality television programmes that showed the lives of the twisted morals, the drug and alcohol abuse, the crime and violence. But like most people that never came from areas like that, I can't help but look down my nose at them, at the way they lived, the aggressive overly defensive street language.

Bloody hell, the end of the world, the zombie apocalypse is upon us and I'm still sneering at the perceived rough common people. I'm not the only one either judging by the comments of "chav city" and "pikey land" being muttered from everyone else.

Then the engine cuts out.

And we all turn to stare at Nick. Nick, who I have personally seen staring down hordes of zombie with a laughing glint in his eye. Facing certain death with barely a tremor. A hardened killer, skilled fighter, tough lad with a skill for electrical and mechanical things. He swam after a ferry and scaled a rope just to stop it getting away. But right now, sitting behind the wheel of a RIB, on a perfectly flat sea a few hundred metres from shore, and with the rest of us staring at him, he holds a look of horror on his face. Frozen in time. Unmoving as the silence descends and the only noise is the gentle lapping of the water from the front as the momentum of the boat pushes us along.

'Shit,' Nick mutters in a high pitched voice, 'shit shit shit.'

'Nick…' Blowers asks softly.

'Shit…shit shit shit,' Nick repeats and grimaces as he twists the key and pushes the start button.

'Nick….' Blowers growls now with an edge to his voice.

'I'm never fucking driving again, you lot can fuck off and drive yourselves from now on, fucking boats cutting out and engines….shit shit shit.'

'Nick!' Clarence's deep voice snaps his head up, 'it's okay mate just calm down.'

'Yeah thanks,' Nick sighs with a look of relief.

'And fix the bloody boat,' Clarence adds and the look of shock on Nick's face sets me off as I burst out laughing. Cookey and Blowers instantly join in, laughing with delight. Nick smiles sheepishly and sticks his fingers up as we clamber our way over to him.

'Don't worry mate, boats just aren't your thing,' Blowers jokes.

'Or piers,' Lani shouts over to a fresh outbreak of giggles.

'There'll be some paddles here somewhere,' Cookey says looking about.

'Paddles? Are we on a hire boat on a canoe lake?' Clarence grumbles, 'you mean oars.'

'Same thing,' Cookey scratches his head, 'aren't they?'

'We've got two,' Lani holds two small oars up.

'What's wrong with it Nick?' I ask the poor lad sat looking dumbstruck on the centre seat with his head in his hands.

'No fuel Mr Howie,' he replies quietly.

'That's not your fault mate; anyone of us could have checked that.'

'Are we paddling along the coast or putting in here at gangsta land?'

'I think we'd better go in here mate, find a vehicle and go by road. It'll take hours to paddle along the coast with so many of us in this boat.'

'Right, I'll take one on this side,' Clarence takes one of the oars and straddles the rubber skirt.

'I'll do the other side,' I reach out to take the oar from Lani, who stares at me with a look of mock defiance.

'I can paddle perfectly well Mr Howie,' she smiles to show she's joking and straddles the skirt. Both of them start moving the paddles through the water and within a couple of minutes it's very clear this is going to be a long job. Two small paddles trying to push a big RIB through the water with several adults, loads of guns, crates of ammunition and a bloody great big machine gun.

We swap over with me and Cookey taking the next turn, and then we keep swapping over, trying to paddle hard and making barely any discernible progress. Sweating freely, panting and drinking bottles of water we lean down and use our hands in the water, frantically paddling and trying to reach the shore.

It does get closer, but painfully slowly and we all become acutely aware of the sun dropping down towards the horizon and the coming night.

'Fucking stuck in chav land in the middle of the night, we'll get mugged...I'm telling you,' Cookey whines looking up at the shore.

'Who is going to mug us? Blowers asks between ragged breaths.

'Those little chav gangsta shits, they'll have more guns than us,' Cookey replies.

'Swear down bruv,' Nick says.

'Innit blood,' Lani says in a brilliant accent, 'swear down my bling blood innit.' Giggles burst out as she continues in a perfect movie accent of council estate speak.

'I was born on a council estate,' Dave says cutting through the laughter instantly.

'Really?' I ask him, suspicious this might be one of his attempts at humour.

'Yes Mr Howie.'

'Where?'

'Hang on, I think we're into the shallows,' Clarence interrupts. He unclips his belt, handing the pistol and magazines to Lani and drops over the side, landing chest deep to a low chorus of cheers. He ducks down and washes the sweat from his face as Dave leans over the front and hands him a rope which looks like a thin bit of string in his big mitts. Then he starts wading and then we all feel the boat start to move faster. As we get closer, Nick and Tom drop over, taking rope and pulling the boat in.

'Pull my beauties, pull me to the shore my servants…swear down innit blood,' Lani stands at the very front, her feet planted wide and her hands on her hips looking down at the lads with a haughty expression. That sets us off again and even Dave smiles at the sight of Lani the queen ordering her subjects. She finds a length of rope and, taking care not to hit anyone, she whips the surface of the water and shouts demonically, 'PULL MY SHIP…PULL IT HARDER MWA HA HA'

Laughing like bloody idiots, with Cookey physically bent over and crying at the sight we gradually make it to the shore and jump down to help pull the boat up the pebble beach.

'Bloody look at that,' Blowers shakes his head at the sight of the broken glass bottles, take away wrapping and litter strewn across the narrow beach.

'We need a vehicle, we can't carry that lot,' I walk up the beach and onto the road, looking up and down for any signs of vehicles. Nothing in sight. With a sigh I walk back, grimacing at the lengthening shadows and the onset of dusk.

'We can't split the group and we don't want to leave that lot here, but then we can't carry it all either.'

'Mr Howie, we could hide some of it in one of those buildings,' Tom points across the road to the row of semi-detached houses. All of them look normal, undamaged and empty.

'Dump some stuff here and come back for it,' Clarence nods in agreement, stripping his boots off and wringing his socks out. In this heat he'll be dry in no time.

'Dave?' I ask, looking at Dave examining the houses.

'It's the best option but we need to move fast otherwise anyone watching us land here will know we delayed for something.'

'Okay, you go and clear one of the houses and we'll bring the stuff over.'

'On it,' Dave answers and jogs over the road, picking a middle house that looks as average as the others. He disappears round the back and less than a minute later the front door opens and he nods for us to come over.

Carrying the crates, boxes and spare rifles we do shuttle runs across the road, securing the load into an upstairs room. We ditch our shotguns too, but keep the axes and knives, then armed with assault rifles we gather back outside while Dave locks the front door from the inside and scoots out the back.

'Bloody hell Clarence, you carrying that?' I turn round to see Clarence stood there holding the GPMG by the top handle, loops of ammunition belts gathered round his neck and making him look even more mercenary than before.

'I always used to carry one of these, back in the day,' Clarence lifted the gun with ease and showed the end of the ammunition belt already fed into the side of the weapon, 'Malcolm and Chris always took the piss but it got us out of some tight spots.'

'Yeah I can imagine,' I reply as Dave joins us. Then we're back. Our group, on foot and armed to the teeth. I did consider waiting the night out in the house but I know we all want to get back to the fort.

'Night is here,' Tom says looking up at the black sky and the stars shining down.

'No howling,' Blowers cocks his head to listen. We all do the same, straining but there is virtually no noise other than the sounds caused by our presence.

'Let's move out find a vehicle, get back here and get our stuff then back to the fort. Stay quiet and keep your eyes and ears open. Dave up front, Clarence at the rear, okay? Let's go.'

Thirteen

The earth spins on its axis as the rays from the sun sweep across the surface. Night becomes dawn, but here, on a motorway in the south of England; day becomes night. A quickening takes place and the ex-taxi driving zombie feels his heart soar as the last of the golden rays plunge below the horizon.

As one, the massed gathering lift their faces and howl into the air, guttural roars that fill the sky and they change instantly from the stumbling, shambling, slow moving things of the day into the evil terrors of the night. Heads become fixed, eyes focus, and limbs twitch less. Steps become easier and controlled and then the exodus starts. Pouring from the embankment they drop down onto the tarmac of the road, gathering round the super zombie, growling and whining with impatience. He waits until most of them are down and then sets off, using the moonlight to pick his way through across the road, over the central reservation, across the other lane and down the embankments. Into the thin fields that border the estate and then they pass through into the urban squalor. Hordes and hordes of zombies pouring into the streets and keeping pace with the intelligent face of the super zombie pacing at the front.

The ex-taxi driver has perfect knowledge of the road layout and knows exactly where to go. Straight down through the estate and then up the main road that leads to the compound. An all-out frontal charge that will over-whelm the tender pieces of meat within the high fences.

His own mouth fills with drool at the pressing urge to feed, saliva spools down his shirt as he quickens his pace.

Fourteen

'Are we all here?' Jeff whispers loudly into the dark shadows of the library. Moonlight and fag ends glinting off the metal nails sticking out of bats and sticks. The medley of weaponry staggered him at first and his face split into a grin at the sight of the savage bastards tooled up and ready for Armageddon.

'Okay now listen, everyone that lives to the east of the centre will attack from that side, everyone that lives west will go from this side. We go up the two side streets and meet at the middle.'

'Which way is east?'

'Am I from east or west?'

'Is that left or right Jeff?'

'Fuc….okay, if you live the other side of the compound then loop round and come in from your side, those of us that live this side will come in from this side.'

'Why are we doing that Jeff?'

'If we go straight up the middle road they'll see us miles off, and in the dark with two big groups coming at them they'll think we've got even bigger numbers and might give up easier.'

'Or fight harder,' a voice calls out to a reply of "Ssshh" from various people.

'So, we give it half hour and then go for it, that gives you plenty of time to loop round, got it?'

'Can we throw our Molotov cocktails?' someone whispers.

'Don't be so bloody stupid, you'll burn all the plants down,' someone replies.

'Oh okay, maybe just at the gates then.'

'No, no fire bombs.'

'None at all.'

'No.'

'Well that's not fair…'

'Hang on,' Jeff whispers frantically, trying to prevent an all-out argument from erupting, 'take them with you, if we need them we'll call for them, got it?'

'What like in the movies, what you gonna yell? Mortars?'

'Er…yeah we'll yell mortars,' Jeff says exasperated.

'Okay…thanks Jeff.'

'That's okay Rodney…now everyone ready? Yes? Good and don't forget that nasty bastard Maddox or whatever his name is, make sure someone gets him quickly. Right let's go.'

Fifteen

'Okay okay,' Maddox waves his arms to settle the crowds of youths gathered round the roaring fire in the pit. 'Now that has been a long day, a very long day and we've everything done that we set out to achieve.' He stands tall and proud. Proud of the tired faces looking up at him. In the course of one day they have gone from being dope smoking faces hiding in hoods to normal fresh faced youngsters, flushed from a day's physical exertion and effort. Maddox made them eat good food too, tinned vegetables, rice and tinned meat, and washed down with plenty of fresh water.

'I'm proud of you guys, I know we all come from the streets and we talk like gangsta's innit bruv…and everyone hated us. We were the pests of the estate; we were the shit that blighted everyone's lives. The schools rejected us, our families rejected us but we had each other. We stood by each other during the bad times and now look at us. We're the ones in a safe place with loads of food while everyone else is shitting themselves. We went out there and killed those things. Us! Children and youths went out and took down the infected and made sure our streets were safe. Now we have a bigger compound with high fences, weapons, a guard tower, houses, food, water and we have each other.' Maddox's voice carries strong across the rear of the compound, and even cynical hardened youths like Darius and Mohammed are stirred by his words.

'Jagger is taking first watch tonight, he volunteered for it. In fact, all the crews volunteered for the first overnight watch and you know what that tells me? That tells me we got each other's backs. We ain't the little gangsta shits they all think we are. We're the future, we got community right here and we made it, and we gonna keep it. We gonna make it bigger and safer. We gonna take this area back and show everyone that if they want to live in our yard, they do it under our rules. No more religion, no more racism, no more stereotypes and thinking we is thick cos we speak different. This is our time now and we gonna make the rules from now on.' Cheering erupts as the children and youths feel filled with pride. Through their own hard work and dedication they've shown what can be achieved.

'We gotta cut back on the weed,' Maddox continued, 'every now and then is cool, but too much fucks you up like Ryker and the Bossman. That is not cool, you get me? We gonna be fit and healthy, fighters and warriors. How can we protect each other if we stoned and doped up? Also, we ain't gonna kill the survivors for not paying no more. We defend ourselves at whatever cost and if that means we have to kill to defend what's ours then that's okay. But those people out there are frightened, just like we were. They scared and don't know nuffin', they ain't hard or tough like we are, they can't figure out how to get food either, so we gonna protect them. And in return they can supply goods for us, food, clothing, whatever they got that they want to share. If they need help and we can help them then we will. We got to set the rules from now on. If we kill them, then they will want to kill us and that puts us all in a constant state of war,' Maddox pressed the point home, remembering the lessons the Bossman taught him.

'The next couple of days we'll get the houses rigged up and you's can move into them, but we also gotta plant food and crops for the winter, so that means digging the ground up and stuff. I don't know how we do that so we might have to go to the library and find a book...unless anyone can get Google working?' A few laughs break out, 'We got plans, and we'll do this together. I got your backs and you got mine, right?' A few murmurs and Maddox shook his head theatrically, 'I said I got your backs so you got mine, right?' Louder response this time, voices shouting out and caught in the moment. The atmosphere of camaraderie bursting through them, the camp fire, the hard work done by all, the good food and the warm weather all combined to make them feel safe, wanted and secure.

'Right it's late, chill out and relax, we'll get a generator on the monitors and Xboxes for a few games, you's earned that but no weed and no booze tonight, you get me?' A chorus of replies, excited about the prospect of playing games but most of them too exhausted to want to do anything other than fall asleep.

'Jagger, you got the watch bruv,' Maddox looked over to the crew chief stood off to one side with his crew stood around him. All of them trying to affect an air of detached toughness. Aloof and ready for action, armed with shotguns and rifles.

'On it,' Jagger replied and headed away with his crew. He led them to the front gates and sent two up the tower, then one into each end house to watch the side roads, one more on the ground at the base of the tower and the rest doing foot patrols around the perimeter. All of them under strict instruction not to start playing games or get talking to the other kids for too long. Keep moving and keep vigilant. The only thing missing was a spotlight on the tower, still to be organised and rigged up by Maddox and Darius.

'That was good speech,' Lenski said softly as they walked back into the units. As soon as they entered the dark shadows they stopped and kissed passionately for a few seconds before breaking away and giggling as they checked to make sure no one had seen them.

'Thanks,' Maddox replied after a few seconds of kissing.

'It is all good now, so much better. I am proud of you,' Lenski murmured.

'Thanks, that means a lot,' and it did. Maddox knew he was doing a good job and knew he had the respect and the love from the youths to get them to what he wanted, but it had been hard earned and came with a cost. Thinking to the deaths of the Bossman, Zayden and Ryker he knew it was the way it panned out, events that he probably had no control over, and if it wasn't for those awful things then this would never be happening.

'So is the king ready for bed yet?' Lenski smiled and ran her hands over his shoulders and down his arms.

'Yeah he is, how about the queen? Is she ready?'

'I not know this, I find Skyla and ask her,' Lenski giggled.

'Skyla?' Maddox scoffed quietly, 'I need a real woman.'

'You think I am the real woman yes?'

'Oh yes,' taking her hand he leads her through the darkened units towards his room and once inside with the door closed the kissing continues. Gentle at first and building up to a passionate frantic embrace with a sense of urgency propelling them both to strip off and fall onto the bed. Moonlight pours through the small grimy window, illuminated the room with just enough light for them to vaguely see the outline of the furniture, but tantalisingly dark so that touch becomes the dominant sense.

'You alright bruv?' Jagger asks the youth staring out the window down the side street. Having already checked the guard on the other side and the two in the tower he now checks on this one before moving off into the compound.

'Yeah sweet Jagger,' the kid answers, his shotgun resting against the wall and a small gas lantern turned low at his feet.

'You got the radio, call me if you need anything or start fallin' asleep, you get me?'

'Swear down I will Jagger,' the grins enthusiastically.

'Nice one.' Jagger quietly slips out, leaving the eleven year old boy staring out the window. His small hands drumming a beat on the windowsill as he glances over and nods at the two kids on the tower. Like most of the youths, he feels no great sense of loss from the infection taking his family and being here with everyone else is more of a family than he's ever known, he's getting fed, given water and nice things to drink and has got a nice bed to sleep in. Humming a tune to himself he drums his hands and lets his mind wander off, staring at the road stretching away opposite him but not really seeing. No street lights or illumination other than the natural moonlight. Deep shadows blend into deeper silhouettes, building lines become muddled with garden walls, the end of the pavement is blurred and indistinct. Stare at anything for too long and it takes on a form of its own, creating horrors within the imagination.

Minutes pass as he sips from a can of Redbull, specially preserved for the night security crews. The syrupy taste is nice and he wants to gulp it down but he knows he'll then have nothing to do, so he sips it gingerly and places it back down on the ground between his feet, then lifts it up and puts it on the windowsill. Turning the can round so the front is facing him, then away, then front again. He adjusts the position of the lamp a few times, then practises reaching for the shotgun. He moves his seat round a little, making small adjustments so that he can reach it with ease, but moving the seat has warped the symmetry of the lamp and the can of Redbull so he sets about adjusting them so they are just right.

Finally and with a contented sigh of satisfaction he looks up and scans the view. His mouth drops open and his heart rate, despite the near toxic ingredients of the energy drink, goes from sedate to panic within a split second. Adrenalin purges through his system and his hands shake as he scrabbles for the radio knocking the can over and kicking the lantern away which instantly puffs out. Cursing and fumbling in the dark he gropes round for the radio, unable to find it he looks back up and realises that there is no time to waste.

He leans out of the window, draws a deep breath and screams one word into the night.

'CONTACT.'

Sixteen

The horde staggers through the estate, a demanding pressure building up as the undead growl at the steady pace they are held at. The need to eat, to feast, to find flesh burns through them and consumes their every ounce of being but the zombie wants them together. He wants a combined attack and the energy levels as high as possible.

The concentrated pack sweep down street after street and every jerky step brings them closer to the goal. Minutes pass as they navigate the now deserted estate. The decomposing bodies left on the ground are trampled by hundreds and hundreds of feet pummelling the squidgy bodies into a pulp. Bare zombie feet get sliced and cut from sharp fragments of broken glass, blood seeps out only to clot and congeal faster than human blood. These bodies are already so more advanced than the human form; having gone days without food or water, drawing off the reserves within their own forms, sucking the nutrients from organs and pumping them round.

Any sense of pain is gone. No remorse, no emotions, no feeling other than a burning desire to eat flesh. That's all that drives them. Vivid images of juicy tender meat being bitten into flash through their rotten minds. Chemicals pumped into their bloodstream build their energy levels up. The dead hearts beat faster and harder, the eyes roll and twitch as they seek food. The ability to smell becomes heightened as they sniff the air in front of them, searching for the smell of fear, the smell of shit, the smell of piss, the smell of anything that means humans are near.

The horde pour round a long corner and start up a slight incline towards the compound. One long straight road now and they'll be there. That fence will fall with the combined weight of so many bodies slamming into it. They might shoot and fire their measly weapons but the taxi super zombie knows he will win the day and before the night is out, his hosts shall feast.

Seventeen

Jeff, after waiting for half an hour and feeling his patience wearing thin listening to the inane and absurd chatter of his fellow estatee's, finally checks his watch and stares at the second hand. Willing it to move round to the twelve. Desperate to be off and moving but knowing they stand no chance without both groups converging at the same time.

'Yeah so I said to our Millie she got to stand by 'im, he's doin' a stretch and that's hardly his fault is it, he's doin' the best he can bless 'im and Millie she gotta wait, course she got the baby now and I know she ain't sure who the baby father is, he don't know that but his dad got a BMW and she ain't gonna find no other boys with dads that got BMW's so she gotta wait...' And it went on. Aimless and pointless talking, wasting perfectly good air. That got Jeff thinking of what's happened to the prisons? Surely they must be safe? Big walls, strong fences, plenty of food and tough men. No one allowed in or out. That would be bloody ironic if the only survivors were the inmates of the world. What if they broke out now? Hundreds of hard men rampaging through the countryside raping and pillaging everything and everyone in sight. That's why he needs this compound now, the security for when the inmates all break out. In his mind, all the inmates are the denim trousers and white vest wearing prisoners of the American movies. Muscles on muscles, huge arms and shoulders, swastikas and random numbers inked into the shaven skulls. With a shudder he checks his watch and whimpers with desperation as the second hand ticks slowly round.

He taps his foot. Smokes a cigarette, taps the stave against his leg. Stares at the night sky, takes his knife out from his belt and puts it back in again. Then, after leaving it for what feels like hours he checks the watch and nods with satisfaction. The time is here. The time for action.

'Let's go, no talking now...we need absolute quiet until I say then we charge like mad, got it?' Faces shining from the moonlight all nod at him, he turns and leads the way. Pacing steadily and feeling the adrenalin purging into his system. Legs feeling a bit shaky and his hand holding the wooden stave trembles so he brings it across his body and pats it up and down in his spare hand.

Estate survivors stretched out behind him, he turns and ushers them to move up and stay close together. Rolling his eyes as clubs get dropped and the nails sticking out of bats dig into other people's legs causing remarks of complaint they move up the street and turn onto the main road that cuts across the front of the compound.

Jeff knows that if this is timed right he will see the other half of the survivors at the junction, if there is a guard positioned there still, then that guard will shout down that there are two large bodies of people coming in from different directions.

Smiling with anticipation, but also feeling scared he wills himself to keep going and lead these idiots. Once the two sides meet and charge at the fence, he can drop back in the chaos and stay safe somewhere deep in the ranks, or maybe even dart into one of the houses and wait it out to charge out triumphantly later when the nasty fighting has been done. That little shit Maddox should never have punched him like that. The little punk gangsta with those hard intelligent eyes, that deep voice and aura of power. Who the fuck does he think he is?

Eighteen

'CONTACT!'

The boy and girl on the top of the tower spin round in alarm at the lad leaning out the window on the right and pointing down the side street. Hearts hammering they lean over desperate to see what's coming.

'CONTACT!' The girl in the window on the left screams out, her high pitched voice sends their stomachs plummeting. Contact from both side streets at the same time? What's going on?

'Oh my fuckin' god Darryl...'the girl lifts her hand to her mouth and points with a shaking arm down the road ahead of them. In the dark shadows a solid mass of staggering forms slowly comes into view. The distance and gloom too great to see the faces, but just from the jerky movements, the almost goosestep walk, the swagger of the upper torso...infected, hundreds of infected.

'CONTACT ON ALL SIDES,' Darryl roars into his radio, then realises he hasn't pressed the button down, his shaking hands fumble and press it down as he repeats the words 'CONTACT ON ALL SIDES CONTACT ON ALL SIDES...'

'Fuck this,' the girl mutters and lifts her rifle, pointing it vaguely in the direction of the army of infected and pulling the trigger. The loud retort bounces round the buildings. The first shot. The first bullet spins through the air and hits nothing but falls gently to the ground far in the distance.

The gunshot sends a signal to all three sides. This thing is happening now. The element of surprise is gone. Charge. Make noise and charge.

They do. Jeff with his half. The other half coming from the opposite direction and the army of infected. They all roar and they all charge.

Nineteen

'CONTACT ON ALL SIDES CONTACT ON ALL SIDES,' the radio clipped to the side of Maddox's trousers lying in a crumpled heap on the floor bursts to life. A gunshot rings out. The unmistakable sound of a rifle shot. With pure instinct flooding through his body, he rolls from the bed, grabs his trousers and starts dressing with lightning speed.

Lenski's heart races as she fumbles around finding her clothes and cursing quietly in Polish.

'EVERYONE TO THE FRONT,' Maddox speaks calmly firmly into the radio, 'GET WEAPONS, GET READY AND GET TO THE FRONT, DON'T WAIT FOR ME.'

'What is it?' Lenski asks.

'Don't know,' Maddox pulls his boots on and grabs the pistol from the cupboard top. Pulling the slide back and checking the ammunition clip as he moves quickly towards the door.

'Get somewhere safe,' Maddox shouts behind him and runs through the units and out into the humid night air. Gunshots sounding out from the gate. Roars and shouts of rage already reaching him as he races towards the gate.

'WHAT IS IT?' Maddox shouts at Jagger already on the top of tower and taking shots with his rifle.

'ALL SIDES MADDOX, THREE GROUPS, INFECTED AND SURVIVORS….FUCKING CHAOS….'

'WHAT THE FUCK?' Maddox replies in shock. He grabs the first scaffold bar and pulls himself up the tower with ease. Reaching the top and staring out. The hardened man's mouth drops open in shock at the sight.

The road ahead is thick with infected pressing forward towards the compound. The road on the right is thick with estate survivors coming towards the compound. The road on the left is the same; survivors tooled up and charging at the gates.

He takes it all in within a split second. The left and right have planned a coordinated attack, planning to meet at this time to attack and take the compound. The infected are charging from the road opposite, also intent on taking the compound. They don't know about each other. The two groups of survivors are screaming as they charge. Weapons held high as they sprint. Looks of confusion as they see the third group emerging from the central road. Who are they? Has Jeff got another group with us? Nope, they're infected.

Maddox watches with horror as the three armies commit themselves. The ones at the front couldn't stop if they wanted due to the momentum of the people behind them.

The last few seconds seem to slow as everyone realises what's about to happen. Even the zombies look confused for a second. They emerge into the open junction keeping the shape of the road they came from. Then, seeing the two groups of humans on both sides they do a literal double take. A zombie in the lead wearing a white shirt, tie and name badge shakes his head in confusion, then smiles. The smile spreads into a grin as he howls. The howls are taken up by every other infected.

The three sides meet in a devastating clash of utter terror. The estate survivors at the back, having no idea of the army of infected, and hearing the start of the battle, and being desperate to join in, all push forward and force the centre to become bogged with scrapping bodies. The rear columns of zombies, all hearing the battle, and all needing to feast, push forward and drive their undead bodies into the melee.

Maddox shakes his head slowly; he raises his pistol to fire then slowly lowers it again. He cocks his head to one side, lifting the pistol again and sweeping it over the battling masses below him.
'Who we shooting?' Jagger asks him.
Maddox turns to see the entire camp stretched out behind him. Bodies leaning out of windows of the houses and staring into the muddle massed battle. The cries of rage, terror, hurt, pain and glory ripping the air apart mere feet from them.
'FUCK THIS...SHOOT EVERYTHING,' Maddox roars out and opens fire with his pistol. Guns blaze out from all sides, behind the gates shooting through the gaps, muzzles flash and rounds pour into the mass of bodies.

'SHOOT EVERYTHING,' Maddox screams again, his eyes ablaze.

Twenty

'Yeah but I really didn't expect there to be no vehicles anywhere,' I reply wiping the sweat from my face and sighing.

'This is a council estate,' Lani continues, 'they would have used them all to get away, or stolen them, or burnt them out.'

'Yeah I guess,' I glance about at the rundown houses on either side. We've spent the last half hour stalking through street after street searching for a vehicle, heading further into the estate. The long straight roads, the potted road surface, houses with peeling facades and windows grimy long before the outbreak started.

We freeze and drop down, raising weapons to our shoulders at the signal from Dave, freezing on the spot and holding one arm up with a clenched fist. To their credit, Lani and Tom respond just as quickly as the rest of us, having been given instruction by Clarence while on the navy supply ship.

Dave opens his fist then closes it again, repeating it several times and waving forward. Multiple contacts ahead. Dave glances round and I shake my head at him.

'Can't hear anything mate,' I whisper across, Dave glances across the line at the rest all shaking their heads.

'Something happening...'Dave cocks his head, 'not sure what though.'

'Keep going,' I whisper back and we start off, moving stealthily behind Dave, weapons at the ready, fingers extended over trigger guards.

Dave reaches the junction at the end of the road before us and instantly drops down to a crouch, lifting his rifle to his shoulder and aiming down to the right.

'Scatter,' I whisper. We crab across the road into the deep shadows on the sides and watch Dave as he stares down along the wider main road on his right. Dave lifts his hand and motions for me to come forward. I step out, keeping low and creep over towards him. As I gain the junction Dave motions down the road and I peer down to see the solid ranks of undead staggering away from us. Stretched fully across the road and taking every available inch, crammed and densely packed they rush forward clearly intent on getting to something ahead of them.

I can smell them now, the stench of death. Decomposition, decay, rotten flesh from the hundreds of walking stiffs that must have staggered past this junction just minutes before. I motion for the others to move up and wait while they shuffle forward and gather round us, all staring down at the backs of the undead down the road to the right.

A single gunshot rings out, followed immediately by the distinct sound of undead howling with an attack. More voices. Human voices that roar out and mingle with the undead roars. Screams and shouts. We look down the road and at each other, wondering what the hell we've bumbled into this time.

The howls and screams bounce and echo of the buildings, the sound funnelling down the streets and coming at us from many directions. A single loud voice bellows out. A deep male voice then shots, many shots.

'Rifles,' Clarence mutters.

'...and shotguns,' Dave adds his head still cocked over and listening intently.

'That lot are going at someone,' Blowers says.

'They are,' I reply staring at the back of the massed horde, 'the dirty fuckers are attacking someone.' My voice comes out in a low growl as I feel the anger start to rise.

'We got an advantage for once,' Nick says clicking his safety off.

'Yeah,' I stand up. We all stand up. I copy Nick and flick my safety off and check my belt for the pouches of spare magazines.

'Are we attacking them?' Tom asks, we all stare at him, at the glint in his eye, at the desire and hunger we can see within him. Lani holds it too. A familiar grimace we've all come to know from so many battles together.

'Yeah,' I reply, 'we are, spread out and form a line. Clarence can you fire that thing on the move?'

'Yes boss,' he answers as he hefts the weapon to waist height and holds the ammunition belt with one hand, ready to feed it in.

'Clarence in the middle then, we hold the line and keep a steady pace.' I step out and sense the others spreading out in a line. Like slow motion we stride across the blackened street, hearts beating, mouths dry, eyes staring hard.

This isn't our fight. We have no idea what's going on. But here there are undead, hundreds of undead and they're attacking something. People are firing back at them which means there are humans. That makes it our business right there. No one invited us to this fight but we're here and we've slaughtered more of your kind than you will ever know.

You have no idea what's behind you. Six outright nasty bastards. One giant and one truly psychotic killer. Seven assault rifles and one big fucking machine gun. Seven men and one girl. Eight of us. Eight that stalk you. Eight that will kill you.

'Dave?'

'Yes Mr Howie.'

'You ready Dave?'

'Yes Mr Howie.'

'Let them know we're here Dave,' we come to a stop and pause while Dave sucks a deep lungful of air in. I smile and glance left and right, we're all smiling. We know what's coming.

'**WE ARE HERE TO KILL YOU,**' Dave's voice penetrates every sound, drowning everything else out. His bellow simply stops everything in its track…

Twenty-One

'What the fuck was that?' Maddox screamed while quickly ejecting the shells from his shotgun and pushing two more in. The intense close quarter fighting has spilled across the junction as zombies and survivors fight, bite and die with utter savageness. The bodies smash into the gates as undead attack the fences and survivors frantically plead to open up and save them. As survivors get bit they drop, then come back a few minutes later.

Maddox and his youths pour fire into them, but for every kill they get, be it human or infected, more pour in. The gates weaken and rattle with each blow as more heavy bodies slam into them. Rifles and shotguns fire, expending ammunition and Maddox knows that within a few minutes they will be out of shells and bullets. Just as he was about to give the order to pull back and try and get over the walls at the back of the compound a voice bellows out. The power and energy from it instantly ceases all action, everything stops, freezes.

'WE ARE HERE TO KILL YOU...HOWIE IS UPON YOU AND HE BRINGS DEATH...TURN AND FACE US...TURN AND SEE THE FACE OF HOWIE...'

'Who the fuck is Howie?' Jagger whispers quietly.

'I don't know, but I hope he's got a big fuckin' gun,' Maddox replies.

Twenty-Two

'WE ARE HERE TO KILL YOU...HOWIE IS UPON YOU AND HE BRINGS DEATH...TURN AND FACE US...TURN AND SEE THE FACE OF HOWIE...'

The hairs on the back of my neck stand up. My breathing becomes faster and my heart beats faster. The wonder drug of adrenalin floods my system. I will talk to Dave later about his choice of taunting words but for now...for now there is us and you.

They turn quickly as Dave's voice staggers everything in sight and hearing. The challenge given, the gauntlet laid. We hold our thin measly line. Fingers pressing lightly on triggers as we face down another army of undead. They start to stagger, faster, quicker, charging. They roar and howl at the sight of the bodies standing calmly and waiting for them. I hold for another few seconds, just long enough to let them get a few feet away from whatever they're attacking.

'Down,' I shout and as one we drop down to the crouch, magazines get placed quickly on the ground in front of us. They charge. They run now. Gathering speed.

'HAVE IT,' my voice roars out and is cut off as seven assault rifles spew lead at them. Fingers squeeze triggers, muzzles flash, rounds spin and zombies die. They fall and die as we fire into their ranks.

Clarence pauses for a second as we empty our first magazines. The timing is perfect and almost as one we shout 'MAGAZINE' as we eject the empty one and snatch a new one up. A quick memory of the battle of Salisbury Plain flashes through my mind.

'MY TURN,' Clarence stands and roars letting rip with the GPMG held one handed and firing into the zombies. We pause and stare in awe as the huge man absorbs the recoil into his massive frame and laughs with maniacal delight. One hand held out to the side feeding the coil of ammunition belt into the side of the machine gun. He takes steady sweeps side to side and nothing survives the sheer fire power of the devastating weapon. Bodies burst apart, limbs sheered off, stomachs ripped out, skulls explode as they fall.

'FIRE,' I scream out as Clarence stops, and the small arms fire of the SA80 assault rifles take up the work. They are nowhere near as powerful as the GPMG but there are seven of them firing at once and that more than makes up the difference.

'ADVANCE,' I shout as we change magazines and Clarence fires for a few seconds taking big strides forwards and sweeping the weapon left to right.

There are hundreds and hundreds of them and they keep coming. Turning and charging and I had no idea how deeply packed they were or how far down the street they were stretched. They die in droves, sent back to the hell they crawled out from. Glancing over at Lani I see her face alive with the glory of battle, the grime from the weapon smearing her face and at this time, at this place I realise I'm in love. As if touched by an invisible hand she glances at me and smiles, a gorgeous big grin full of white teeth.

Once again, there is nowhere else I would rather be right now.

Twenty-Three

'GET DOWN AND BRACE THE GATES,' Maddox screams out, ordering his youths to lie down on the ground. The experience of knowing that bullets can fly for miles, especially when they're fired from assault rifles and heavy machine guns. With no idea who the new group of attackers are, but with a suspicion that maybe they're not here to attack the compound too, Maddox stares down at the junction in front of the gates and the terrific battle still being waged.

More bodies slam into the gates and he looks down to see his youths stacked up against the inside, holding low but pushing their bodies against them.

The two groups from the side roads still pour into the middle, roaring and screaming as they fight to join the battle, having no idea of the slaughter taking place just yards in front of them. The undead easily over power the survivors, tearing them apart with a frenzied and sustained attack. Biting and ripping flesh open, transmitting the deadly infection into the blood stream and launching off to take more down. The zombies fight and claw their way into the ranks of the survivors, the darkness of the night and the confusion of the battle masking their routes. Legs, arms, stomachs and arses get bit. Survivors fall and die, writhing in agony for seconds before dying. Inside their bodies the infection pours through every cell and brings them back, re-starting the heart and bringing the host back in the new perfect form. The survivors twitch and sit up, opening red bloodshot eyes and howling out as they launch and surge into the ranks of humans.

The firing continues. Small arms from machine guns then a heavy machine gun for a few seconds. Maddox strains his eyes and can just make out the muzzle flashes in the distance of the road ahead.

'Darius get the weapons up into the windows and fire down, keep firing everything we got. Jagger, get everyone else tooled up with hand weapons, anything they want.'

Maddox turns back to the front, watching the battle and knowing the estate survivors are fucked. They don't stand a chance. The infected are too fast and too powerful for them. Watching between the distant muzzle flashes and the battle underneath him he senses that instead of running away they may need to fight. If they run now, they'll always be running.

'Sometimes Maddox, sometimes you can run away, retreat or withdraw and survive to fight another day. Every once in a while though son, you have to man up and stand your ground. Stand and fight son. Whatever the outcome, whatever the cost. Let them know your name and what you stand for. Be beholden to no man. Stand and fight son.'

The Bossman's words sound through his mind, the great and powerful lord brought down by smoking a plant. But he was right and this is that time.

Twenty-Four

'MAGAZINE,' I shout and eject the old one, quickly pushing it into the pouch on my belt and slamming a new one in. We've advanced enough to be reaching the first bodies felled by our bullets. But still they come and still we mow them down. Holding at times, then advancing a couple of steps but all the time taking ground and despatching these foul things back to hell.

Lucky bastards is what we are. Finding such a big horde to play with. And at the point of being tooled up to high heaven too. New guns with lots and lots of shiny bullets to throw at them. Clarence is clearly having a great time doing his whole Rambo thing, I'm going to get him a bandana for his bald head and smear some black lines across his nose.

Our incessant fire rate whittles them down and the bodies pile up. As with many times before I notice the bodies act as trip hazards and obstacles to the oncoming zombies and a couple of times I smile at the sight of the stupid things tripping and falling over.

'HOLD,' Dave shouts out and we drop down while he works to clear a blockage in his weapon. Clarence lays down flat and uses the front tripod to steady the weapon as he fires into the pressed ranks. The obliteration is immense and before long we've got a nice big gap in front of us.

'CLEARED,' Dave shouts and we rise up to advance again, marking our steps and holding the line. I notice some of our lads have switched to single shots and are going for head shots, calling out when they get one. Dave joins in but again, he gets discounted as every one of his shots is a head shot. We're all getting better though and we're getting more heads now than we we're before. Apart from Lani and Tom who are still quite new to the assault rifle experience.

Picking them off one by one and letting Clarence do a sweep every couple of minutes with the GPMG, we conserve ammunition and make steady progress and before long we looking through the pressed ranks at some kind of high fencing and a scaffold tower erected behind it. A fortified commune, this must be what the undead were attacking. From this distance I can just make out a single figure stood on the top of the tower. I raise my hand and wave, hoping he can see us and be re-assured that we are making headway towards them.

He waves back just as muzzle flashes and shots ring out from the windows of houses behind the fence. Shotguns and rifles firing down into the junction beneath them.

'Dave shout for them to hold their fire,' I shout, worried that they will fire into us if we keep advancing.

'HOLD YOUR FIRE, LET US WORK OUR WAY TO YOU,' Dave bellows out and I can vaguely see as the man on the tower waves his arms and after a couple of seconds the shotguns and rifles cease.

'MOVE UP,' I shout and we advance, firing into the undead as they still turn and charge at us. There is a ferocious battle taking place ahead of us but the gates to that commune look closed and secure so who is fighting outside the gates?

'PEOPLE IN THE MIDDLE,' Lani shouts, 'THERE ARE PEOPLE IN THE JUNCTION,' she adds. We peer down and look in horror at men and women fighting out with sticks, battling away at the undead and being taken down by the ferocious attacks.

'We'll shoot them if we keep firing,' Blowers shouts. Then aims and fires into a zombie breaking away to charge at us.

'Dave, get their attention, tell them to pull back into the side streets.'

'MOVE BACK, MOVE AWAY FROM THE JUNCTION. WE WILL FIRE ON YOU, MOVE AWAY NOW,' Dave bellows but despite his enormous voice he has little effect as the fighting is too intense for anyone to try and back away or turn to flee.

'What now?' Tom asks in alarm at seeing more people being savaged down.

'We go in with hand weapons,' I draw my axe wedged into the gap between my back and my rucksack, then twist the assault rifle round out of the way, 'form a circle, we stay tight and fight to the gates, maybe draw the zombies away from the other survivors and give them a chance to get away.'

No arguments and they can all see the sense in the planning. Clarence pushes the heavy machine gun to rest behind him on the long shoulder strap and pulls his axe out. We form up in a circle with Dave at the front and start advancing down towards the open junction.

Within a few steps we get contacts as the undead see us pushing out into the open ground and start charging. Axes swing as we cut and strike them down. Our close phalanx stays tight as we lash out, swiping and lunging. Lani making neat swipes with her meat cleaver and Dave just killing anything that looks at him the wrong way.

'This is carnage,' I shout at the sight of many small fights taking place. People pressed against the gates lashing out with sticks and bats with nails through the ends. The two roads leading away to the left and right are packed with bodies fighting and rolling about on the ground. Too dark and too confusing to see if they are undead or people.

'OPEN THE GATE,' I shout up and wave at the man on the top of tower. He hesitates and sweeps his arm round at the junction, clearly telling me he's worried about breaching his own entry point.

'WE'LL KEEP IT SAFE, OPEN THE GATE, THEY WON'T GET IN.'

'THEY MIGHT,' the man shouts down in a deep but youthful voice.

'WHY ARE YOU IN THERE IF YOUR PEOPLE ARE OUT HERE FIGHTING?'

'THEY AIN'T MY PEOPLE, THEY CAME TO ATTACK US AND TAKE OUR COMPOUND. THOSE INFECTED CAME AT THE SAME TIME,' He shouts back.

'Shit, that was bad timing,' Cookey jokes to a few sniggers from everyone else.
'HOW MANY YOU GOT IN THERE?'

Twenty-Five

Maddox stares down at the fighting still raging in the junction and watching the small group of mercenaries stalking down the road slaughtering everything in their path. He watches as they get close to the junction and then one of them shouts for him to cease fire.

'STOP SHOOTING.' Maddox waves his arms and hears his order repeated as the rifles and shotguns suddenly stop.

Incredibly, the mercenaries then push their guns away and take bloody big axes out and get into a small circle before walking out into the junction. Maddox watches with keen interest, his heart in his mouth as he observes the strange mix of people killing everything that steps close to them. A small man with two knives at the front, a giant man with a bald head, a Thai girl, some young lads and a bloke with curly dark hair.

'How the fuck…' he mutters to himself as the infected seem to drop instantly at the tight little swings and lunges these people lash out.

The man with the curly dark hair shouts up to open the gates. Maddox refuses, pointing to the fierce fighting still taking place. He shouts down that these ain't his people and someone says something funny within the circle as they all snigger.

'HOW MANY YOU GOT IN THERE?' the man shouts up. Maddox hesitates. If he tells them they are just children it will show them as weak and they are heavily armed with machine guns and assault rifles and they look like soldiers.

'THEY ARE JUST CHILDREN IN HERE,' Lenski shouts as she scrambles to the top of the tower to stand next to Maddox.

'KIDS? JUST KIDS?' The man with the curly dark hair asks.

'YEAH JUST KIDS,' Maddox shouts back as Lenski grips his hand in terror at the sight of the carnage taking place.

'HOW MANY?' The man asks.

'OVER ONE HUNDRED,' Lenski shouts down in reply and Maddox watches as every face in that circle glances up. Hard looks on tough faces.

'STAY THERE AND KEEP THAT GATE CLOSED, WE'LL SORT THIS LOT OUT,' the man with the curly dark hair shouts. He says something to the rest of his group and they instantly push their axes and knives away and pull their guns back round. At another order they split into two lines of four standing back to back. They raise their weapons to their shoulders.

'GET DOWN GET DOWN GET DOWN, DROP TO THE GROUND NOW DROP TO THE GROUND NOW.' The small man roars out and Maddox leans over to see people dropping down and covering their faces. The small group pauses a few seconds then opens up. The hammering retorts boom out as the infected get shot to pieces. The heavy machine gun rips them apart like hot knives through butter and within a few seconds it's over.

Everything that was standing is now dead.

RR Haywood

Twenty-Six

We didn't hesitate when the woman said it was just kids inside and we knew this had to end now. Why these adults were attacking a compound was beyond me, but that didn't manner. What mattered was ending this.

So we did.

Ruthlessly.

Anything left standing after Dave gave the warning was shot down. We poured rounds into those things and I have no doubt in my mind that we killed people too. But the way it was going they would have been bitten and turned anyway, so they had it coming. There were so many undead in amongst them we could never have ended it cleanly. This wasn't our fight and maybe we had no right to get involved. But I know if I was behind a high fence with over a hundred children I'd want someone to come and kill the nasty monsters for me.

As the smoke cleared we ejected our emptied magazines and quickly pushed new ones home. Clicks and metallic noises filled the air. Clarence threaded his last coil of ammunition belt into the GPMG as we stepped out drawing our axes and started moving between the corpses, using our torches to seek out the still living zombies. Their groaning and shuffling noises made them easy to find and we stalked through the bodies chopping heads off and cutting throats open.

'Mr Howie,' Nick calls my attention and points to the gate opening up. All of us turn and stand ready as a well-built young man walks out. He looks round at the bodies and then straight at me. Walking steadily with a pistol in his hand down at his side. A young woman steps out behind him and walks forward. More young people gather in the gap created by the open gate but they hold there.

'Hey, you the man from the tower?' I call out.

'Yeah,' he replies, his voice low and deep. His tone as wary as his movements which are fluid and powerful but aloof and ready for action.

'I'm Howie, nice to meet you?' I step towards him and hold my hand out. He pauses looking me up and down, then across at the rest of my group. A decision made and he steps in closer, extending his hand to shake.

'Maddox,' he nods and up close I see how young he is, maybe eighteen or nineteen at the most but his eyes are deeply intelligent and his grip has power.

'This is Lenski,' he nods behind him at the very attractive young lady stepping carefully over the bodies, she stops next to Maddox and I extend my hand to her.

'Lenski, I'm Howie these people are with me. We mean you no harm, we are not a threat to you, we're just passing through.' I want to re-assure them quickly knowing that with over a hundred terrified children inside they must be deeply worried.

'It good to meet you Howie,' she replies with in a clipped Polish accent.

'So are you the only adults here?' I ask.

'Kind of,' Maddox replies and I can see he's still very wary.

'Listen mate, we're going to sort these out and make sure they're all dead. There might be some injured people out here. Have you got a first aid station or medical bay here?'

'No,' he replies simply.

'Okay, have you got bandages and clean water, something we can use to patch them up, maybe some lights?'

'We have these, I get them and make the lights ready,' Lenski says with a pointed look at Maddox.

'I'll get some of my lot out here to help clear this up,' Maddox says. He turns back to the open gate. 'Jagger, take the left side, Mohammed take the right, Sierra and Liam I want your crews down the main road ahead. Ryland get into the units and get some lights out here bruv, Skyla find Lenski and get water and bandages up here into the street.'

'Bloody hell,' Cookey exclaims at seeing groups of youths pour from the gates. Young kids armed to the teeth with knives and sharp sticks, bats, swords and poles. A few bigger kids direct them with short words of order and they move about in sections. Dropping down and shoeing bodies over, slitting throats, clubbing heads and bursting skulls apart. They rifle pockets and loot the bodies, searching for anything usable.

We all stand shocked and stunned, unable to take our eyes off these children doing the bloody work of killers. The fact that they're ordered really stands out. They smile and joke with each other and the banter remind me of how we are when we operate and move together. And I notice they keep staring and glancing at us, but the faces become hard and unsmiling when they look at us. Not scared, not terrified little children but the same wary aloofness that Maddox had.

'What the fuck...' Nick mutters.

'This is one strange day,' Lani adds in the same muted tone. A proud looking girl leads a group of children across the junction heading into the shadows of the street opposite, one of the smaller children stares in awe at Clarence as he passes by.

'You is hench bruv,' the child says in a strong confident tone and turns away as the others start sniggering and pointing at Clarence.

'Did we just save a bunch of gangsta kids from a nice group of survivors being eaten by a horde of zombies?' Cookey asks.

'Possibly...' I reply quietly, not quite believing what my eyes are showing me. Within minutes there are injured bodies being dragged past us through the open gates and dumped on the street beyond. The children dragging them race back out and grab more injured people. The youths on the street inside the gates examine each body closely with torches, checking for bite wounds. Any that are suspicious are killed instantly and without any sign of mercy or pity.

Generators get carried into the street, then lighting units plugged in and glowing bright as soon as the generators are started. The street floods with light and I see Lenski and other girls carrying bottles of water and dumping them down onto the road, boxes filled with sealed bandages get brought up along with boxes of disposable gloves.

'Howie,' Maddox walks back out the gates straight towards me, 'my crews will sort this out from here, we'll get the injured cared for.'

'Er...that's good mate, what's in your compound?'

'How do I answer that?' Maddox replies bluntly.

'What? I mean what is in there that these people wanted so badly? They launched an attack at a base full of children? Why Maddox?'

'We didn't ask for your help Howie,' he replies with a defiant stare.

'Maddox mate, we're not here to take anything from you. We got a place down the coast from here; we got food, medicines and safety. Now why were these people attacking you?'

'Who are you bruv?' Maddox flares up with an angry tone his voice making the other seven members of my group take a step towards him, the response was a hundred or so children, tooled up and looking mean, gathering quickly and quietly all around us. Looking round I saw my group sliding their axes away and slowly pulling assault rifles round.

'Stand easy,' I wave them down, 'we are not shooting children, Dave listen to me we are not shooting children got it?'

'Yes Mr Howie,' he answers quickly as I know he won't hesitate if he thinks the group is threatened. He'd drown kittens if he felt any of us were at risk.

'Maddox, I asked you a simple and open question. We are not a threat to you, and we do not need anything from you but after what we just did I feel we are owed an explanation as to why these adults were attacking a compound full of children.'

'We didn't ask your help, go home, this is our place,' he stands full on and stares hard.

'Don't tell me to go home mate,' I can feel the first bite of anger rising up, 'I'm not after your place or anything that's inside it. I want to know why they were attacking you? What do you have that they need?'

'You get me bruv? This is our place, who are you to come here and demand answers, you ain't nuffin'. Yeah thanks for the help but we got this now.'

'Do not fucking dismiss me like I'm some idiot,' my voice to rises in volume and I start walking towards him, 'what did you do to make them come at you like this?'

'Who the fuck are you to question us? You passing through? So pass through, go home and leave us,' he walks towards me a few steps, showing me his open hands.

'Why are they attacking you Maddox? What did you do to them?'

'Don't question me bruv, go home.'

'You will answer my fucking question or I will tear this place apart with my bare hands, what did you do to them? Did you rob them? Did you take their food and supplies? Answer me!'

'I answer to no one,' he bellows back, 'this is my place and I make the rules here, you ain't no one.'

'I want to know why we just fired on people, not just those things but people. You got kids here so why are these people attacking you?'

'We didn't ask for your help,' he roars back at me, spittle flying from his mouth.

'But we gave it thinking you have scared kids in here, you took these peoples things didn't you? You took their food and supplies didn't you?'

'Get fucked,' he sneers, 'this conversation is over, go about your business.' He turns to walk away and the fury erupts from me as I stride towards him. He spins round pulling a pistol from his belt. Instinctively I grab mine and lift it up as I side step out. Two men holding pistols at each other from a few feet away. Assault rifles get cocked behind me, voices call out. The distinctive sound of rifle bolts being racked back. A cacophony of sound as everyone gears up for a fight.

'Stand down Maddox,' I growl at him.

'You stand down,' he growls back.

'No, stop this,' Lenski screams from behind Maddox.

'Boss, this isn't our fight,' Clarence shouts, 'these are just kids boss.' I get the pleading tone in his voice and I glance round to see him holding the heavy machine gun pointing at masses of children. Rifles and shotguns are pointed at my group, kids with knives and bats all converging and creeping in.

'Howie, we need to go,' Lani shouts with alarm in her voice. Maddox and I face off with our pistols pointing at each other. If I drop my aim he'll shoot me and then everyone will open up and then everyone will be dead.

'Maddox listen to me...'

'No you listen, this is our place and you don't come here in our back yard making demands. You ain't the feds bruv, we got this place now.'

'We don't want your fucking place Maddox...'

'Then go!'

'Okay, take it easy...we'll go...everyone listen up, we are going so nobody shoot,' I shout to make everyone hear me, backing away but keeping the pistol raised, honestly believing that if I lower it he'll go for a shot. The prize of our weapons for his compound would be too tempting.

'Yeah you go,' Maddox stalks after me, 'keep going and don't come back here.'

'This doesn't have to be this way Maddox, we got a community too, few miles down the coast at Fort Spitbank, we got food, doctors, medicines, safety and order, you don't have to live like this.'

'Like what?' he smiles, 'you see us struggling bruv? We got food, medicines and safety right here.'

'You can't kill other survivors for food Maddox, there's no way back from that mate. Look at what you did here, these people attacked a secure compound full of children for fucks sake, the only reason they did that was because of what you did to them.'

'You don't know this,' he shouts, 'these people are vermin, they want to take the food from children, they is greedy.'

Backing away I reach my group and we start walking back down the road we came from, all of us pointing our weapons at the children as they stalk after us. Some of them smiling and laughing like it's a game, goading each other and shouting insults.

'Maddox, we are leaving, call your people off.'

'Just keep going bruv; don't tell me what to do.'

'Maddox, listen to Howie, back off and stand down son, your kids are itching to start and we've got bloody big guns here son, don't risk it,' Clarence shouts, his deep voice carrying clearly down the road.

'Maddox let them go now,' Lenski pushes through the crowd of kids and reaches out to pull Maddox back, his arm still extended with the pistol pointing at me. Surprisingly he stops and allows the girl to pull him back. She looks angry and scared.

'Lenski, we're going,' I shout over to her, 'we're at Fort Spitbank, remember that...Fort Spitbank, we've got doctors and safety. We can take people in.'

'I remember this,' she shouts back, 'you go and I remember this.'

'Lenski, we need a vehicle,' Clarence shouts.

'A what?'

'Car, we need a car or a van, anything.'

'I not know this,' she implores then turns to whisper fiercely at Maddox. A heated exchange of words takes place but watching Maddox I can see he is clearly listening to her.

'Maddox, do the right thing mate, we'll be gone quicker with a vehicle.'

'Behind the shops two roads over, there's a dog shit bin there, the keys are in the bin, you got twenty minutes to go. You still here after that we comin' for you, you get me?'

'Take it easy Maddox, we're going mate, no one needs to get hurt now,' I shout back.

'You's the ones getting' fucked up innit, swear down we'll fuck you up,' another youth shouts over, more join in, catcalls, whistles and goading. These kids are fearless and it makes us back away quickly. Taking care not to trip over the bodies of the undead we felled just a short time earlier.

A few minutes later and we're walking steadily along in our group, weapons still at the ready but the youths now long gone.

'What the fuck was that?' Clarence says quietly.

'Different rules I guess, fucking hell, did you see them kids? Tooled up and just itching for a scrap?' I reply with a shake of my head.

We move in silence after that. All of shocked at the turn of events. We saw a horde of undead attacking something and charged in, but the boundaries have been blurred. Feral kids killing people and taking their stuff. Now those people are dead and those kids are secure within a gated commune. We all know we just played a part in helping the bad guys win. But then they're still just kids.

'Shit this is confusing,' I sigh, 'I don't know if we did a bad thing or a good thing.'

'We killed lots of those things, that's a good thing,' Dave says flatly.

'But did we just give more power to little gangsta shits that are already fucking everyone over?' Cookey asks seriously.

Dave stares ahead then seem to realise that Cookey was asking him the question. 'I don't know Alex,' Dave says, 'we saw the zombies and we killed them. That's it. The rest is just people being people. We can't be everywhere and make everyone have the same values as us.'

'Good words Dave,' I add with respect, 'now let's get the fuck out of here and quickly before those shits change their mind and decide they want our guns.'

Twenty-Seven

'What in your head?' Lenski says with worry lines etched onto her face. Maddox stares into the dark road. Every member of the compound gathered behind him as he searches the shadows for any sign of them. A contrary feeling rises in his soul; that everything was going right, he was on the right track. They saved the compound so why didn't he show gratitude, why didn't he back down and welcome them. Show them what they were planning and what ideas he had. They said they had another commune with doctors and food and that meant stability. They had proper weapons and moved like a unit too. He could have joined forces with them, traded supplies for weapons.

But that attitude. That instant assumption that they were feral little gangsta chav shits running riot and killing everyone. That had been true but it wasn't now. Maddox felt conflicted and a sense of shame. But more than anything he knew this had ended badly. If they were good people then they would come back under the misguided banner of trying to save the kids, or trying to save the people on the estate.

If they weren't good people they would see that the compound held food and supplies. Either way. They'll come back.

That righteous attitude, demanding answers, white men with guns trying to throw their weight around and be the new law and order. Those days were gone. Maddox was going to change the way they did things, and it wasn't his fault the survivors decided to attack tonight. This was new times, new rules.

'Maddox, I ask what in your head?' Lenski asked again. He turned to look at her, seeing the fear and confusion in her face. He knew what needed to be done. Whatever it cost to survive. New times. New rules.

'Darius, take three crews and go left, go after them...Jagger you take three more and go right, Mohammed you go straight and keep behind them. Liam, you stay and hold the base secure. We go after them. I want them weapons. Take them at the shops where all the roads meet,' Maddox barked the orders out, hardly believing he was doing this. But the way that man shouted at him, the sneer on his face and the anger in his eyes. He wouldn't forget and he would come back with more men. This had to end here.

'No Maddox, this wrong, you not do this...' Lenski grabbed his arm begging him to stop the youths as they instantly split and went off different directions. Melting into the shadows and racing after the armed group.

'Go back to the compound and wait there,' Maddox pulled his arm free.

'No, they help you, they save us Maddox, why you do this? They have safe place with doctors and medicine. We should work with them not fight.'

'They'll come back and try to take this Lenski; they'll see these kids as a threat and try to end what we have. They'll tell people we're here and others will come. The compound with a hundred children. Every survivor with a gun will try and get in. We got to stop that.

'This wrong, these men they try to help you, they help us Maddox...'

'Go back Lenski,' Maddox pulled free and jogged after Mohammed and his crew moving quickly down the road. Lenski fell to her knees, hands clutching her face. Tears rolling down her cheeks as the sobs wracked her body. They were so close, so close to doing it properly. Good people came to help them. She knew the way Maddox and the others viewed outsiders and any form of authority. But these were good people, she could tell by the way they worked together; they were clean and healthy with good clothes and good weapons. They had a safe place with doctors. These children needed that kind of help. What happens when one of them breaks a leg, gets the measles, cuts themselves on a rusty nail? Those things meant death without medicine and trained people.

Everything they worked for, everything they planned was going...unless she did something, persuaded Maddox to listen, made him listen. Got that man Howie to listen...she had to try. Rubbing the tears from her face she gets to her feet and starts moving off.

'Lenski, Maddox said you had to go back,' Liam quickly called out, watching her from a few feet away and feeling confused and worried at seeing her cry.

'Liam, go to the compound now!' Lenski turned and shouted. Her harsh tone stopped him in his tracks as she fled into the dark shadows.

Twenty-Eight

'Shops,' Dave pointed ahead to a collection of commercial buildings set into the side of the road next to a large junction.

'Bout bloody time,' Cookey muttered. We ran forward using the moonlight to pick our route. Reaching the shops we hunted round and found a small service road running behind them. Taking the road we jogged to the back of the shops and a long line of cars and vans parked up tight behind the shops.

'Look at that,' Blowers said shining his torch on the wall at the spray painted letters. BOSSMAN VEHICLES TOUCH AND DIE.

'Nice,' Nick shook his head.

'I thought you couldn't read,' Cookey asked innocently.

'I can't read very well but I can read that,' Nick replied without any offence.

'Dog shit bin is here,' Blowers said from across the road, shining his light on the distinctive red plastic refuse bin. He lifted the lid gingerly, clearing expecting to find the thing full of shit. Someone had taped the keys to the underside of the lid, all of them hanging down.

'Bloody hell, these kids have got some influence leaving them here with the keys right there,' Blowers said.

'We need a van,' I called out scanning the vehicles, 'there's a few here press the clickers and see which one lights up.'

'On it,' Blowers reached his hand in and started pushing the raised nodules. Indicators flashed with clunking noises as cars were unlocked.

'That one,' Lani shouts as a white van clunks open with the orange lights flashing.

'Get in, I'll drive,' I call out as Lani and Tom start pulling the side and rear doors open. Running over I clamber into the driver's seat as Blowers passes me the keys.

'CONTACT,' Dave roars. A shot rings out. A rifle shot from somewhere at the front of the shops, immediately followed by shotgun blasts and more rifles. The windows of the vehicles start exploding as I ram the ignition key in and twist it round. The van lurches forward, slamming into the vehicle in front.

'Fuck it was in gear, sorry,' I say through gritted teeth and turn the key back round then press the clutch down as I start it again. The van ticks over for a few seconds then fires up with the noisy diesel engine sputtering into the night.

'Dave get in,' I shout through the open door watching as he runs down the service road and dives into the open rear doors. 'Are we all in?'

'Yes go!' Blowers and Clarence both shot. I select reverse and slam the van backwards, impacting into the vehicle behind. Twisting the wheel over hard I start to ease forward as more shots rings out and the windscreen implodes, showering me in glass fragments. Leaning over to the side I press the pedal down and scrape the van out from its position.

Shots impact into the side of the van as I drive down the service road and I feel a wheel blowing out causing the van to tilt down and veer off to the side. Fighting to control the vehicle I navigate the corner and glance up to look out the hole where the windscreen was. My heart sinks at the sight of youths spread all over the place. Missiles start thudding against the vehicle as rocks, stones and bricks get launched at us.

'They're fucking everywhere,' I scream out.

'Keep going,' Dave shouts back, then his head appears between the seats, assault rifle in hand. He glances up and quickly scans the route ahead.

'Go faster Mr Howie,' he urges.

'I can't mate, wheels blown out, this is top speed,' my foot is pressed down and the van is roaring with power but the rubber must have been shredded from the wheel, causing the drum to spin and gouge into the tarmac. We're going no faster than walking pace.

'Get ready, we'll have to fight our way out,' Dave shouts at the figures lying in the back of the van.

'I'm not shooting kids,' Clarence shouts.

'Clarence, they are going to kill us,' Dave shouts.

'I can't shoot kids,' he replies.

'I can,' Dave says bluntly, I look down and lock eyes with the small quiet men. An absolute killer stares back at me. A monster. But he's our monster.

'They're not negotiating Clarence, they're fucking shooting at us,' Blowers shouts.

'I can't do it,' he roars, 'I won't do it; I'll fucking die before I shoot a child. I'm a fucking soldier not a murderer and so are you, this isn't our way.'

Shots ping into the sides of the van, fewer now but more missiles get thrown as loud thunks bang of the metal sides.

'Then suggest something,' I plead with him.

'Let me fire,' Dave growls.

'NO!' Clarence roars, 'If you fire on those kids I'll fucking shoot you Dave.'

'What then?' I scream in desperation.

'We give up and give them what they want, surrender,' Clarence spits the last word out.

'NEVER,' Dave roars.

'Dave we are not shooting children, we give up and let them have the weapons.'

'They'll kill us,' he shouts in reply, 'they'll kill the lads and Mr Howie. Clarence this isn't the army, this is different times. Mr Howie has to survive.'

'Why? Why me?'

'Because,' Dave roars and I swear the van shakes from the emotion in his voice.

'Because what?' I shout back.

'Clarence you do this and I swear I'll fucking kill 'em all,' Dave roars.

'Dave, this isn't the way mate,' Clarence shouts back, his tone softer now, 'we are not child killers, we don't do that.'

'Dave, please listen to him,' Lani shouts, 'we can't kill them.'

'They are fucking shooting at us,' Cookey shouts.

'Mr Howie, you're the boss...' Blowers cuts everyone else down, 'what you say goes, if you say we fight then we fight, if you say surrender than we do that without argument.'

'Dave?' Clarence prompts him, 'do you hear that? Howie is boss here, what he says goes.'

'I will not let them kill him that will not happen.'

'It's my choice Dave...You abide my order you hear me?'

'Mr Howie,' he growls in reply.

'Dave! You abide my order DO YOU HEAR ME?'

'Yes Mr Howie,' he barks.

'We surrender, you shout that now, you shout it loud Dave and make them hear.'

He pauses, our eyes locked and then he draws breath and bellows out, 'CEASE FIRING! WE SURRENDER, CEASE FIRING, WE SURRENDER...'

Shouts from outside and gradually the shots and thumps end as the word is spread. I ease my foot of the pedal and the van instantly stops and cuts out. The only sounds are the engine cooling down with light clicks and clunks.

'Mr Howie, I'll charge and distract them, you run and get away,' Dave pleads with me, his eyes wide and it's the first time I've ever seen fear in his face.

'No Dave,' I smile back, 'Clarence is right, we don't kill kids.'

'I won't kill them I promise…I'll fight with my hands and I promise I won't kill any…'

'Dave they'll tear you apart, there's over a hundred of them.'

'That's fine with me Mr Howie, but you got to get away, you have to survive,' his eyes beg me, his tone soft and pleading.

'I'll fight with him Mr Howie,' Blowers adds.

'Me too,' Cookey says.

'And me,' Nick says softly.

'What? What the fuck has got into you? We do this together; I'm not running and leaving you to die.'

'This isn't your day to die Mr Howie,' Dave continues, 'you must survive and…and…'

'And what Dave? Blowers what is this?'

'You have to live Mr Howie,' Blowers says matter of fact, 'you lead and others follow. We wouldn't have that fort without you; we wouldn't have survived without you. It's not us Mr Howie, it's you. Others will follow you and you can lead them….you have to survive.'

'Fuck off,' I spit the words out in shock.

'Boss, you do one and get away, we've got this,' Clarence adds.

'Not you too Clarence, you just you wouldn't kill kids.'

'I won't kill' em but I can fucking batter them about for a bit.'

'You're all nuts, no...no...not happening...we stay together.'

'If they go for you I swear I'll end them,' Dave curses.

'No you won't Dave, you promised me and that means something.'

'COME OUT WITH YOUR HANDS UP,' Maddox's voice screams out.

'COMING...DO NOT SHOOT,' I shout back, 'DO NOT SHOOT WE WILL NOT FIRE ON YOU.'

'Boss, take the chance and go,' Clarence urges.

'Don't ask me that again, any of you, not ever do you hear me? Do you hear me?' I get murmurs of reply and look back to see Lani staring at me with an intense expression. Suddenly, the thought of them hurting her bites me inside. I want to ask her to go, to run away like they said I should but I know what the response will be.

'Come on, weapons down,' I shrug my pistol from my belt and lay it on the seat and push the door open slowly before clambering out with my hands held high.

'WE ARE NOT ARMED...' I shout clearly and walk slowly round to the side door, pulling it back and watching as my group files out one at a time, hands held high.

'Dave, did you leave your knives?' I ask him quietly.

'Yes,' he answers sulkily.

'All of them?'

'I've got one,' he answers instantly, 'small one in my boot.'

'Okay, keep that one then.' I only say it for fear of him suddenly reaching down to his boot and causing a reaction from the youths.

Maddox strides forward, the pistol held high and pointing at us. Youths gather behind him, pointing rifles and shotguns in our direction. We stay quiet as they converge, coming in close and surrounding us.

'You will shoot each other,' Clarence says.

'What?' Maddox snaps the pistol round to point it up at the big man.

'You've got guns surrounding us, if you all fire you will shoot each other, you need one line in front and none behind.'

'What the fuck?' Maddox looks confused.

'He's right,' Dave adds, 'arcs of fire, basic skills.'

'Move to the front,' Maddox gives the order and waits while everyone shuffles round.

'Shit, look at this bitch,' a stocky lad pulls the heavy machine gun from the van, holding it in both hands while the youths stare in awe.

'Be careful son, the safety might not be on, please check it.' Clarence rumbles.

'Why you doing this?' Maddox suddenly demands.

'Doing what?' I ask him, knowing full well what he means.

'Why you giving up bruv? You got guns, you got weapons and skills, you could fight.'

'We don't kill children,' Clarence replies for me, 'that's not our way son.'

'Stop calling me son,' Maddox shouts.

'I'm old and you are young, it's a natural thing for me to say. I don't shout when you call me bruv do I?'

'We would have killed you; I told them to kill you…' He says with anger still in his voice.

'So kill us,' I reply, 'we're here without weapons, you got the guns, go ahead.'

'This ain't some movie,' Maddox says through gritted teeth, 'ain't no smart speech gonna save you now. Get down on your knees all of you.'

'No,' I reply with a dull tone.

'Get down,' he shouts and waves the pistol an inch from my face.

'No, we won't kill children so we surrendered but not one of us will beg or kneel in front of you.'

'That bitch is well fit,' one of the lads shouts from the massed ranks, clearly meaning Lani.

'Watch your manners,' Maddox turns and shouts surprising all of us, 'Was that you Jermaine? You're on toilet duty for the next week.'

'Sorry Maddox,' the lad replies in a humbled tone while the rest of us cast confused glances at each other.

'Maddox, we have been fighting every day since this thing started, that's ten solid days of fighting. We've killed tens of thousands of those things, we've slaughtered 'em with guns and with our bare hands…if we wanted to fight you would all be dead, all of you,' my voice snaps his attention round, 'but we didn't because you are children. Nasty little shits yes, but still children. We have honour and integrity and we draw a line at that.'

'Im not a child,' he sneers.

'No Maddox, you are clearly not a child mate, but the rest are and even if we killed you it would mean having to kill them, which we won't do.'

'How old are you?' Blowers asks.

'Eighteen,' Maddox answers quickly.

'You look older,' Nick adds.

'You been to prison?' Cookey asks.

'What? What the fuck is this?' he spits.

'You're massive for an eighteen year old; I heard they got good gyms in prison.'

'Cos I'm black you think I been in prison,' he shouts.

'No mate, cos your big, packed with muscle, and you're from a council estate, it figures,' Cookey replies with an easy tone.

'Did he go to prison then?' Maddox waves the pistol at Clarence.

'Nah he's just a freak,' Cookey jokes, 'eats everything.'

'And snores like a fucking bear too,' Nick adds as I smile at the disarming banter, one of the lads best weapons and they know it.

'I bet Blowers would like prison,' Cookey says softly.

'Oh fuck off!' Blowers sighs.

'All them men in showers,' Nick joins in, 'oh did I drop the soap…let me bend over and pick it up.'

'Fuck off,' Blowers exclaims rolling his eyes, 'I get this every bloody day,' he shakes his head at Maddox.

'Where's Lenski?' Lani asks.

'What? What the...'

'I am here,' she pushes through the youths to stand just behind Maddox.

'Hi,' Lani nods at the woman.

'Hello,' she replies then stares at Maddox with her arms folded.

'Well? You kill them now yes? That is what we do now yes? We kill everyone. So kill,' she shrugs at him, her face blank.

'Lenski,' he says.

'What?' she snaps, 'look at them, they surrender without the fight, look at their guns they could kill all of us. Why didn't they do this?'

'Are you two a couple?' Lani asks.

'Yes,' Lenski replies quickly and I notice the youths looking at each other in surprise, 'we are, but maybe not for long...' her voice trails off as Maddox stares at her.

'What are you worried about Maddox?' I ask him, 'that we'll come back and get revenge? That we'll try and save these kids? Mate, these kids can look after themselves and as for revenge, no offence but that's not on our plan. There's probably hundreds of communes and places like this round the country. We're going back to our fort, and the only thing we're interested in is killing those things.'

'I couldn't take that risk,' he replies, 'everyone will see us as weak, a base full of kids...'

'Maddox, we've been all over the place. Those things are everywhere, all over the country. People are the rare species now. We've got no interest in your compound. We got a bloody great big fort of our own. I was trying to tell you before.'

'You were demanding to know why those people attacked us.'

'Yeah and maybe I was wrong to do that, but mate...killing people for their food is bad...'

'Maddox was not in charge at this time no? The Bossman he make these rules and he give the children the drugs. The Bossman he try to kill Maddox but Maddox kill him and now he in charge. He say yesterday no more killing, no more of the drugs, he made the fence out there, he stop the children taking the drugs, he say to plant the food and make the crops yes? The Bossman he did the bad things but Maddox he try to fix this but only in last day, we need time to fix this.' Lenski implored, looking between Maddox and I.

'This true?' I ask him.

'Yeah,' he replies.

'Why didn't you say before?'

'Not your business,' he shrugs.

'Maddox, these are new times. I understand your suspicion and concern but I think we've proved ourselves now.'

'Yeah,' he suddenly looks defeated and slumps his shoulders. I realise the youths are looking at him with concerned expressions, their leader lost for words, the fight gone out of him. I glance over at Clarence, nodding at him to say something.

'Er...so what you benching?' He asks, I stare at him with a look of horror and mouth "what the fuck" he shrugs apologetically, "I don't know" he mouths back.

'What?' Maddox shakes his head and looks at Clarence.

'Must be well over hundred kilos, big lad like you.'

'Yeah,' his voice trailed off 'let them go, give them their weapons back and let them go.' He waves at the youths holding our assault rifles who suddenly look crestfallen.

'Aah Maddox...' One of them whines and gets a sharp look from Lenski. Reluctantly the youths hand the weapons back and I watch my group taking their rifles and checking magazines, pushing pistols back into their belt holsters. Dave moves into the van and starts pushing his knives back into his belt. Rucksacks get pulled out and swapped about. I take mine and shove my axe down the back before taking my assault rifle from Nick. All the time watching Maddox slouch away quietly with Lenski at his side.

'Wait here,' I say to the others and start moving after him, 'Maddox, wait up mate.'

'What?' He turns quickly to watch me approaching.

'You okay? You look like shit.'

'Tired,' he replies gruffly.

'Take it easy mate; if what Lenski said was true then you're doing the right thing. But you can't give up and sulk in front of everyone like that.'

'What I ain't sulking,' he replies quickly.

'Just can't do it. Everyone looks up to you mate, you got to lead them. They look confused now.'

'It's hard,' he answers quietly showing just how young he really is, 'I thought I was doing the right thing but then I sent them after you...that was a bad decision, so maybe I'm not doing the right thing.'

'Everyone makes mistakes mate, that was a bad one admittedly, but it's done now and you've recovered it. Move on and stick to the plan you had, it sounded a good one to me. Anyway, your estate is now pretty much cleared out; more might come but keep patrols out on the perimeters and keep checking. Have fall back points and make sure you got an escape route out of your compound. Go through the houses and secure everything you need. If you find other survivors protect them, they'll be older and can teach you things. I don't know everything but I got a good team and they help with everything we do. Also,' I'm warming up now, 'get those vehicles closer to your compound, they are a valuable commodity now. Don't waste ammunition either, and get some medical books or something, you can't leave it to chance with all those kids in one place. We're a few miles down the coast, you send someone if you need help. If we can spare it we'll send what we can, ask for Howie or Big Chris.'

'Yeah...thanks,' he nods, 'er you too, if we can help with anything then just ask.'

'That might just happen mate, you got a huge estate here that could easily be fenced in and secured. Just don't be alarmed if that happens and people come here...and don't kill them.'

'We won't Howie and I'm sorry for attacking you.'

'It's done, but for the record, you don't know how close you came to losing everything mate. Those people in my group are nasty bastards if they get pissed off.'

'It was good to meet you Maddox,' I hold my hand out which he takes in a firm grip and smiles at me. A smile full of youth and future...and white teeth.

'You too Lenski,' I shake hands with the woman who stares with rapture at Maddox.

'Take it easy,' I turn and walk away, back to my group, 'oh and can we have another vehicle?'

'Yeah, take what you need, just bring it back!' Maddox laughs.

'That's a deal mate,' I nod and head over to my group stood talking to the youths. The lads all trading jokes and banter with the kids, Clarence talking to some stockier lads about weight training and Lani staring with revulsion at a sixteen year old girl with a huge cleavage poking out from her low cut top.

'We're off,' I shout over.

'Again?' Lani smiles.
'Yeah again.'

Twenty-Nine

Maddox watches Howie walking away and glances over to the crews crowding round the men with guns. Shaking his head he sighs deeply and feels an overwhelming sense of shame at what almost happened. How he misread the situation and nearly risked the lives of so many more people.

'Shit, this stuff is complicated,' he says to Lenski.

'Yes,' she replies simply.

'I'm sorry,' he adds. Twice now in the last few minutes he's apologised for his actions. Something he very rarely does.

'I know,' again she replies simply. He terrified her with his actions, with his thirst for action and violence only it wasn't that. He was terrified too. Scared of those men coming back and hurting the kids. Lenski knows that's why he went after them and for that loyalty to the kids she can forgive the dangerous and stupid action he took.

'What now?' She asks.

'We carry on I guess,' he scratches the side of his head with the end of the pistol, then realises what he's doing and quickly shoves the gun away, tutting at himself. 'That Howie had some good advice, perimeters and stuff.'

'We should find their base so we know the place it is in yes? If we need doctor or something we can get there quickly then.'

'Okay,' he nods back, staring down at the ground. She moves in close and entwines her fingers in his and waits until he lifts his head. Then she kisses him. In full view of nearly every crew from the compound they kiss passionately, breaking away and looking round at the sea of young faces watching them quietly.

'Wot you lot lookin' at?' Maddox shouts suddenly making them jump, he grins quickly then laughs at the surprised looks on their faces, 'everyone back, we got a lot of work to do.'

'What's up?' Darius asks, stepping in next to Maddox as they walk slowly back to the compound.

'Nuffin', you?'

'Nuffin',' Darius pauses for a minute then looks over at his friend, 'I'm glad we didn't kill them.' He adds quietly.

'Me too,' Jagger says from behind them both, Maddox turns to see Mohammed and more crew chiefs all nodding agreement.'

'Then why did you shoot at them? Why go after them?'

'Coz you said so bruv, you the Bossman now Maddox, wot you says it goes innit,' Mohammed says.

Maddox stops and stares at the chiefs, 'I got it wrong you get me? I fucked up and read it wrong, if I do that again you got to say something. I ain't the Bossman; this ain't no tyranny with a ruler at the top who always gets what he wants. You's got to step up and say something if you think I'm wrong. I might not agree but I'll listen, you get me? I can't do everything.'

'Yeah we get you Maddox,' Sierra replies in a serious tone, 'so are you and Lenski going out now?' She asks. Still showing the need to know the structure and the hierarchy.

'Yeah we are,' Maddox replies with a smile.

'That's sweet Maddox,' Sierra beams at him, 'so is she still number two, or is she number one with you?'

'What?' Maddox shakes his head at the convoluted logic.

'If she's number one then that means Darius is number two and I'm wiv Darius so that makes me number two too, so someone got to be number three...'

'And four,' Jagger added.

Maddox shook his head for a few long seconds, staring as the chiefs started talking about who the number three and four should be. The funny thing was he could see the reasoning and knew they'd want the numbers all the way to the bottom.

'We gotta get back,' he says, 'Liam needs to be told he's now number three...' He turned with a big smile as the chiefs, stunned into silence for a second, erupted into loud arguments.

'Oh you a bad man,' Lenski laughed. Taking his hand they walked side by side back towards the compound.

Their compound.

Thirty

We take another van from behind the shops and load up. I drive again but this time Lani sits up front in the passenger seat. Making idle chat we get lost several times and bicker our way through the confusing estate, making comments that even taxi drivers must find this place confusing. Eventually we find our way back to the shore and our RIB sat forlorn on the beach.

Dave gets us back into the house and we load the van up with our looted gear, finally, a few hours before dawn we move off. Driving back through the estate and getting lost a few more times until we find a motorway on the northern edge. After that it's a sedate pace and the conversation becomes muted and quiet.

'What happened here?' Lani asks as we drive slowly down the country lane towards the ruined landscape of the housing estate bordering the wide open flatlands.

'Dave,' Cookey says with a smile, 'he blew it up.'

'Really?' She asks Dave who stares back and nods once. We still haven't talked about that conversation we had in the van. Why I'm so special and need to survive. But we will.

For now though, the fort is only a few miles away. Safety and comfort, food and rest. Big Chris and Doc Roberts, Sergeant Hopewell and Ted.

'Look at that,' Lani exclaims leaning forward. The lads group behind the seats and we look in silence at the soft lights on the fort in the distance. Just small orange glows that seem to hover in the air. It fills us all with a profound sense of coming home.

>To our compound.
>Our fort.
>Home.

Printed in Great Britain
by Amazon.co.uk, Ltd.,
Marston Gate.